VIRAGO
MODERN CLASSICS
543

Barbara Pym

BARBARA PYM (1913–1980) was born in Oswestry, Shropshire. She was educated at Huyton College, Liverpool, and St Hilda's College, Oxford, where she gained an Honours Degree in English Language and Literature. During the war she served in the WRNS in Britain and Naples. From 1958–1974 she worked as an editorial secretary at the International African Institute. Her first novel, *Some Tame Gazelle*, was published in 1950, and was followed by *Excellent Women* (1952), *Jane and Prudence* (1953), *Less than Angels* (1955), *A Glass of Blessings* (1958) and *No Fond Return of Love* (1961).

During the sixties and early seventies her writing suffered a partial eclipse and, discouraged, she concentrated on her work for the International African Institute, from which she retired in 1974 to live in Oxfordshire. A renaissance in her fortunes came in 1977, when both Philip Larkin and Lord David Cecil chose her as one of the most underrated novelists of the century. With astonishing speed, she emerged, after sixteen years of obscurity, to almost instant fame and recognition. *Quartet in Autumn* was published in 1977 and was shortlisted for the Booker Prize. *The Sweet Dove Died* followed in 1978, and *A Few Green Leaves* was published posthumously. Barbara Pym died in January 1980.

Also by Barbara Pym

EXCELLENT WOMEN

Barbara Pym

Introduced by Alexander McCall Smith

virago

VIRAGO

This paperback edition published in 2009 by Virago Press
Reprinted 2009 (twice), 2010 (twice), 2011, 2012 (twice),
2013 (twice)

Published in hardback in 2008 by Virago Press
First published in Great Britain in 1952 by Jonathan Cape Limited

A CIP catalogue record for this book
is available from the British Library.

ISBN 978-1-84408-451-7

Typeset in Goudy by M Rules
Printed and bound in Great Britain by
Clays Ltd, St Ives plc

Papers used by Virago are from well-managed forests
and other responsible sources.

MIX
Paper from
responsible sources
FSC® C104740

Virago Press
An imprint of
Little, Brown Book Group
100 Victoria Embankment
London EC4Y 0DY

An Hachette UK Company
www.hachette.co.uk

www.virago.co.uk

To My Sister

INTRODUCTION

James Thurber once remarked on the difference between English and American humour that whereas American consists of making the extraordinary seem ordinary, English humour turns on transforming the ordinary into the extraordinary. Readers of Jane Austen will perhaps agree with this, as will those who enjoy E. F. Benson's timeless Mapp and Lucia novels. Barbara Pym belongs in this company; indeed she, more than the others, illustrates Thurber's point about English humour. It delights in tiny little things; and by that standard, *Excellent Women* stands as one of the most endearingly amusing English novels of the twentieth century.

Like Jane Austen, Barbara Pym painted her pictures on a small square of ivory, and covered much the same territory as did her better-known predecessor: the details of smallish lives led in places that could only be in England. Neither used a megaphone; neither said much about the great issues of their time. In *Excellent Women* the reader is made aware of the fact that not long before, there had been a war, but what that war was about is not touched upon. With Jane Austen the fact that there was a major war raging hardly impinges upon the consciousness of the characters. And yet although Barbara Pym's novels are about as far away as it is possible to imagine from engagement with the great political and social issues, they are powerful reminders of the fact that one of the great and proper concerns of literature is that motley cluster of small concerns that makes up our day-to-day lives. This is what gives her novels their permanent appeal.

Excellent Women was Barbara Pym's second published novel, and in the view of many it is her best. She had written her first book, *Young Men in Fancy Dress*, at the age of sixteen. The wonderful title of this teenage work perhaps gave a hint of what was to come – men, young and otherwise, were to form a major focal point of her writing; men, wryly and sometimes wistfully observed by a single female character, bring both excitement and disappointment – and mostly the latter – to the heroines of all her books. *Excellent Women* is as much about men as it is about women; the excellent women who populate this novel are excellent because they have been described as such by men.

The first novel Barbara Pym wrote as an adult, *Some Tame Gazelle*, was initially turned down by a number of publishers. That is to be expected: few novelists have the good fortune of their work being accepted with open arms by the first publisher to whom they show it. Many, no doubt, are sufficiently discouraged by initial rejection to give up there and then. Barbara Pym did not, and eventually, in 1950, *Some Tame Gazelle* saw the light of day. Two years later, *Excellent Women* was accepted for publication.

Over the next eleven years Barbara Pym continued to write her highly individual, small-scale novels, each of them a little gem. Her reputation grew, although she remained a modest writer, working in a rather dull job at the International African Institute, a setting which provided her with considerable inspiration for some of her novels. Then, in 1963, disaster struck. Barbara Pym sent off the manuscript of her new novel, *An Unsuitable Attachment*, to Jonathan Cape, her usual publisher, who replied with a letter of rejection. There are various possible reasons for this, but the explanation that the author herself chose was that her writing – and the world it portrayed – was considered old-fashioned. That has the ring of truth about it: even if the 1960s were years of intellectual experiment and rapid social change, they were also years of some shallowness and silliness. Of course Barbara Pym would be considered old-fashioned in the decade of flower power and drugs, and publishers, like anyone else, might have been carried away by the heady atmosphere of the times. But the brute fact remains: this unfortunate act of pursuit of the zeitgeist, along with the numerous rejections that followed it, silenced an important author for some fourteen years. She continued to write, but not as much, perhaps, as she might have done had her manuscripts been published. And during this period, of course, her public was deprived of all the pleasure that her novels might have brought to them.

The long-overdue rectification came in 1977 with the famous championing of her books by Philip Larkin and David Cecil in the *Times Literary Supplement*. Now at last she was given her due, and was showered with invitations and expressions of interest from those who had previously ignored her. How satisfying it must have been, if not to her, then at least to her friends. What wonderful embarrassment for those who believed that an unmitigated diet of gritty social realism, graphically described sexual couplings and sadistic violence was what readers really wanted – and all they should get. The entire time the reading public, or quite a large section of it, was really yearning for the small-scale delights, the beautiful self-deprecating humour and the brilliant miniaturisation of Barbara Pym's novels. It was the same in children's literature: what children were being given was an offering of improving, pious and very dull tales; what they actually wanted to read was adventure and excitement and, believe it or not, boarding school stories. Eventually Miss Rowling was allowed to give them that.

There has been no diminution of Barbara Pym's reputation after her death; indeed it has been steadily enhanced. An indication of this is the fact that she has become an adjective, the finest compliment that posterity can pay any writer. There are very few novelists to whom this has happened – notably to Graham Greene, who became not only an adjective but also a territory, Greeneland, a land of seedy hotels and forgotten colonial corners. It also happened to Hemingway – a life described as Hemingwayesque is one filled with bull-fighting, hunting, and deep-sea fishing. To say that a moment is 'very Barbara Pym' is to say that it is a moment of self-observed, poignant acceptance of the modesty of one's circumstances, of one's peripheral position. A Barbara Pym moment also occurs when one realises that for those whom one is observing, one will never be an object of love. Tolerant affection, perhaps, but never deep, passionate love. Indeed, one is not really entitled to expect such an emotion, although it is ennobling, some say, to observe it in others.

The world portrayed in *Excellent Women* is a world of shortages and genteel drabness. It is not a world of real poverty – that is not Barbara Pym's territory at all. The characters in this book have all known better days in one way or another: they come from a vicarage background but are now in shared accommodation; they appreciate better fare than the tinned food they eke out; their lives might have had more light in them.

Is this a world that the contemporary reader can recognise? I think that it is. Certainly London is a very different city from the city described in this novel. It is more cosmopolitan and more dangerous, more alienated from its hinterland than ever before, but it is still recognisable in this book. And *Excellent Women* transcends its particular historical setting, as do all of the Pym novels, because it says something about human aspirations that is as true today as it was when it was written: we all have our hopes; we are all, to an extent, and unless we are very lucky, unfulfilled in some parts of our life; we would all like things to be just a little bit better for us. That world of vague longing is described in this novel in a way which not only shows us the poignancy of such hopes, but allows us to smile at them. One does not laugh out loud while reading Barbara Pym; that would be too much. One smiles. One smiles and puts down the book to enjoy the smile. Then one picks it up again and a few minutes later an unexpected observation on human foibles makes one smile again.

It is these asides, I think, that make *Excellent Women* so beguiling. The plot itself is not without interest, but it is the narrator's comments on her world and on the scraps of pleasure it allows her that are so utterly engaging; as where Mildred says, right at the beginning of the book: "'I have to share a bathroom," I had so often murmured, almost with shame, as if I personally had been found unworthy of a bathroom of my own.' To be found unworthy of having one's own

CHAPTER ONE

'Ah, you ladies! Always on the spot when there's something happening!' The voice belonged to Mr Mallett, one of our churchwardens, and its roguish tone made me start guiltily, almost as if I had no right to be discovered outside my own front door.

'New people moving in? The presence of a furniture van would seem to suggest it,' he went on pompously. 'I expect *you* know about it.'

'Well, yes, one usually does,' I said, feeling rather annoyed at his presumption. 'It is rather difficult not to know such things.'

I suppose an unmarried woman just over thirty, who lives alone and has no apparent ties, must expect to find herself involved or interested in other people's business, and if she is also a clergyman's daughter then one might really say that there is no hope for her.

'Well, well, *tempus fugit*, as the poet says,' called out Mr Mallett as he hurried on.

I had to agree that it did, but I dawdled long enough to see the furniture men set down a couple of chairs on the pavement, and as I walked up the stairs to my flat I heard the footsteps of a person in the empty rooms below me, pacing about on the bare boards, deciding where each piece should go.

Mrs Napier, I thought, for I had noticed a letter addressed to somebody of that name, marked 'To Await Arrival'. But now that she had materialised I felt, perversely, that I did not want to see her, so I hurried into my own rooms and began tidying out my kitchen.

I met her for the first time by the dustbins, later that afternoon. The dustbins were in the basement and everybody in the house shared them. There were offices on the ground floor and above them the two flats, not properly self-contained and without every convenience. 'I have to share a bathroom,' I had so often murmured, almost with shame, as if I personally had been found unworthy of a bathroom of my own.

I bent low over the bin and scrabbled a few tea leaves and potato peelings out of the bottom of my bucket. I was embarrassed that we should meet like this. I had meant to ask Mrs Napier to coffee one evening. It was to have been a gracious, civilised occasion, with my best coffee cups and biscuits on little silver dishes. And now here I was standing awkwardly in my oldest clothes, carrying a bucket and a wastepaper basket.

Mrs Napier spoke first.

'You must be Miss Lathbury,' she said abruptly. 'I've seen your name by one of the door-bells.'

'Yes, I live in the flat above yours. I do hope you're getting comfortably settled in. Moving is such a business, isn't it? It seems to take so long to get everything straight. Some essential thing like a teapot or a frying-pan is always lost ...'

Platitudes flowed easily from me, perhaps because, with my parochial experience, I know myself to be capable of dealing with most of the stock situations or even the great moments of life – birth, marriage, death, the successful jumble sale, the garden fête spoilt by bad weather . . . 'Mildred is such a help to her father,' people used to say after my mother died.

'It will be nice to have somebody else in the house,' I ventured, for during the last year of the war my friend Dora Caldicote and I had been the only occupants, and I had been quite alone for the past month since Dora had left to take up a teaching post in the country.

'Oh, well, I don't suppose I shall be in very much,' said Mrs Napier quickly.

'Oh, no,' I said, drawing back; 'neither shall I.' In fact, I was very often in, but I understood her reluctance to pledge herself to anything that might become a nuisance or a tie. We were, superficially at any rate, a very unlikely pair to become friendly. She was fair-haired and pretty, gaily dressed in corduroy trousers and a bright jersey, while I, mousy and rather plain anyway, drew attention to these qualities with my shapeless overall and old fawn skirt. Let me hasten to add that I am not at all like Jane Eyre, who must have given hope to so many plain women who tell their stories in the first person, nor have I ever thought of myself as being like her.

'My husband will be coming out of the Navy soon,' said Mrs Napier, almost in a warning tone. 'I'm just getting the place ready.'

'Oh, I see.' I began to wonder what could have brought a naval officer and his wife to this shabby part of London, so very much the 'wrong' side of Victoria Station, so definitely *not* Belgravia, for which I had a sentimental affection, but which did not usually attract people who looked like Mrs Napier. 'I suppose it's still very difficult to find a flat,' I went on, driven by curiosity. 'I've been here two years and it was much easier then.'

'Yes, I've had an awful time and this isn't really what we wanted. I don't at all like the idea of sharing a bathroom,' she said bluntly, 'and I don't know what Rockingham will say.'

Rockingham! I snatched at the name as if it had been a precious jewel in the dustbin. Mr Napier was called Rockingham! How the bearer of such a name would hate sharing a bathroom! I hastened to excuse myself. 'I'm always *very* quick in the mornings, and on Sundays I usually get up early to go to church,' I said.

She smiled at this, and then seemed to feel bound to add that of course she had no use for churchgoing.

We walked upstairs in silence with our buckets and wastepaper baskets. The opportunity for 'saying a word', which was what our vicar always urged us to do, came and went. We had reached her flat, and much to my surprise she was asking me if I would like to have a cup of tea with her.

I don't know whether spinsters are really more inquisitive than married women, though I believe they are thought to be because of the emptiness of their lives, but I could hardly admit to Mrs Napier that at one point during the afternoon I had arranged to be brushing my flight of stairs so that I could peer through the banisters and watch her furniture being brought in. I had noticed then that she had some good things – a walnut bureau, a carved oak chest

4

and a set of Chippendale chairs, and when I followed her into her sitting-room I realised that she also possessed some interesting small objects, Victorian paperweights and snow-storms, very much like those I had on my own mantelpiece upstairs.

'Those are Rockingham's,' she said, when I admired them. 'He collects Victoriana.'

'I have hardly needed to collect them,' I said. 'My old home was a rectory and full of such objects. It was quite difficult to know what to keep and what to sell.'

'I suppose it was a large, inconvenient country rectory with stone passages, oil lamps and far too many rooms,' she said suddenly. 'One has a nostalgia for that kind of thing some-times. But how I'd hate to live in it.'

'Yes, it was like that,' I said, 'but it was very pleasant. I sometimes feel rather cramped here.'

'But surely you have more rooms than we have?'

'Yes, I've got an attic, too, but the rooms are rather small.'

'And there's the shared bathroom,' she murmured.

'The early Christians had all things in common,' I reminded her. 'Be thankful that we have our own kitchens.'

'Oh, God, yes! You'd hate sharing a kitchen with me. I'm such a slut,' she said, almost proudly.

While she made the tea I occupied myself by looking at her books, which were lying in stacks on the floor. Many of them seemed to be of an obscure scientific nature, and there was a pile of journals with green covers which bore the rather stark and surprising title of *Man*. I wondered what they could be about.

'I hope you don't mind tea in mugs,' she said, coming in with a tray. 'I told you I was a slut.'

'No, of course not,' I said in the way that one does, thinking that Rockingham would probably dislike it very much.

'Rockingham does most of the cooking when we're together,' she said. 'I'm really too busy to do much.'

Surely wives shouldn't be too busy to cook for their husbands? I thought in astonishment, taking a thick piece of bread and jam from the plate offered to me. But perhaps Rockingham with his love of Victoriana also enjoyed cooking, for I had observed that men did not usually do things unless they liked doing them. 'I suppose the Navy has taught him that?' I suggested.

'Oh, no, he's always been a good cook. The Navy hasn't taught him anything, really.' She sighed. 'He's been Flag Lieutenant to an Admiral in Italy and lived in a luxurious villa overlooking the Mediterranean for the past eighteen months, while I've been trailing round Africa.'

'*Africa?*' I echoed in amazement. Could she be a missionary, then? It seemed very unlikely and I suddenly remembered that she had said she never went to church.

'Yes, I'm an anthropologist,' she explained.

'Oh.' I was silent with wonder, and also because I was not at all sure what an anthropologist was and could think of no intelligent comment to make.

'Rockingham hasn't had to do anything much but be charming to a lot of dreary Wren officers in ill-fitting white uniforms, as far as I can make out.'

'Oh, surely . . .' I began to protest, but then decided that this was, after all, a work well worth doing. Clergymen were often good at it; indeed, so many of their flock wore drab, ill-fitting clothes that it came as second nature to them. I had not realised that it might also be among the accomplishments of naval officers.

'I've got to write up my field notes now,' Mrs Napier went on.

'Oh, yes, of course. How interesting . . .'

'Well, well . . .' she stood up and put her mug down on the tray. I felt that I was being dismissed.

'Thank you for the tea,' I said. 'You must come and see me when you get settled. Do let me know if there's anything I can do to help.'

'Not at the moment, thank you,' she said, 'but there may be.'

I thought nothing of her words at the time. It did not seem then as if our lives could ever touch at any point beyond a casual meeting on the stairs and of course the sharing of a bathroom.

This last idea may have occurred to her too, for when I was halfway up the stairs to my own flat she called out, 'I think I must have been using your toilet paper. I'll try and remember to get some when it's finished.'

'Oh, that's quite all right,' I called back, rather embarrassed. I come from a circle that does not shout aloud about such things, but I nevertheless hoped that she would remember. The burden of keeping three people in toilet paper seemed to me rather a heavy one.

When I got into my sitting-room I found to my surprise that it was nearly six o'clock. We must have talked for over an hour. I decided that I did not like Mrs Napier very much, and then began to reproach myself for lack of Christian charity. But must we always like everybody? I asked myself. Perhaps not, but we must not pass judgement on them until we have known them a little longer than one hour. In fact, it was not our business to judge at all. I could hear Father Malory saying something of the kind in a sermon, and at that moment St Mary's clock began to strike six.

I could just see the church spire through the trees in the square. Now, when they were leafless, it looked beautiful, springing up among the peeling stucco fronts of the houses, prickly, Victorian Gothic, hideous inside, I suppose, but very dear to me.

There were two churches in the district, but I had chosen St Mary's rather than All Souls', not only because it was nearer, but because it was 'High'. I am afraid my poor father and mother would not have approved at all and I could imagine my mother, her lips pursed, shaking her head and breathing in a frightened whisper, '*Incense*.' But perhaps it was only natural that I should want to rebel against my upbringing, even if only in such a harmless way. I gave All Souls' a trial; indeed I went there for two Sundays, but when I returned to St Mary's, Father Malory stopped me after Mass one morning and said how glad he was to see me again. He and his sister had been quite worried; they feared I might have been ill. After that I had not left St Mary's again, and Julian Malory and his sister Winifred had become my friends.

I sometimes thought how strange it was that I should have managed to make a life for myself in London so very much like the life I had lived in a country rectory when my parents were alive. But then so many parts of London have a peculiarly village or parochial atmosphere that perhaps it is only a question of choosing one's parish and fitting into it. When my parents had died, within two years of each other, I was left with a small income of my own, an assortment of furniture, but no home. It was then that I had joined forces with my old school friend Dora Caldicote, and while she was teaching I worked in the Censorship, for which, very fortunately, no high qualifications appeared to be necessary, apart from patience, discretion and a slight tendency towards eccentricity. Now that Dora had gone I looked forward to being alone once more, to living a civilised life with a bedroom and a sitting-room and a spare room for friends. I have not Dora's temperament which makes her enjoy sleeping on a camp bed and eating off plastic plates. I felt that I was now old enough to become fussy and spinsterish if I wanted to. I did part-time work at an organisation which helped impoverished gentlewomen, a cause very near to my own heart, as I felt that I was just the kind of person who might one day become one. Mrs Napier, with her gay trousers and her anthropology, obviously never would.

I was thinking about her as I changed to go out to supper at the vicarage, and was glad that I was wearing respectable clothes when I met her on the stairs with a tall, fair man.

'You'll have to drink gin out of a mug,' I heard her say. 'The glasses aren't unpacked.'

'It doesn't matter,' he answered rather stiffly as if it mattered a great deal. 'I suppose you haven't got things straight yet.'

Not Rockingham, I felt; no, it could hardly be when he was in Italy being charming to Wren officers. Perhaps a fellow anthropologist? The bell of St Mary's began to ring for Evensong and I realised that it was none of my business who he was. It was too early to go to the vicarage, so I hurried into church and took my place with the half-dozen middle-aged and elderly women who made up the weekday evening congregation. Winifred Malory, late as always, came and sat by me

CHAPTER TWO

Julian Malory was about forty, a few years younger than his sister. Both were tall, thin and angular, but while this gave to Julian a suitable ascetic distinction, it only seemed to make Winifred, with her eager face and untidy grey hair, more awkward and gaunt. She was dressed, as usual, in an odd assortment of clothes, most of which had belonged to other people. It was well known that Winifred got most of her wardrobe from the garments sent to the parish jumble sales, for such money as she had was never spent on herself but on Good – one could almost say Lost – Causes, in which she was an unselfish and tireless worker. The time left over from these good works was given to 'making a home' for her brother, whom she adored, though she was completely undomesticated and went about it with more enthusiasm than skill.

'If only I could paint the front door!' she said, as the three of us went into the vicarage after Evensong. 'It looks so dark and drab. A vicarage ought to be a welcoming sort of place with a bright entrance.'

Julian was hanging up his biretta on a peg in the narrow

hall. Next to it hung a rather new-looking panama hat. I had never seen him wearing it and it occurred to me that perhaps he had bought it to keep until its ribbon became rusty with age and the straw itself a greyish yellow. My father had worn just such a hat and it always seemed to me to epitomise the wisdom of an old country clergyman, wisdom which Julian could not hope to attain for another twenty or thirty years.

'A welcoming sort of place with a bright entrance,' Julian repeated. 'Well, I hope people do get a welcome even if our front door is dark and I hope Mrs Jubb has got some supper for us.'

I sat down at the table without any very high hopes, for both Julian and Winifred, as is often the way with good, unworldly people, hardly noticed what they ate or drank, so that a meal with them was a doubtful pleasure. Mrs Jubb, who might have been quite a good cook with any encouragement, must have lost heart long ago. Tonight she set before us a pale macaroni cheese and a dish of boiled potatoes, and I noticed a blancmange or 'shape', also of an indeterminate colour, in a glass dish on the sideboard.

Not enough salt, or perhaps *no* salt, I thought, as I ate the macaroni. And not really enough cheese.

'Do tell me about this anonymous donation,' I asked. 'It sounds splendid.'

'Yes, it's really most encouraging. Somebody has sent me ten pounds. I wonder who it can be!' When Julian smiled the bleakness of his face was softened and he became almost good-looking. There was usually something rather forbidding about his manner so that women did not tend to fuss over him as they might otherwise have done. I am not even sure whether anyone had ever knitted him a scarf or pullover. I suppose he was neither so handsome nor so conceited as to pretend a belief in celibacy as a protection, and I did not really know his views on the matter. It seemed a comfortable arrangement for the brother and sister to live together, and perhaps it is more suitable that a High Church clergyman should remain unmarried, that there should be a biretta in the hall rather than a perambulator.

'I always think an anonymous donation is so exciting,' said Winifred with adolescent eagerness. 'I'm longing to find out who it is. Mildred, it isn't you, is it? Or anyone you know?'

I denied all knowledge of it.

Julian smiled tolerantly at his sister's enthusiasm. 'Ah, well, I expect we shall know soon enough who has sent it. Probably one of our good ladies in Colchester or Grantchester Square.' He named the two most respectable squares in our district, where a few houses of the old type, occupied by one family or even one person and not yet cut up into flats, were to be found. My flat was in neither of these squares, but in a street on the fringe and at what I liked to think was the 'best' end.

'It doesn't seem like them, somehow,' I said. 'They don't usually do good by stealth.'

'No,' Julian agreed, 'their left hand usually knows perfectly well what their right hand is doing.'

'Of course,' said Winifred, 'a lot of new people have moved here since the war ended. I've noticed one or two strangers at church lately. It may be one of them.'

'Yes, it probably is,' I agreed. 'The new people moved into my house today and I met Mrs Napier for the first time this afternoon. By the dustbins, too.'

Julian laughed. 'I hope that isn't an omen, meeting by the dustbins.'

'She seemed very pleasant,' I said rather insincerely. 'A bit younger than I am, I should think. Her husband is in the Navy and is coming home soon. He has been in Italy.'

'Italy, how lovely!' said Winifred. 'We must ask them in. Don't you remember, dear,' she turned to her brother, 'Fanny Ogilvy used to teach English in Naples? I wonder if he met her.'

'I should think it very unlikely,' said Julian. 'Naval officers don't usually meet impoverished English gentlewomen abroad.'

'Oh, but his wife told me that he spent his time being charming to dull Wren officers,' I said, 'so he sounds rather a nice person. She is an anthropologist, Mrs Napier. I'm not quite sure what that is.'

'Really? It sounds a little incongruous – a naval officer and an anthropologist,' said Julian.

'It sounds very exciting,' said Winifred. 'Is it something to do with apes?'

Julian began to explain to us what an anthropologist was, or I suppose he did, but as it is unlikely that any anthropologist will read this, I can perhaps say that it appeared to be something to do with the study of man and his behaviour in society – particularly among 'primitive communities', Julian said.

Winifred giggled. 'I hope she isn't going to study *us*.'

'I'm very much afraid that we shan't see her at St Mary's,' said Julian gravely.

'No, I'm afraid not. She told me that she never went to church.'

'I hope you were able to say a word, Mildred,' said Julian, fixing me with what I privately called his 'burning' look. 'We shall rely on you to do something there.'

'Oh, I don't suppose I shall see anything of her except at the dustbins,' I said lightly. 'Perhaps her husband will come to church. Naval officers are often religious, I believe.'

'*They that go down to the sea in ships: and occupy their business in great waters; These men see the works of the Lord: and His wonders in the deep*,' Julian said, half to himself.

I did not like to spoil the beauty of the words by pointing out that as far as we knew Rockingham Napier had spent most of his service arranging the Admiral's social life. Of course he might very well have seen the works of the Lord and His wonders in the deep.

We got up from the table and Julian went out of the room. There was to be some kind of a meeting at half-past seven and I could already hear the voices of some of the 'lads' in the hall.

'Let's go into the den,' said Winifred, 'and I'll make some coffee on the gas ring.'

The den was a small room, untidily cosy, looking out on to the narrow strip of garden. Julian's study was in the front on the same side, the drawing-room and dining-room on the other side. Upstairs there were several bedrooms and attics and a large cold bathroom. The kitchen was in the basement. It was really a very large house for two people, but Father Greatorex, the curate, a middle-aged man who had been ordained late in life, had his own flat in Grantchester Square.

'We really ought to do something about letting off the top floor as a flat,' said Winifred, pouring coffee that looked like weak tea. 'It seems so selfish, *wrong*, really, just the two of us living here when there must be so many people wanting rooms now. I do hope this coffee is all right, Mildred? You always make it so well.'

'Delicious, thank you,' I murmured. 'I'm sure you'd have no

15

difficulty in getting a nice tenant. Of course you'd want somebody congenial. You might advertise in the *Church Times*.' At this idea a crowd of suitable applicants seemed to rise up before me – canons' widows, clergymen's sons, Anglo-Catholic gentlewomen (non-smokers), church people (regular communicants) . . . all so worthy that they sounded almost unpleasant.

'Oh, yes, we might do that. But I suppose you wouldn't think of coming here yourself, Mildred?' Her eyes shone, eager and pleading like a dog's. 'You could name your own rent, dear. I know Julian would like to have you here as much as I should.'

'That's very kind of you,' I said, speaking slowly to gain time, for fond as I was of Winifred I valued my independence very dearly, 'but I think I'd better stay where I am. I should be only one person and you'd really have room for two, wouldn't you?'

'A couple, you mean?'

'Yes, or two friends. Something like Dora and me, or younger people, students, perhaps.'

Winifred's face brightened. 'Oh, that would be lovely.'

'Or a married curate,' I suggested, full of ideas. 'That would be very suitable. If Father Greatorex does get somewhere in the country, as I believe he wants to, Julian will be wanting another curate and he may very well be married.'

'Yes, of course, they don't all feel as Julian does.'

'Does he?' I asked, interested. 'I didn't realise he had any definite views about it.'

'Well, he's never actually said anything,' said Winifred vaguely. 'But it's so much nicer that he hasn't married, nicer for me, that is, although I should have liked some nephews and nieces. And now,' she leapt up with one of her awkward impulsive movements, 'I must show you what Lady Farmer's sent for the jumble sale. Such *good* things. I shall be quite set up for the spring.'

Lady Farmer was one of the few wealthy members of our congregation, but as she was over seventy I was doubtful whether her clothes would really be suitable for Winifred, who was much thinner and hadn't her air of comfortably upholstered elegance.

'Look,' she shook out the folds of a maroon embossed chenille velvet afternoon dress and held it up against her, 'what do you think of this?'

I had to agree that it was lovely material, but the dress was so completely Lady Farmer that I should have hated to wear it myself and swamp whatever individuality I possess.

'Miss Enders can take it in where it's too big,' said Winifred. 'It will do if people come to supper, you know, the Bishop or anybody like that.'

We were both silent for a moment, as if wondering whether such an occasion could possibly arise.

'There's always the parish party at Christmas,' I suggested.

'Oh, of course. It will do for that.' Winifred sounded relieved and bundled the dress away again. 'There's a good jumper suit, too, just the thing to wear in the mornings. How much ought I to give for them?' she asked anxiously. 'Lady Farmer said that I could have anything I wanted for myself, but I must pay a fair price, otherwise the sale won't make anything.'

We discussed the matter gravely for some time and then I got up to go.

There were lights in Mrs Napier's windows as I approached

the house, and from her room came the sound of voices raised in what sounded like an argument.

I went into my little kitchen and laid my breakfast. I usually left the house at a quarter to nine in the morning and worked for my gentlewomen until lunchtime. After that I was free, but I always seemed to find plenty to do. As I moved about the kitchen getting out china and cutlery, I thought, not for the first time, how pleasant it was to be living alone. The jingle of the little beaded cover against the milk jug reminded me of Dora and her giggles, her dogmatic opinions and the way she took offence so easily. The little cover, which had been her idea, seemed to symbolise all the little irritations of her company, dear kind friend though she was. 'It keeps out flies and dust,' she would say, and of course she was perfectly right, it was only my perverseness that made me sometimes want to fling it away with a grand gesture.

Later, as I lay in bed, I found myself thinking about Mrs Napier and the man I had seen with her. Was he perhaps a fellow anthropologist? I could still hear voices in the room underneath me, raised almost as if they were quarrelling. I began to wonder about Rockingham Napier, when he would come and what he would be like. Cooking, Victorian glass paperweights, charm . . . and then there was the naval element. He might arrive with a parrot in a cage. I supposed that, apart from encounters on the stairs, we should probably see very little of each other. Of course there might be some embarrassment about the sharing of the bathroom, but I must try to conquer it. I should certainly have my bath *early so* as to avoid clashing. I might perhaps buy myself a new and more becoming dressing-gown, one that I wouldn't mind being seen in, something long and warm in a rich colour . . . I must have dropped off to sleep at this point, for the next thing I knew was that I had been woken up by the sound of the front door banging. I switched on the light and saw that it was ten minutes to one. I hoped the Napiers were not going to keep late hours and have noisy parties. Perhaps I was getting spinsterish and 'set' in my ways, but I was irritated at having been woken. I stretched out my hand towards the little bookshelf where I kept cookery and devotional books, the most comforting bedside reading. My hand might have chosen *Religio Medici*, but I was rather glad that it had picked out *Chinese Cookery* and I was soon soothed into drowsiness.

CHAPTER THREE

It was several days before I saw Mrs Napier again, although I heard her going in and out and there seemed to be voices coming from her room every evening. I had an idea that I might ask her in to coffee sometime but hesitated about it because I did not quite know how to convey the impression that it was not, of course, to become a regular thing. I wanted to appear civil rather than friendly. One day a new roll of toilet paper of a rather inferior brand appeared in the lavatory, and I also noticed that an attempt had been made to clean the bath. It was not as well done as I should have liked to see it; people do not always realise that cleaning a bath properly can be quite hard work.

'I suppose *she* did it,' said Mrs Morris, my 'woman', who came twice a week. 'She doesn't look as if she could clean anything.'

Mrs Morris was a Welshwoman who had come to London as a girl but still retained her native accent. I marvelled as always at her secret knowledge, when, as far as I knew, she had not yet set eyes on Mrs Napier.

'Kettle's boiling, miss,' she said, and I knew that it must be eleven o'clock, for she made this remark so regularly that I should have thought something was wrong if she had forgotten.

'Oh, good, then let's have our tea,' I said, making the response expected of me. I waited for Mrs Morris to say, 'There's a drop of milk in this jug,' as she always did on discovering the remains of yesterday's milk, and then we were ready for our tea.

'I was cleaning at the vicarage yesterday, those rooms they're going to let,' said Mrs Morris. 'Miss Malory was saying how she wanted you to go there.'

'Yes, I know, but I think it's really better for me to stay here,' I said.

'Yes, indeed, Miss Lathbury. It wouldn't be right at all for you to live at the vicarage.'

'Well, Father Malory and Miss Malory are my friends.'

'Yes, but it wouldn't be right. If Miss Malory was to go away now . . .'

'You think it wouldn't be quite respectable?' I asked.

'Respectable?' Mrs Morris stiffened, and straightened the dark felt hat she always wore. 'That isn't for me to say, Miss Lathbury. But it isn't natural for a man not to be married.'

'Clergymen don't always want to,' I explained, 'or they think it better they shouldn't.'

'Strong passions, isn't it,' she muttered obscurely. 'Eating meat, you know, it says that in the Bible. Not that we get much of it now. If he was a *real* Father like Father Bogart,' she went on, naming the priest of the Roman Catholic Church in our district, 'you could understand it.'

'But Mrs Morris, you're a regular churchwoman. I thought you liked Father Malory.'

'Oh, yes, I've nothing against him really, but it isn't right.' She finished her tea and went over to the sink. 'I'll just wash up these things.'

I watched her stiff uncompromising back which hardly seemed to bend even though the sink was a low one.

'Has something upset you?' I asked. 'Something about Father Malory?'

'Oh, miss,' she turned to face me, her hands red and dripping from the hot water. 'It's that old black thing he wears on his head in church.'

'You mean his biretta?' I asked, puzzled.

'I don't know what he calls it. Like a little hat, it is.'

'But you've been going to St Mary's for years,' I said. 'You must have got used to it by now.'

'Well, it was my sister Gladys and her husband, been staying with us they have. I took them to church Sunday evening and they didn't like it at all, nor the incense, said it was Roman Catholic or something and we'd all be kissing the Pope's toe before you could say knife.'

She sat down with the drying-cloth in her hands. She looked so worried that I had to stop myself smiling.

'Of course,' she went on, 'Evan and I have always been to St Mary's because it's near, but it isn't like the church I went to as a girl, where Mr Lewis was vicar. He didn't have incense or wear that old black hat.'

'No, I don't suppose he did,' I agreed, for I knew the seaside town she came from and I remembered the 'English' church, unusual among so many chapels, with the Ten Commandments in Welsh and in English on either side of the altar and a special service on Sunday morning for the visitors. I did not remember that they had expected or received 'Catholic privileges'.

'I was always church,' said Mrs Morris proudly. 'Never been in the chapel, though I did once go to the Ebenezer social, but I don't want to have anything to do with some old Pope. Kissing his toe, indeed!' She looked up at me, half laughing, not quite sure if Gladys and her husband had been joking when they said it.

'There's a statue in St Peter's Church in Rome,' I explained, 'and people do kiss the toe. But that's only *Roman* Catholics,' I said in a loud clear voice. 'Don't you remember Father Malory explaining about the Pope in his Sunday morning sermons last year?'

'Oh, Sunday morning, was it?' she laughed derisively. 'That's all very fine, standing up and talking about the Pope. A lot of us could do that. But who's going to cook the Sunday dinner?'

No answer seemed to be needed or expected to this question, and we laughed together, a couple of women against the whole race of men. Mrs Morris dried her hands, fumbled in the pocket of her apron and took out a squashed packet of cigarettes. 'Let's have a fag, any road,' she said cheerfully. 'I'll just tell Gladys what you said, Miss Lathbury, about it being some old statue.'

I did not feel that I had done as well as I might have in my attempt to instruct Mrs Morris in the differences between the Roman Church and ours, but I did not think that Julian Malory could have done much better.

After she had gone I boiled myself a foreign egg for lunch and was just making some coffee when there was a knock on the kitchen door.

It was Mrs Napier.

'I've come to ask something rather awkward,' she said, smiling.

'Well, come in and have a cup of coffee with me. I was just making some.'

'Thank you, that would be nice.'

We went into the sitting-room and I switched on the fire. She looked around her with frank interest and curiosity.

'Rather nice,' she said. 'I suppose this is the best from the country rectory?'

'Most of it,' I said, 'and I've bought a few things from time to time.'

'Look,' she said abruptly, 'I was wondering if your woman, the one who's been here this morning, could possibly do for me at all? Perhaps on the mornings when you're not here?'

'I dare say she would be glad to have some more work,' I said, 'and she's quite good. She does go to the vicarage occasionally.'

'Oh, the vicarage.' Mrs Napier made a face. 'Will the vicar call?'

'I can ask him to, if you like,' I said seriously. 'He and his sister are friends of mine.'

'He isn't married then? One of *those* . . . I mean,' she added apologetically as if she had said something that might offend me, 'one of the kind who don't marry?'

'Well, he isn't married and as he's about forty I dare say he won't now.' I seemed to have spent so much time lately in talking about the celibacy of the clergy in general and Julian Malory in particular that I was a little tired of the subject.

'That's just when they break out,' laughed Mrs Napier. 'I always imagine that clergymen need wives to help them with

24

their parish work, but I suppose most of his congregation are devout elderly women with nothing much to do, so that's all right. Holy fowl, you know.'

I felt that I did not like Mrs Napier any more than I had at our first meeting, and she was dropping ash all over my newly brushed carpet.

'Will your husband be coming back soon?' I asked, to break the rather awkward silence that had developed.

'Oh, soon enough,' she said casually. She stubbed out her cigarette in a little dish that wasn't meant to be an ashtray and began walking about the room. 'I know it sounds awful', she said, standing by the window, 'but I'm not really looking forward to his coming very much.'

'Oh, that's probably because you haven't seen him for some time,' I said, in a bright sensible tone.

'That doesn't really make any difference. There's more to it than that.'

'But surely it will be all right once he is here and you've had a little time together?' I said, beginning to feel the inadequacy that an unmarried and inexperienced woman must always feel when discussing such things.

'Perhaps it will. But we're so different. We met at a party during the war and fell in love in the silly romantic way people did then. You know . . .'

'Yes, I suppose people did.' In my Censorship days I had read that they did and I had sometimes wanted to intervene and tell them to wait a little longer, until they were quite sure.

'Rockingham is rather good-looking, of course, and everyone thinks him charming and amusing. He has some money of his own and likes to dabble in painting. But you see,' she

25

turned to me very seriously, 'he knows nothing about anthropology and cares less.'

I listened in bewildered silence. 'Why, ought he to?' I asked stupidly.

'Well, I did this field trip in Africa when he was away and I met Everard Bone, who was in the Army out there. He's an anthropologist too. You may have seen him on the stairs.'

'Oh, yes, I think I have. A tall man with fair hair.'

'We've done a lot of work together, and it does give one a special link with a person, to have done any academic work with him. Rockingham and I just haven't got that.'

Did she always call him Rockingham? I wondered irrelevantly. It sounded so formal, and yet it was difficult to know how to abbreviate it unless one called him Rocky or used some other name.

'Surely you and your husband have other things in common, though, perhaps deeper and more lasting than this work?' I asked, feeling that I must try to take my part in this difficult conversation. I hardly liked to think that she might also have these other things with Everard Bone. Indeed, I did not think that I liked Everard Bone at all, if he was the person I had seen on the stairs. His name, his pointed nose, and the air of priggishness which fair men sometimes have, had set me against him. Also, and here I was ready to admit that I was old-fashioned and knew nothing of the ways of anthropologists, I did not think it quite proper that they should have worked together while Rockingham Napier was serving his country. Here the picture of the Wren officers in their ill-fitting white uniforms obtruded itself, but I resolutely pushed it back. Whatever he may have had to do, he had been serving his country.

'Of course,' Mrs Napier went on, 'when you're first in love, everything about the other person seems delightful, especially if it shows the difference between you. Rocky's very tidy and I'm not.'

So he could be called Rocky now. Somehow it made him seem more human.

'You should see my bedside table, such a clutter of objects, cigarettes, cosmetics, aspirins, glasses of water, *The Golden Bough*, a detective story, any object that happens to take my fancy. Rocky used to think that so sweet, but after a while it maddened him, it was just a mess.'

'I suppose it does get like that,' I said. 'One ought to be careful of one's little ways.' Dora's beaded cover on the milk jug, her love of Bakelite plates, and all the irritating things I did myself and didn't know about . . . perhaps even my cookery books by my bed might drive somebody mad. 'But surely that's only a detail,' I said, 'and it ought not to affect the deeper relationship.'

'Of course you've never been married,' she said, putting me in my place among the rows of excellent women. 'Oh, well . . .' she moved towards the door. 'I suppose we shall go our own ways. That's how most marriages turn out and it could be worse.'

'Oh, but you mustn't say that,' I burst out, having all the romantic ideals of the unmarried. 'I'm sure everything will be all right really.'

She shrugged her shoulders. 'Thank you for the coffee, anyway, and a sympathetic hearing. I really ought to apologise for talking to you like this, but confession is supposed to be good for the soul.'

I murmured something, but I did not think I had been particularly sympathetic and I certainly had not felt it, for people like the Napiers had not so far come within my range of experience. I was much more at home with Winifred and Julian Malory, Dora Caldicote, and the worthy but uninteresting people whom I met at my work or in connection with the church. Such married couples as I knew appeared to be quite contented, or if they were not they did not talk about their difficulties to comparative strangers. There was certainly no mention of them 'going their own ways', and yet how did I really know that they didn't? This idea raised disquieting thoughts and doubts, so I turned on the wireless to distract me. But it was a women's programme and they all sounded so married and splendid, their lives so full and yet so well organised, that I felt more than usually spinsterish and useless. Mrs Napier must be hard up for friends if she could find nobody better than me to confide in, I thought. At last I went downstairs to see if there were any letters. There was nothing for me, but two for Mrs Napier, from one of which I learned that her Christian name was Helena. It sounded rather old-fashioned and dignified, not at all the kind of name I should have imagined for her. Perhaps it was a good omen for the future that she should have such a name.

CHAPTER FOUR

It was certainly unfortunate that Helena Napier should be out when the telegram came. Wives ought to be waiting for their husbands to come back from the wars, I felt, though perhaps unreasonably, when a few hours by aeroplane can transport a husband from Italy to England.

I heard her bell being rung and then mine, and when I opened the door and saw the boy standing there with the telegram I knew at once as if by instinct what its news must be. The question was, when would he arrive? It sounded as if it might be that very evening and I had heard Mrs Napier go out about six o'clock. She was probably meeting Everard Bone somewhere. Ought I to try to find out where she was and let her know? I felt that I ought to make an attempt and began searching through the telephone directory to see if I could find his number. If I couldn't, so much the better – I should be saved from interfering in something which didn't really concern me. But there it was, a Chelsea address – there would hardly be two Everard Bones. I dialled the number fearfully and heard it ring. 'Hello, hello, who is that?' a querulous elderly woman's voice answered. I was completely taken aback, but before I could speak the voice went on, 'If it's Miss Jessop I can only hope you are ringing up to apologise.' I stammered out an explanation. I was not Miss Jessop. Was Mr Everard Bone there? 'My son is at a meeting of the Prehistoric Society,' said the voice. 'Oh, I see. I'm so sorry to have bothered you,' I said. 'People are always bothering me – I never wanted to have the telephone put in at all.'

After a further apology I hung up the receiver, shaken and mystified but at the same time relieved. Everard Bone was at a meeting of the Prehistoric Society. It sounded like a joke. I could hardly be expected to pursue my enquiries any further, so I decided that I was an interfering busybody and went upstairs to get my supper. I opened a tin of baked beans, thinking that it would be easy and quick, for I could not rid myself of the feeling that Rockingham Napier might arrive at any moment and that I might have to go down and open the door. He would certainly have no latch-key and he might not have had supper. I now began to feel almost agitated; I hurried about the kitchen, eating the baked beans in ten minutes or less, quite without dignity, and then washing up. I had made a cup of coffee and taken it into the sitting-room when I heard a taxi draw up and then Mrs Napier's bell ringing.

I hesitated at the top of the stairs, feeling nervous and stupid, for this was a situation I had not experienced before, and my training did not seem to be quite equal to it. Also, I suddenly thought of the parrot in a cage and that was distracting.

I opened the door rather timidly, hoping that he would not be too disappointed when he saw that I was not his wife.

'I'm afraid Mrs Napier is out,' I said, 'but I heard the bell and came down.'

It was a good thing he began talking, for I am not used to meeting handsome men and I am afraid that I must have been staring at him rather rudely. And yet it was his manner that charmed me rather than his looks, though he was dark and elegant and had all those attributes that are usually considered to make a man handsome.

'How very nice of you to come down,' he said, and I could see, though it is impossible to put into words, exactly what Helena had meant when she talked about him putting the awkward Wren officers at their ease. 'It's lucky for me you were in. I think you must be Miss Lathbury.'

'Yes, I am,' I said, surprised. 'But how did you know?'

'Helena mentioned you in a letter.'

I could not help wondering how she had described me. 'Yes, we have met once or twice,' I said, 'I live in the flat above you.'

We were going upstairs now, I leading the way and he following with his suitcases. Fortunately the doors of their flat were unlocked and I showed him into the sitting-room.

'Oh, my things, how good it is to be with them again!' he exclaimed, going over to the bookcase and picking up one of the paperweights which were arranged on the top. 'And my chairs, too. Don't you think they're beautiful?'

'Yes, they are lovely,' I said, hovering in the doorway. 'Do let me know if there's anything I can do, won't you?'

'Oh, please don't go, unless you have to, that is . . .?' He turned his charming smile full on me and I felt a little dazed.

'Have you had anything to eat?' I asked.

'Yes, thank you. I had dinner on the train. It isn't wise to drop in on Helena and expect to find a meal ready or even anything in the larder. I'm afraid we don't always agree about the importance of civilised eating.' He looked round the room. 'Quite pleasing, isn't it? I rather feared the worst when Helena told me where we were going to live.'

'I'm afraid it isn't one of the best parts of London,' I said, 'but I'm fond of it.'

'Yes, I believe it may have a certain *Stimmung*. If you live in an unfashionable district you have to find at least that to make it tolerable.'

I was not quite sure what he meant. 'I like to think of it when it was a marsh and wild boars roamed over it,' I ventured, remembering something I had read in the local weekly paper. 'And Aubrey Beardsley lived here once, you know. There is a plaque marking his house.'

'Oh, perfect!' He seemed pleased. 'That does make things rather better. Those exquisite drawings.'

Personally I thought them disgusting, but I made a noncommittal reply.

'It's going to be very cold after Italy, though.' He shivered and rubbed his hands together.

'I don't know whether you would like to come up to my flat for a while?' I suggested. "I have a fire and was just going to make some coffee. But perhaps you'd rather unpack?'

'No, I should love some coffee.'

'What a charming room,' he said when we were in it. 'You are obviously a person of taste.'

I could not help being pleased at the implied compliment but felt bound to explain that most of the furniture had come from my old home.

'Ah, yes,' he paused, as if remembering something, 'from the old rectory. Helena told me that, too.'

I went into the kitchen and busied myself making more coffee.

'I hope you've had your meal?' he said, coming in and watching me. 'I've arrived at rather an awkward time.'

I explained that I had just finished supper and added that I found it rather a bother cooking just for myself. 'I like food,' I said, 'but I suppose on the whole women don't make such a business of living as men do.' I thought of my half-used tin of baked beans; no doubt I should be seeing that again tomorrow.

'No, and women don't really appreciate wine either. I suppose you wouldn't dream of drinking a bottle of wine by yourself, would you?'

'Of course not,' I said, rather primly, I am afraid.

'That's what's so wonderful about living out of England,' he said, pacing round the small kitchen, 'such a glorious feeling of well-being, sitting at a table in the sun with a bottle of whatever it happens to be – there's nothing to equal that, is there?'

'Yes, I like sitting at a table in the sun,' I agreed, 'but I'm afraid I'm one of those typical English tourists who always wants a cup of tea.'

'And when it comes, it's a pale straw-coloured liquid . . .'

'And the tea's in a funny little bag . . .'

'And they may even bring *hot* milk with it . . .'

We both began laughing.

'But even that has its own kind of charm,' I said stubbornly; 'it's all part of the foreign atmosphere.'

'The English tourists certainly are,' he said, 'though there weren't any in Italy, of course. I think that was what was lacking, what made life so unnatural. The sightseers were all in uniform, there were no English gentlewomen with Baedekers and large straw hats. I missed that.'

33

We went on talking about Italy and then somehow I was telling him about the neighbourhood, Julian Malory and his sister and the church.

'High Mass – with music and incense? Oh, I should like that,' he said. 'I hope it is the *best* quality incense? I believe it varies.'

'Yes, I've seen advertisements,' I admitted, 'and they have different names. Lambeth is *very* expensive, but Pax is quite cheap. It seems as if it ought to be the other way round.'

'And have you dozens of glamorous acolytes?'

'Well . . .' I hesitated, remembering Teddy Lemon, our Master of Ceremonies, with his rough curly hair and anxious face, and his troop of well-drilled, tough-looking little boys, 'they are very nice good boys, but perhaps you should go to a Kensington church if you want to see glamorous acolytes. I hope you will come to our church sometimes,' I added more seriously, for I felt that Julian would expect me to 'say a word' here.

'Oh, yes, I shall look in. I'm very fond of going to church, but I don't like doing anything before breakfast, you know. That's always seemed to me to be the great snag about religion, don't you agree?'

'Well, one feels that a thing is more worth doing if it's something of an effort,' I attempted.

'You mean virtue goes out of you? Ah, yes, how it does, or rather how it would if there was any to go out of me,' he sighed. 'I'm sure you have so much.'

I did not altogether like his frivolous attitude, but I could not help liking him. He was so easy to talk to and I could see him at any social gathering, using his charm to make people feel at home, or rather not consciously using it, for the exercise of it seemed natural to him as if he could not help being charming.

We were still talking about churches when we heard voices on the stairs.

'Do excuse me,' he said, 'that must be Helena. Thank you so much for being so kind to me. I hope we shall be meeting often.' He ran out on to the landing and down the stairs.

I put the coffee cups on to a tray and took them into the kitchen. It was a pity, I felt, that Everard Bone should intrude on the Napiers' reunion. Still, Helena would no doubt be capable of managing the two of them and it was to be hoped that Everard Bone would have the tact to go away quickly and leave them alone. I was just starting to wash the cups when there was a knock at the door. Rockingham stood there with a straw-covered flask of wine in his hand.

'We feel this is an occasion,' he said, 'and should like you to join us. That is, if you approve of drinking wine at this hour.'

'Oh, but surely you'd rather be by yourselves . . .'

'Well, the anthropologist is with us, so it seemed a good idea to make it a party,' he explained.

I began taking off my apron and tidying my hair, apologising as I did so, in what I felt was a stupid, fussy way, for my appearance. As if anyone would care how I looked or even notice me, I told myself scornfully.

'You look very nice,' said Rockingham, smiling in such a way that he could almost have meant it.

Helena and Everard Bone were in the sitting-room, she putting glasses out and he standing over by the window. I was able to study his profile with its sharp-pointed nose and decide that I disliked it, until he turned towards me and stared with what seemed to be disapproval.

35

'Good evening,' I said, feeling very silly.

'You do know each other, don't you?' said Helena.

'Yes, at least I've seen Mr Bone on the stairs,' I explained.

'Oh, yes, I do remember meeting somebody on the stairs once or twice,' he said indifferently. 'Was it you?'

'Yes.'

'How marvellous that you were here when Rocky arrived,' said Helena in a quick nervous tone, 'too awful for him, coming home to an empty house, but he said you were marvellous and I don't believe he's missed me at all, have you, darling?'

She did not wait for him to answer but ran back into the kitchen to fetch something. Rockingham was pouring the wine, so that I was left standing awkwardly with Everard.

'I believe you're an anthropologist,' I said, making what I felt was a brave attempt at conversation. 'But I'm afraid I don't know anything about anthropology.'

'Why should you?' he asked, half smiling.

'It must be fun,' I floundered, 'I mean, going round Africa and doing all that.'

'"Fun" is hardly the word,' he said. 'It's very hard work, learning an impossibly difficult language, then endless questionings and statistics, writing up notes and all the rest of it.'

'No, I suppose it isn't,' I said soberly, for he had certainly not made it sound fun. 'But there must be something satisfying in having done it, a sort of feeling of achievement?'

'Achievement?' He shrugged his shoulders. 'But what *has* one done really? I sometimes wonder if it isn't all a waste of time.'

'It depends what you set out to do,' I said rather crossly, feeling like Alice in Wonderland. I was doing very badly here and was grateful when Rockingham came to the rescue.

'Oh, they hate you to think they get any enjoyment out of it,' he said rather spitefully.

'But I do enjoy it,' said Helena; 'we aren't all as dreary as Everard. I simply loved it. And now we've got to do all the writing up; that's what we've been discussing this evening. We're to give a paper before one of the learned societies. Miss Lathbury,' she turned to me with unnatural animation, 'you simply must come and hear it.'

'Yes, Miss Lathbury, you and I will sit at the back and observe the anthropologists,' said Rockingham. 'They study mankind and we will study them.'

'Well, the society is in many ways a primitive community,' said Everard, 'and offers the same opportunities for fieldwork.'

'When is it to be?' I asked.

'Oh, quite soon, next month even,' said Helena.

'We must *get on*,' said Everard in an irritable tone. 'The thing will never be ready if we don't hurry.'

'It must take a lot of work putting it all together,' I said. 'I should be very nervous at the thought of it.'

'Oh, well, it isn't that. Our stuff is quite new but one wants it to be good.'

'Oh, certainly,' I agreed.

'Well, darling . . .' Helena looked at her husband and raised her glass. 'Isn't it lovely to have him back again?' she said to nobody in particular.

Everard said nothing but raised his glass politely, so I did the same.

'More to drink!' said Rockingham with rather forced gaiety. He came towards me with the straw-covered flask and I let him refill my glass, although it was by no means empty. I began to see how people could need drink to cover up

37

embarrassments, and I remembered many sticky church functions which might have been improved if somebody had happened to open a bottle of wine. But people like us had to rely on the tea-urn and I felt that some credit was due to us for doing as well as we did on that harmless stimulant. This party, if such it could be called, was not going well and I did not feel socially equal to the situation. My experience, which had admittedly been a little narrow, had not so far included anything in the least like it. I wished that Everard Bone would go, but he was talking seriously to Helena about some aspect of their paper, ignoring or not noticing the awkwardness. At last, however, he said he must be going, and said goodnight quite pleasantly to Rockingham and me and rather more coldly to Helena, mentioning that he would be ringing her up within the next few days about the kinship diagrams.

'We must *get on*,' he repeated.

'I shall look forward to hearing your paper,' I said, feeling that some effort was required and that it was up to me to make it.

'Oh, you will find it deadly dull,' he said. 'You mustn't expect too much.'

I forebore to remark that women like me really expected very little – nothing, almost.

'Well, well,' said Rockingham as we heard the front door close, 'so that is the great Everard Bone.'

'Great?' said Helena, surprised. 'I'm afraid he was at his worst tonight. Don't you think he's intolerably pompous and boring, Miss Lathbury?' She turned to me, her eyes shining.

'He seems very nice and he's certainly rather good-looking.'

'Oh, do you think so? I don't find fair men at all attractive.'

It seemed pointless to follow up that line, so I admitted that

I had found him difficult to talk to, but that that was not surprising since I was not used to meeting intellectuals.

'Oh, he's impossible!' she burst out.

'Never mind, wait till you see what I've brought for you,' said Rockingham in a soothing tone as if speaking to a child. 'I've got some majolica and a pottery breakfast set packed up with my other luggage, and the usual trifles here.' He opened one of his suitcases and took out a bottle of perfume, several pairs of silk stockings and some small pottery objects. 'And you mustn't go yet, Miss Lathbury,' he called, seeing me moving uncertainly towards the door. 'I should like you to have something.'

He put a little china goat into my hand. 'There, let it go among the bearded archdeacons and suchlike.'

'Oh, it's charming – thank you so much . . .'

I went upstairs and put it on the table by my bed. Had he been a little drunk? I wondered. I believed the wine had made me feel a little unsteady too, but then I was not used to it and the whole evening had a fantastic air about it, as if it couldn't really have happened.

I lay awake feeling thirsty and obscurely worried about something. Well, there was really no need for me to see very much of the Napiers. Circumstances had thrown us together this evening but tomorrow we should all be keeping to ourselves. I did not suppose that Helena would remember her invitation to me to hear their paper at the learned society, so I would not expect it. I would ask Dora to stay in the Easter holidays. I couldn't see her getting on very well with Rockingham, or Rocky as I now thought of him. He was not at all the sort of person either of us had been used to meeting, yet I seemed to have found it quite easy to talk to him, I thought smugly. But then I remembered the Wren officers and I knew what it was that was worrying me. It was part of his charm that he could make people like that feel at ease. He must be rather a shallow sort of person really. Not nearly so worthwhile as Julian Malory, or Mr Mallett and Mr Conybeare our churchwardens, or even Teddy Lemon, who had no social graces . . . as I dozed off I remembered that I had forgotten to say my prayers. There came into my mind a picture of Mr Mallett, with raised finger and roguish voice, saying, 'Tut, tut, Miss Lathbury . . .

CHAPTER FIVE

The next afternoon I was helping Winifred to sort out things for the jumble sale.

'Oh, I think it's *dreadful* when people send their relations to jumble sales,' she said. 'How *can* they do it?' She held up a tarnished silver frame from which the head and shoulders of a woman dressed in Edwardian style looked out. 'And here's another, a clergyman, too.'

'A very young curate, just out of the egg, I should think,' I said, looking over her shoulder at the smooth beardless face above the high collar.

'It might almost be somebody we know,' lamented Winifred. 'Imagine if it were and one saw it lying on the stall! What a shock it would be! I really think I must take the photographs out – it's the frames people will want to buy.'

'I don't suppose their own relatives send them,' I said comfortingly. 'I expect the photographs have been in the boxroom for years and nobody knows who they are now.'

'Yes, I suppose that's it. But it's the idea of being unwanted, it's like sending a *person* to a jumble sale – do you see? You feel it more as you get older, of course. Young people would only laugh and think what a silly idea.'

I could see very well what she meant, for unmarried women with no ties could very well become unwanted. I should feel it even more than Winifred, for who was there really to grieve for me when I was gone? Dora, the Malorys, one or two people in my old village might be sorry, but I was not really first in anybody's life. I could so very easily be replaced . . . I thought it better not to go into this too deeply with Winifred, for she was of a romantic, melancholy nature, apt to imagine herself in situations. She kept by her bed a volume of Christina Rossetti's poems bound in limp green suede, though she had not, as far as I knew, had the experience to make those much-quoted poems appropriate. I feel sure that she would have told me if there had been someone of whom she could think when she read

> *Better by far you should forget and smile,*
> *Than that you should remember and be sad . . .*

'Well, you'll never be unwanted,' I said cheerfully. 'Goodness knows what Julian would do without you.'

'Oh, my goodness!' She laughed as if she had suddenly remembered something. 'You should just see him now! He had the idea that he'd distemper the rooms we're going to let and he's got into such a mess. I started to help, but then I remembered I had to do these things, so Miss Statham and Miss Enders and Sister Blatt are up there giving helpful advice.'

'Oh, dear, I should think he needs more practical help than that,' I said. 'May I go up and see?'

'Yes, do. I'll go on sorting out these things. You know, I

think I shall buy this skirt for myself,' I heard her murmuring; 'there's a *lot* of wear in it yet.'

The sound of women's voices raised in what seemed to be a lamentation led me to a large room on the top floor, where I found Julian Malory sitting on top of a stepladder, holding a brush and wearing an old cassock streaked with yellow distemper. Standing round him were Miss Statham and Miss Enders, two birdlike little women whom I tended to confuse, and Sister Blatt, stout and rosy in her grey uniform, with a blunt no-nonsense manner.

They were all staring at a wall which Julian had apparently just finished.

'Well, I hope it's going to dry a different colour,' said Sister Blatt; 'the one it is now would drive anyone mad.'

'It said Old Gold on the tin,' said Julian unhappily. 'Perhaps I mixed it too thickly.'

'Of the consistency of thin cream,' said Miss Enders, reading from the tin. 'That's how it should be.'

'Of course it's difficult to remember what cream was like,' said Miss Statham. 'I suppose *thin* cream might be like the top of the milk.'

'Oh, Mildred,' Julian waved his brush towards me in a despairing gesture, showering everybody with drops of distemper, 'do come to the rescue!'

'What can I do?'

'Nothing,' said Sister Blatt, almost with satisfaction. 'I'm afraid Father Malory has done the wall the wrong colour. The only thing will be to wait till it's dry and then do it over again with a lighter shade. And it looks so streaky, too,' she bent down and peered closely at the wall. 'Oh dear, oh dear, I'm afraid *I* shouldn't care to live with walls that colour.'

'I believe it *does* dry lighter,' I said hopefully.

'I wish I'd got the boys' club to do it,' said Julian. 'I'm afraid I'm no good at practical things. I always think it must be such a satisfying feeling, to do good work with one's hands. I'm sure I've preached about it often enough.'

'Ah, well, we aren't meant to be satisfied in this world,' said Sister Blatt; 'perhaps that's what it is.'

Julian smiled. 'It seems a little hard that I shouldn't be allowed even this small satisfaction, but I've certainly learnt humility this afternoon, so the exercise will have served some purpose. It looked so easy, too,' he added sadly.

'Oh, well, things are never as easy as they seem to be,' said Miss Statham complacently.

'No, they certainly are not,' agreed Miss Enders, who was a dressmaker. 'People often say to me that they're just going to run up a cotton dress or a straight skirt, but then they find it isn't as easy as it looks and they come running to me to put it right.'

'I wish you could put this right, Miss Enders,' said Julian, drooping on the top of his ladder.

'Look,' I called out, 'it *is* drying lighter, and quite evenly too. I suppose it would naturally be darker when it was wet.'

'Why, so it is,' said Sister Blatt. 'It's quite a nice colour now.'

'Mildred, how clever of you,' said Julian gratefully. 'I knew you would help.'

'Well, well, now that we've seen you on your way we may as well be going on ours,' said Sister Blatt good-humouredly.

'Thank you for your help and advice,' said Julian with a touch of irony.

'Is Father Malory going to attempt the ceiling?' asked Miss Statham in a low voice.

'That's the most difficult part,' said Miss Enders.

'Oh, well, as a clergyman he will naturally wish to make the attempt,' said Sister Blatt, with a jolly laugh. 'Perhaps Miss Lathbury will help him. I'm afraid the ladder would hardly bear my weight,' she added comfortably, looking down at her grey-clad bulk. 'In any case, I believe the ceiling should have been done *before* the walls. If you do the ceiling now, Father, the walls will get splashed with white.'

'So they will,' said Julian patiently. 'Excellent women,' he sighed, when they had gone. 'I think we will knock off for tea now, don't you?'

'You could ask for volunteers from the choir or the boys' club to finish it,' I suggested. 'I'm sure Teddy Lemon would be good at that kind of thing. Men love messing about with paint and distemper.'

'I suppose I am not to be considered as a normal man,' said Julian, taking off his yellow-streaked cassock and draping it over the stepladder, 'and yet I do have these manly feelings.'

We found Winifred in the hall with a case of stuffed birds.

'Look,' she said, 'from Mrs Noad – the usual.'

'The house must be quite bare of birds considering that she sends some to every sale,' I remarked.

'Oh, there are plenty more,' said Julian. 'I believe these come from the lumber-room. There are even finer specimens in the hall, some quite menacing with raised wings. These are *very* small ones, almost like sparrows.'

'Oh, they'll go like hot cakes,' said Winifred; 'there's always competition to buy them. Let's go and have tea.'

Tea at the vicarage was a safer meal than most and today there was even a rather plain-looking cake.

'I must ask the Napiers if they have any jumble,' I said. 'He

45

may have some old civilian suit that he doesn't want or even a uniform with the buttons and braid removed.'

'One hears that so many husbands coming back from the war find that their civilian clothes have been devoured by *moth*,' said Winifred seriously. 'That must be a dreadful shock.'

'Oh, the women should look after that sort of thing,' said Julian. 'Mothballs, camphor and so on,' he added vaguely. 'I believe it's perfectly possible to keep the moth at bay. Do you think Mrs Napier has done her duty in that respect?'

'I don't know,' I said slowly, for it occurred to me that perhaps she had not. I could not imagine her doing these methodical wifely things.

'Have you met *him* yet?' Winifred asked.

'Oh, yes, he's charming. Good-looking, amusing and so easy to talk to. I'm very much taken with him.'

'It sounds almost as if you have fallen in love with him,' said Julian teasingly, 'if he has made such a favourable first impression.'

'Oh, that's ridiculous!' I protested. 'I've only met him once and he's probably younger than I am. Besides, he's a married man.'

'I'm very glad to hear you say that, Mildred,' said Julian more seriously. 'So many people nowadays seem to forget that it should be a barrier.'

'Now, Julian, we don't want a sermon,' said Winifred. 'You know Mildred would never do anything wrong or foolish.'

I reflected a little sadly that this was only too true and hoped I did not appear too much that kind of person to others. Virtue is an excellent thing and we should all strive after it, but it can sometimes be a little depressing.

'Pass Mildred something to eat,' said Winifred.

'I hope she knows us well enough to help herself without being asked,' said Julian, 'otherwise I'm afraid she would get very little.'

I took another piece of cake and there was a short lull in the conversation, during which I considered Julian's suggestion that I might have fallen in love with Rockingham Napier. It was of course quite impossible, but I certainly felt the power of his charm, and I should often have to remind myself of the awkward Wren officers and how he had made them feel at ease in the Admiral's villa. But I have never been very much given to falling in love and have often felt sorry that I have so far missed not only the experience of marriage, but the perhaps even greater and more ennobling one of have loved and lost. Of course there had been a curate or two in my schooldays and later a bank clerk who read the Lessons, but none of these passions had gone very deep.

'And now,' said Julian, taking advantage of the silence, 'I have an announcement to make.'

'Oh, what is it?' we both exclaimed.

'I believe I have found a tenant for out flat.'

'Oh, Julian, how exciting!' Winifred waved her hands in an impulsive movement and knocked over the hot-water jug. 'Do tell us who it is!'

'Is it somebody really suitable?' I asked.

'Most suitable, I think,' said Julian. 'She is a Mrs Gray, a widow.'

'That sounds excellent. A Mrs Gray, a widow,' I repeated. 'I can just imagine her.'

'Oh, so can I!' said Winifred enthusiastically. 'A neat little person of about sixty, rather nicely dressed.'

'Well, I'm afraid you're quite wrong,' said Julian. 'I should think she is very little older than Mildred. And she is tall, but nicely dressed, I dare say; you know I don't really notice such things.'

'But where did you find her?' I asked. 'Did you advertise in the *Church Times?*'

'No, that was not necessary. She is actually living in this parish, in furnished rooms at the moment. You may have seen her in church, though she told me she always sat at the back.'

'Oh, really? I wonder . . .' Winifred began to enumerate all the strangers she had noticed lately, but somehow we did not seem to be able to identify Mrs Gray. Julian's description was vague enough to fit any of two or three women we could remember having noticed as strangers.

'How did she know about the flat?' I asked.

'She went to Miss Enders to have a dress altered and I suppose they got talking. Then she mentioned the matter to Father Greatorex and he told me. She felt she did not like to approach me directly. She is a clergyman's widow, you see,' Julian added, as if this would explain a delicacy not usually displayed by people engaged in the desperate business of flat-hunting.

'Oh, *good*,' I exclaimed involuntarily, for I had an inexplicable distrust of widows, who seem to be of two distinct kinds, one of which may be dangerous. I felt that Mrs Gray sounded very definitely of the safer kind.

'I gather that she hasn't much money,' said Julian, 'so I hardly know what would be a fair rent to ask. I found I couldn't bring myself to mention it, and neither, apparently, could she.'

'Well, really, I should have thought that would have been her first question,' I said, thinking what a remarkable delicate conversation they must have had. 'She can hardly expect to get three rooms for nothing. You must be careful she doesn't try to do you down.'

'Oh, Mildred,' Julian looked grieved, 'you wouldn't say that if you had seen her. She has such sad eyes.'

'No; I'm sorry,' I mumbled, for I had been forgetting that she was a clergyman's widow.

'Of course we don't want to make any profit out of it,' said Winifred, 'so I'm sure we can come to some friendly arrangement. Perhaps I could discuss it with her; it might be less embarrassing with a woman.'

Julian looked at his sister doubtfully and then at me. 'Of course Mildred would be the ideal person,' he said.

'You mean because I'm used to dealing with impoverished gentlewomen?' I asked. 'But I'm afraid it's made me develop a rather suspicious attitude. You see, we sometimes get people who aren't genuine and every case has to be carefully investigated.'

'Really, how distressing! I had no idea people would try that sort of thing.'

'How terrible!' said Winifred. 'It always saddens me when I hear of wickedness like that. Especially among gentlewomen.'

'Yes, perhaps one does expect rather more of them,' I agreed, 'but I can assure you it does sometimes happen.' The Malorys often gave me a feeling that I knew more of the wickedness of the world than they did, especially as I had learned much of the weaknesses of human nature in my Censorship work, but so much of my knowledge was at second hand that I doubted whether there was much to choose between us in worldly wisdom. But I did feel that they were simpler and more trusting by nature than I was.

'Oh, I expect I shall be able to manage it quite satisfactorily,' said Julian. 'It would hardly be fair to expect Mildred to deal with something that doesn't concern her at all.'

'I will if you like,' I said doubtfully, 'but of course it's not really my business.' I did not then know to the extent I do now that practically anything may be the business of an unattached woman with no troubles of her own, who takes a kindly interest in those of her friends.

'We must look out for Mrs Gray in church,' said Winifred. 'I *think* I know who she is. I believe she sometimes wears a silver fox fur.'

'I thought Julian said she hadn't much money,' I said, 'though of course the fur might have been left over from more prosperous days.'

'It's a rather *bushy* fur,' said Winifred. 'Perhaps it isn't silver fox at all. I don't know much about these things.'

'I don't think she was wearing a fur when I saw her,' said Julian, 'but she did appear to be nicely dressed.'

'I hope she won't distract you from writing your sermons, Julian,' I said jokingly. 'We shall probably notice a marked falling off in your preaching when Mrs Gray moves in.'

Julian laughed and got up from the table. 'I must go back to my distempering,' he said, 'or the place won't be habitable. I shall enjoy it now that I know the colour dries lighter. I have certainly learnt something this afternoon.'

Winifred smiled affectionately after him as he left the room. 'Men are just children, really, aren't they. He's as happy as a sandboy when he's doing something messy. Now, Mildred, perhaps we could get on with pricing these things for the sale?'

We spent a contented half hour going through the jumble and speculating about Mrs Gray.

'Julian didn't *really* tell us what she was like,' lamented Winifred.

'No, but I suppose women of my sort and age are difficult to describe, unless they're strikingly beautiful, of course.'

'Oh, wouldn't that be lovely,' Winifred pushed back her untidy grey hair, 'if she were strikingly beautiful!'

'Oh, I don't know,' I said. 'Perhaps it would if she could be nice as well, but one feels that beautiful people aren't always.'

'But she's a clergyman's widow . . .'

'Oh, dear,' I laughed, 'I'd forgotten that.' It seemed like a kind of magic formula. 'So she's to be beautiful as well as good. That sounds almost *too* much. We don't know how her husband died, do we? She may have driven him to his grave.'

Winifred looked rather shocked, so I stopped my foolish imaginings and went on pricing the worn garments, stuffed birds, old shoes, golf clubs, theological books, popular dance tunes of the thirties, fenders and photograph frames – jumble in all its glory.

'I wonder . . .' said Winifred thoughtfully, 'I wonder what her *Christian* name is?'

CHAPTER SIX

Lent began in February that year and it was very cold, with sleet and bitter winds. The office where I dealt with my impoverished gentlewomen was in Belgravia, and it was my custom to attend the lunchtime services held at St Ermin's on Wednesdays.

The church had been badly bombed and only one aisle could be used, so that it always appeared to be very full with what would normally have been an average congregation crowded into the undamaged aisle. This gave us a feeling of intimacy with each other and separateness from the rest of the world, so that I always thought of us as being rather like the early Christians, surrounded not by lions, admittedly, but by all the traffic and bustle of a weekday lunch hour.

On Ash Wednesday I went to the church as usual with Mrs Bonner, one of my fellow workers, who was drawn more by the name of the preacher than by anything else, for, as she confessed to me, she loved a good sermon. We had hurried over our lunch – a tasteless mess of spaghetti followed by a heavy steamed pudding, excellent Lenten fare, I felt – and were in our seats in good time before the service was due to begin. We had made our way through the ruins, where torn-down wall tablets and an occasional urn or cherub's head were stacked in heaps, and where, incongruous in the middle of so much desolation, we had come upon a little grey woman heating a saucepan of coffee on a Primus stove.

Mrs Bonner settled herself down comfortably with the anticipation of enjoyment and peered round at the people coming in, as if she were at a fashionable wedding. I am afraid that she cannot have found them very interesting, for they were a mixed collection of office workers and passers-by, together with the elderly ladies and dim spinsters who form a proportion of church congregations everywhere. The vicar stood at the door, a gaunt figure in his rusty black cassock, while his wife fussed over the new arrivals, trying to prevent them from following their natural inclination to crowd into the back of the church, leaving no room for late-comers.

I sat quietly, sometimes turning my head, and it was on one of these occasions that, to my surprise and dismay, I found myself looking straight at Everard Bone, who was coming in at that moment. He looked back at me but without any sign of recognition. I suppose I was indistinguishable from many another woman in a neutral winter coat and plain hat and I was thankful for my anonymity. But he was unmistakable. His tall figure, his well-cut overcoat, his long nose and his fair hair were outstanding in this gathering of mediocrity. I felt that I could almost understand the attraction he might have for the kind of person who is drawn to the difficult, the unusual, even the unpleasant.

'What a handsome man – though his nose is a shade too

long,' said Mrs Bonner in a loud whisper, as Everard took his seat a few rows in front of us.

I did not answer but I found that I could not help thinking about him. He was certainly the last person I should have expected to see here. I suppose I was ignorant enough to imagine that all anthropologists must be unbelievers, but the appearance of Everard Bone had shaken my complacency considerably. And yet, of course, it might be that he was here in a professional capacity, observing our behaviour with a view to contributing a note on it to some learned journal. I should have to ask Helena about it the next time I saw her.

A grey little woman – perhaps the same one who had been brewing coffee in the ruins – took her seat at the harmonium and played the first line of a Lenten hymn. The singing was hearty, if a little ragged, and as I sang I began to feel humble and ashamed of myself for my unkind thoughts about Everard Bone. He was certain to be a much nicer person and a better Christian than I was, which would not be difficult. Besides, what reason had I for disliking him? His pointed nose and the fact that I had found him difficult to talk to? His friendship or whatever it was with Helena Napier? The last, certainly, was none of my business.

The preacher was forceful and interesting. His words seemed to knit us together, so that we really were like the early Christians, having all things in common. I tried to banish the feeling that I should prefer not to have all things in common with Everard Bone but it would keep coming back, almost as if he was to be in some way my Lenten penance, and I was quite upset to find myself near him as we crowded out of the church.

'Oh dear, oh *dear*,' whispered Mrs Bonner loudly, 'a very

interesting sermon, but what a lot of talk about *sin*. I suppose it's only to be expected at the beginning of Lent, but it's all so *miserable*, don't you think?'

I could think of no suitable comment and her loud whispering embarrassed me, for I was afraid that Everard Bone's attention would be attracted and that he might recognise me. But I need not have feared, for after standing uncertainly outside the church for a second or two, he walked quickly away in the opposite direction from the one we were taking.

'I can understand that man packing the churches,' went on Mrs Bonner. 'He certainly has a forceful personality, and yet I can't believe we're really so wicked.'

'No, but we have to be made to realise it,' I said unconvincingly, for we certainly seemed harmless enough, elderly and middle-aged people with one or two mild-looking younger men and women. Indeed, Everard Bone had been the only person one would have looked at twice.

'Of course a lot of very *good* people aren't religious in the sense of being churchgoers,' persisted Mrs Bonner.

'No, I know they aren't,' I agreed, feeling that at any moment she would begin talking about it being just as easy to worship God in a beech wood or on the golf links on a fine Sunday morning.

'I must admit I always feel the presence of God much more when I'm in a garden or on a mountain,' she continued.

'I'm afraid I haven't got a garden and am really never on a mountain,' I said. Was it perhaps likely though, that one might feel the presence of God more in Whitehall or Belgrave Square, than say, Vauxhall Bridge Road or Oxford Street? No doubt there was something in it.

'*A garden is a lovesome thing, God wot,*' said Mrs Bonner

rather half-heartedly. 'Well, we must certainly go next week. It's interesting having a different preacher every time – one never knows what will turn up.'

When I got home it occurred to me that I might ask the Napiers whether they had anything suitable for the jumble sale, which was to be held the next Saturday. It also occurred to me that I might find out something about Everard Bone and why he had been at the service. Of course it was nothing to do with me but I was curious to know. Perhaps if I did know I should understand and like him better.

As I walked upstairs past the Napiers' flat I could hear that they were in, for they always seemed to keep their doors half open. Now their voices were raised in what seemed to be an argument.

'Darling, you are *filthy*,' I heard Rocky say, 'putting down a hot greasy frying-pan on the linoleum!'

'Oh, don't fuss so!' came her voice from the sitting-room.

I was just creeping slowly and guiltily past, feeling as if I had been eavesdropping, when Rocky came out of the kitchen with a cloth in his hand and invited me in to have some coffee with them.

I went into the sitting-room where Helena was sitting writing at a desk. Pieces of paper covered with diagrams of little circles and triangles were spread around her.

'That looks very learned,' I said, in the feeble way that one does.

'Oh, it's just kinship diagrams,' she said rather shortly.

Rocky laughed and poured out the coffee. I had the impression that Helena was annoyed with him for having invited me in.

'You mustn't mind if I get on with this,' she said. 'Our paper is due to be read soon and there's a lot to do.'

'I expect you'll be quite relieved when it's over,' I said.

'I shall be,' said Rocky. 'At the moment I have to do all the cooking and washing up. I'm worn out.'

'Well, you're not in the Admiral's villa now, and anyway it won't be long. I thought you *liked* cooking, darling,' said Helena in an edgy voice.

I felt rather uncomfortable. I suppose married people get so used to calling each other 'darling' that they never realise how false it sounds when said in an annoyed or irritable tone.

'I wonder if you could let me have anything for the jumble sale on Saturday?' I asked quickly. 'Old clothes, shoes or anything?'

'Oh, I've always got lots of junk. It will be a good chance to get rid of it,' said Helena without looking up from her writing. 'I'll look out some things this evening.'

'I've got a pair of shoes and a suit that the moth got,' said Rocky, with a glance at his wife. 'I'll bring them to you tonight. Everard Bone is coming to talk to Helena about the paper.'

'Oh, I saw him today,' I said in what I hoped was a casual tone.

'*Did* you?' Helena turned round from her desk, her face animated.

'Yes, I've been to the Lent service at St Ermin's and I saw him there. I was quite surprised. I mean,' I added, not wanting to sound smug, 'I was surprised because one doesn't usually see anyone one knows there.'

'You mean you don't expect anthropologists to go to church, Miss Lathbury,' said Helena. 'But Everard is a convert, quite ardent, you know.'

'I thought converts always were ardent,' said Rocky. 'Surely that's the point about them? The whole set-up is new and interesting to them. Did he get converted in Africa, seeing the missionaries going about their work? One would have thought it might have the opposite effect.'

'Oh, *no*,' I protested, 'they do such splendid work.'

'Splendid work,' Rocky repeated, savouring the words, 'how I love that expression! It has such a very noble sound. Perhaps Miss Lathbury is right – it may have been the sight of his fellow anthropologists that sent him over to the other side.'

'Well, it wasn't in Africa,' said Helena, not sounding amused. 'I think it happened when he was at Cambridge, though he never talks about it.'

'Perhaps it is rather an awkward thing,' said Rocky. 'In many ways life is easier without that.'

'Of course it is more of an intellectual thing with him,' said Helena. 'He knows all the answers.'

'We certainly want people like that,' I said. 'The Church needs intelligent people.'

'I should think so,' said Helena scornfully. 'All those old women swooning over a good-looking curate won't get it anywhere.'

'But our curate isn't good-looking,' I said indignantly, visualising Father Greatorex's short stocky figure in its untidy clothes. 'He isn't even young.'

'And anyway, why should the Church want to get anywhere?' said Rocky. 'I think it's much more comforting to think of it staying just where it is.'

'Wherever that may be,' Helena added.

I made a faint murmur of protest, but it *was* rather faint, for between the two of them I hardly knew where I was, though Rocky's attitude seemed the more sympathetic. 'I'm afraid we aren't all very intelligent about our religion,' I said, slightly on the defensive, 'we probably don't know many of the answers and can't argue cleverly. And yet I suppose there's room for the stupid as well,' I added, for I was thinking of the lines in Bishop Heber's hymn,

> *Richer by far is the heart's adoration,*
> *Dearer to God are the prayers of the poor.*

Though obviously He must be very pleased to have somebody as clever as Everard Bone.

'Did he speak to you?' Helena asked.

'Oh, no, I don't think he saw me, or if he did he didn't recognise me. People don't, you know. I suppose there's really nothing outstanding about me.'

'*Dear* Miss Lathbury,' Rocky smiled, 'how completely untrue!'

Once more I was transported to the terrace of the Admiral's villa and took my place among the little group of Wren officers. Naturally, I did not know what to say.

'Why shouldn't we call you Mildred?' said Rocky suddenly. 'After all, we shall probably be seeing a lot of each other and I think we're going to be friends.'

I felt a little embarrassed but could hardly refuse him.

'And you must call us Helena and Rocky? Could you do that?'

'Yes, I think so,' I said, wondering when I should begin.

'And you can call Everard Bone Everard,' said Helena, suddenly laughing.

'Oh, no,' I protested; 'I can't imagine that ever happening.'

'You should have spoken to him after the service,' she said, 'made some comment on the sermon or something. He's very critical.'

'He hurried away,' I explained, 'so I had no chance to, even if he had recognised me.'

'Oh, it is nice having you living above us,' said Helena surprisingly. 'Just think who we might have had, some dreary couple, or "businesswomen" or a family with children, too awful.'

I hurried upstairs feeling light-hearted and pleased. I was a little amused to think that my having seen Everard Bone at the Lent service should have made me into a nice person to have living above them. For Helena's sake, if not for my own, I ought perhaps to make some friendly overture if he were there next week. I could make it a Lent resolution to try to like him. I began imagining the process, what I should say and how he would respond. Some comment on the preacher or the weather, or a friendly enquiry about the progress of his work would be an obvious beginning.

I stood by the window, leaning on my desk, staring absent-mindedly at my favourite view of the church through the bare trees. The sight of Sister Blatt, splendid on her high old-fashioned bicycle like a ship in full sail, filled me with pleasure. Then Julian Malory came along in his black cloak, talking and laughing with a woman I had not seen before. She was tall and rather nicely dressed but I could not see her face. It suddenly occurred to me that she must be Mrs Gray, who was coming to live in the flat at the vicarage. I watched them out of sight and then went into the kitchen and started to wash some stockings. I had a feeling, although I could not have said why, that she was not quite what we had expected. A clergyman's widow . . . she has such sad eyes . . . Perhaps we had not imagined her *laughing* with Julian, I could not put it more definitely than that.

CHAPTER SEVEN

I was formally introduced to Mrs Gray at the jumble sale on the following Saturday afternoon. She was behind one of the stalls with Winifred, who was looking very pleased and animated, rather reminding me of a child who has asked 'Will you be friends with me?' and has been accepted.

Mrs Gray was, as I had supposed from my first brief glimpse of her, good-looking and nicely dressed, rather *too* nicely dressed for a clergyman's widow, I felt, remembering many such whom I had met before. Her quiet manner suggested self-sufficiency rather than shyness and there was something secret about her smile, as if she saw and thought more than she would ever reveal.

'You will have to tell me what to do,' she said, addressing Winifred and me, 'though I suppose jumble sales are the same the world over.'

'Oh, we get a tough crowd,' said Winifred gaily. 'This isn't a very *nice* part, you know, not like Belgravia. I'm afraid a lot of the people who come to our sales never put their noses inside the church.'

'Do you think they have jumble sales in Belgravia?' asked Mrs Gray; 'that hadn't occurred to me.'

'I believe St Ermin's has one occasionally,' I said.

'One likes to think of Cabinet Ministers' wives attending them,' said Mrs Gray, with what seemed to me a rather affected little laugh.

Winifred laughed immoderately and began rearranging the things on the stall. She and Mrs Gray were in charge of the odds-and-ends or white elephant stall. The stuffed birds made a magnificent centrepiece, surrounded by books, china ornaments, pictures and photograph frames, some with the photographs still in them. Winifred had removed the Edwardian lady and the young clergyman, but others had escaped her and now seemed to stare out almost with indignation from their elaborate tarnished settings, an ugly woman with a strained expression – perhaps a governess – a group of bearded gentlemen in cricket clothes, a wayward-looking child with cropped hair.

'Oh, look,' I heard Winifred exclaiming, 'those poor things! I thought I'd taken them all out.'

'Never mind,' Mrs Gray said in a soothing tone as if she were speaking to a child, 'I think the people who buy the frames don't really notice the photographs in them. I remember in my husband's parish . . .'

So her husband had had a parish, I thought. Somehow I had imagined him an Army chaplain killed in the war. Perhaps he had been elderly, then? After this I could hear no more, for Mrs Gray's voice was quiet and Sister Blatt was upon me. I was glad that I should have her help at the clothing stall, always the most popular. Each garment had been carefully priced, but even so there would be arguments and struggles among the buyers and the usual appeals for one of us to arbitrate.

The sale was being held in the parish hall, a bare room with green-painted walls, from which an oil painting of Father Busby, the first vicar, looked down to bless our activities. At least, we liked to think of him as doing that, though if one examined the portrait carefully it appeared rather as if he were admiring his long bushy beard which one hand seemed to be stroking. A billiard table, a darts board and the other harmless amusements of the boys' club stood at one end of the hall. Behind the hatch near the door Miss Enders, Miss Statham and my Mrs Morris, apparently no longer troubled about birettas and Popes' toes, were busy with the tea urns. Julian Malory, in flannels and sports jacket, supported by Teddy Lemon and a few strong 'lads', waited near the doors to stem the rush when they should be opened. Father Greatorex, wearing a cassock and an old navy blue overcoat of the kind worn by Civil Defence workers during the war, stood uncertainly in the middle of the room.

Sister Blatt looked at me and clicked her teeth with irritation. 'Oh, that man! How he gets on my nerves!'

'He certainly is rather useless at jumble sales,' I agreed, 'but then he's so good, saintly almost,' I faltered, for I really had no evidence to support my statement apart from the fact that his habitual dress of cassock and old overcoat seemed to indicate a disregard for the conventions of this world which implied a preoccupation with higher things.

'Saintly!' snorted Sister Blatt. 'I don't know what's given you that idea. Just because a man takes Orders in middle age and goes about looking like an old tramp! He was no good in business so he went into the Church – that's not what we want.'

'Oh, come now,' I protested, 'surely you're being rather hard? After all, he *is* a good man . . .'

'And Mr Mallett and Mr Conybeare, just look at them,' she went on in a voice loud enough for our two churchwardens to hear. 'It wouldn't do them any harm to soil their hands with a little honest toil. Teddy Lemon and the boys put up all the trestles and carried the urns.'

'Yes, Sister, we found everything had been done when we put in an appearance,' said Mr Mallett, a round jolly little man. 'It was quite a blow, I can tell you. We had hoped to be able to help you ladies. But they also serve who only stand and wait, as the poet says.'

'You certainly came early enough,' said Sister Blatt with heavy sarcasm.

'The early bird catches the worm,' said Mr Conybeare, a tall stringy man with pince-nez.

'Now, Mr Conybeare, I hope you're not suggesting that there're any worms here,' giggled Miss Statham from behind the hatch. 'You'll catch something else if you don't get out of the way. And don't think I'm going to give you a cup of tea till you've earned it . . .'

But at that moment, Julian, watch in hand, ordered the doors to be opened. The surging crowd outside was kept in check by Teddy Lemon and his supporters, while Julian took the threepences for admission; but once past him they rushed for the stalls.

'Talk about landing on the Normandy beaches,' said Sister Blatt, 'some of our jumble sale crowd would make splendid Commandos.'

The next few minutes needed great concentration and firmness. I collected money, gave change and tried at the same time to rearrange the tumbled garments, settle arguments and prevent the elderly from being injured in the crush.

Sister Blatt was free with advice and criticism. 'You'll never get into that, Mrs Ryan,' she called out derisively to a stout Irishwoman, a Roman Catholic incidentally, who was always in the front of the queue for our sales.

Mrs Ryan laughed good-humouredly and clutched the flowered artificial silk dress she had picked up. Her soft brogue beguiled me, as always, so that I listened, fascinated, not knowing what she said. I just caught the words 'a lovely man' as she went off with her dress.

Sister Blatt was laughing in spite of herself. 'Well, really, that woman has a nerve, inviting me over to *their* jumble sale next week and telling me that their new priest, Father Bogart, is a lovely man! As if that would attract me!'

'Oh, but think how it does and how it has done, that kind of thing. Whence would the Church be if it hadn't been for a "lovely man" here and there? It's rather nice to think of churches being united through jumble sales,' I suggested. 'I wonder if the Methodists are having one too?'

'Churches united through jumble sales?' said Julian, coming up to our stall. 'Well, we might do worse.' He glanced round at the crowd, less struggling than it had been half an hour ago, with satisfaction. 'You didn't persuade your friends the Napiers to come?' he asked me.

'I'm afraid I didn't try,' I admitted. 'They sent some things but somehow I just couldn't imagine them here. It wouldn't be the right kind of setting for them.'

Julian glanced round at the dingy green walls. 'Well, I suppose we all of us think that we're worth a better one.'

'Except for Father Greatorex,' said Sister Blatt spitefully.

'He's quite in his place here. He hasn't done a thing all afternoon. And why doesn't he take his coat off? He must be boiled.'

'Oh, look,' I said, 'he's taking tea to Miss Malory and Mrs Gray.'

'Well, that completely out of character,' said Sister Blatt.

'You can hardly blame him for wanting to do it,' said Julian, watching the little group with interest. 'I wonder if they have cakes? He would hardly be able to carry everything at once. I think I had better go and help.'

I saw him go to the hatch, come away with a plate of brightly coloured iced cakes and then offer one to Mrs Gray.

Sister Blatt and I looked at each other.

'Well,' I began rather doubtfully, 'the vicar is always charming to new parishioners, or he ought to be. That's a known thing.'

'But *we* hadn't got any tea,' she pointed out indignantly. 'I think it was extremely rude of him to ignore us like that. All because of a new face.

> *Make new friends but keep the old,*
> *One is silver, the other gold . . .'*

she recited. 'Perhaps we shouldn't value ourselves as highly as that, but all the same . . .'

'Yes, I think he did rather forget his manners,' I agreed. 'Of course, Mrs Gray is going to live in his house, you know, so perhaps he feels that the relationship between them should be especially cordial.'

'Oh, rubbish! I never heard such far-fetched excuses.'

67

'Oh-ho, jealous are you, Sister?' said Mr Mallett roguishly. 'You'd better go and get your tea before all the cakes go.'

'You mean before you and Mr Conybeare eat them all,' said Sister Blatt. 'I expect you've been tucking in for hours.'

'Now you ladies, run along. I'll look after the stall,' said Mr Mallett, picking up a dress and holding it up against himself in a comic manner. 'I'll guarantee that business will look up now that I'm in charge.'

'Yes, I think we can safely leave the stall now,' I said, with a backward glance at the tumbled garments lying on the bare boards of the table. An old velvet coat trimmed with moth-eaten white rabbit, a soiled pink georgette evening dress of the nineteen-twenties trimmed with bead embroidery, a mangy fur with mad staring eyes priced at sixpence – these things were 'regulars' and nobody ever bought them.

At the tea hatch, too, trade had slackened and we were able to talk as we ate and drank. Mrs Morris's sing-song voice could be heard above the others: 'Lovely *antique* pieces they've got. I said what about giving them a bit of polish and *he* said oh yes a good idea, but *she* said not to bother, it was the washing up and cleaning that was the main thing.'

I knew that she was talking about the Napiers, but though my natural curiosity would have liked to hear more, I felt I could hardly encourage her. Is it a kind of natural delicacy that some of us have, or do we just lack the courage to follow our inclinations?

'Of course he's been in the Navy,' said Mrs Morris.

'Yes, Lieutenant-Commander Napier was in Italy,' I said in a rather loud clear voice, as if trying to raise the conversation to a higher level.

'How nice,' said Miss Enders. 'My sister once went there on

68

a tour, my married sister, that is, the one who lives at Raynes Park.'

'Such a nice young man, he is, Mr Napier,' said Mrs Morris. 'Too good for her, I shouldn't wonder.'

My efforts had obviously not been very successful but I did not feel I could try again.

'The Italians are very forward with women,' declared Miss Statham. 'Of course it's unwise to walk about after dark in a foreign town anywhere when you're alone.'

'Pinch your bottom they would before you could say knife,' burst out Mrs Morris, but the short silence that followed told her that she had gone too far. Strictly speaking, she was socially inferior to Miss Enders and Miss Statham; it was only her participation in parish activities that gave her a temporary equality.

'Of course my sister had her husband with her,' said Miss Enders stiffly, 'so there couldn't be anything like that.'

Sister Blatt let out a snort of laughter.

'Excuse me . . .' Julian came up behind us with some empty cups and saucers which he put down on the hatch.

'Did you get some of my home-made sandwich cake, Father?' asked Miss Statham anxiously. 'I particularly wanted you to try it.'

'Yes, thank you, delicious,' he murmured absently.

'I don't think he did, you know,' said Miss Enders to me in a low tone. 'He only took a plate of fairies and iced buns.'

'Perhaps Father Greatorex did,' I suggested.

'If you ask me, I think Mr Mallett and Mr Conybeare had most of it. They were the first to have their tea. And I did see Teddy Lemon take a piece.'

'I'm sure he deserved a good tea,' I said. 'He worked very hard.'

'Oh, yes, Mr Mallett and Mr Conybeare didn't do a hand's turn. Just got in everybody's way as usual.'

The group started to break up and we went back to the stalls to tidy them. Another jumble sale was over.

Winifred came up to me, her eyes shining. 'Oh, Mildred,' she breathed, '*what* do you think her name is?'

I said I had no idea.

'Allegra!' she told me. 'Isn't that lovely? Allegra Gray.'

I found myself wondering if it was really Mrs Gray's name, or if she had perhaps adopted it instead of a more conventional and uninteresting one. 'Wasn't Allegra the name of Byron's natural daughter?' I asked.

'Byron! How splendid!' Winifred clasped her hands in rapture.

'I'm not sure that it was splendid,' I persisted.

'Oh, but Byron was such a splendid romantic person,' said Winifred, 'and that's the main thing, isn't it?'

'Is it really?' I asked, still determined that I would not be forced to admire Mrs Gray. 'Doesn't one look for other qualities in people?'

'Oh, Mildred, you're so practical,' laughed Winifred. 'Of course I've always been silly and romantic – it's just how you're made.'

I thought of the Christina Rossetti in its limp green suede cover. *When I am dead, my dearest* . . . when there had perhaps never been a dearest. Weren't we all a little like that? I began to consider the people I knew in terms of splendour and romance. I had certainly known very few who could be described as splendid and romantic. Clergymen could and should be left out of it straight away, I felt, and that didn't leave many others. Only Rocky Napier and Everard Bone, perhaps, who were both good-looking in their different styles. Rocky had charm, too, and must have seemed a splendidly romantic person to a great many women.

I crept quietly up to my flat and began to prepare supper. The house seemed to be empty. Saturday night . . . perhaps it was right that it should be and I sitting alone eating a very small chop. After I had washed up I would listen to *Saturday Night Theatre* and do my knitting. I wondered where the Napiers were, if they were out together, or if Helena was with Everard Bone. *My son is at a meeting of the Prehistoric Society* . . . I began to laugh, bending over the frying-pan. There was certainly nothing romantic about *him*, but was he perhaps just a little splendid?

CHAPTER EIGHT

During the next few weeks the weather improved and suddenly it was almost spring. The time came round for my annual luncheon with William Caldicote, the brother of my friend Dora. This was always something of a ceremonial occasion and dated from the days when Dora, and perhaps even William himself, had hoped that 'something might come of it'. But as the years had passed our relationship had settled down into a comfortable dull thing. I do not remember when it was that I first began to realise that William was not the kind of man to marry, and that I myself did not mind in the very least. It now seemed so natural that if we were in a taxi together he should express the emotion that it was a relief to sit down rather than that it was pleasant to be alone with me. His care for his food and drink, too, was something I accepted and even found rather endearing, especially as I benefited from it myself. I could always be sure of a good meal with William.

He worked in a Ministry somewhere near Whitehall and was now a rather grey-looking man in the late thirties, with surprisingly bright beady eyes. We always met in a restaurant, one in Soho where he was known, and as I hurried towards it – for I was a little late – I began thinking that William wasn't really the most suitable person to be having luncheon with on this fresh spring day. Surely a splendid romantic person was the obvious companion? The blue sky full of billowing white clouds, the thrilling little breezes, the gay hats of some of the women I met, the mimosa on the barrows – all made me feel disinclined for William's company, his preoccupation with his health and his food and his spiteful old-maidish delight in gossip.

He was in a fussy mood today, I could see, as he went rather petulantly through the menu. The liver would probably be overdone, the duck not enough done, the weather had been too mild for the celery to be good – it seemed as if there was really nothing we could eat. I sat patiently while William and the waiter consulted in angry whispers. A bottle of wine was brought. William took it up and studied the label suspiciously. I watched apprehensively as he tasted it, for he was one of those men to whom the formality really meant something and he was quite likely to send the bottle back and demand another. But as he tasted, he relaxed. It was all right, or perhaps not that, but it would do.

'A tolerable wine, Mildred,' he said, 'unpretentious, but I think you will like it.'

'Unpretentious, just like me,' I said stupidly, touching the feather in my brown hat.

'We really should have a tolerable wine today. Spring seems to be almost with us,' he observed in a dry tone.

'Nuits St Georges,' I read from the label. 'How exciting that sounds! Does it mean the Nights of St George? It conjures up the most wonderful pictures, armour and white horses

73

and dragons, flames too, perhaps a great procession by torch-light.'

He looked at me doubtfully for a moment and then, seeing that I had not yet tasted my wine, began to explain that Nuits St Georges was a place where there were vineyards, but that not every bottle bearing the name on its label was to be taken as being of the first quality. 'It might,' he said seriously, 'be an *ordinaire*. Always remember that. A *little learning is a dangerous thing*, Mildred.'

'*Drink deep, or taste not the Pierian spring*,' I went on, pleased at being able to finish the quotation. 'But I'm afraid I shall never have the chance to drink deep so I must remain igno-rant.'

'Ah, Pope at Twickenham,' sighed William. 'And now Popesgrove is a telephone exchange. It makes one feel very sad.' He paused for a moment and then began to eat with great enjoyment.

It was certainly an excellent luncheon and what we were having did not appear to be on the menu. After we had been eating for some time and had satisfied our first brutish hunger, he began to ask me about myself, what I had been doing since the last time we met, whether there had been any interesting cases before my committee.

'How I should love to do work of that kind,' he said, 'I feel that I almost have a natural gift for it. You see, I would under-stand so well what these unfortunate gentlepeople had lost. The great house in Belgrave Square with the servants bringing up trays from the basement, the Edwardian country house par-ties with visiting foreign royalties, the villa at Nice or Bordighera for the winter months . . .'

'Oh, but the people we have to deal with aren't usually as

74

grand as that,' I said, marveling at William's understanding, when he and Dora, the children of a doctor, had been brought up in a Birmingham suburb. 'They are gentlepeople, of course, but more like us, daughters of clergymen or professional people, who may have been comfortably off but never really wealthy.'

'A pity, I mean that you don't get the grander kind, because the greater the fall the more poignant the tragedy.'

'Yes, I suppose so.' I remembered reading something of the kind at school when we had been studying Shakespeare's tragedies. 'But we do have some very tragic cases,' I said, 'and I'm afraid there is nothing at all dramatic about them, poor souls.'

'Ah, yes.' He became serious, but then seemed to brighten up. 'Tell me about the new people who have come to live in your house.'

I began to describe the Napiers, rather hesitantly, for I did not want to make too much of their disagreements as I knew that William with his love of gossip and scandal would seize eagerly on any scrap. Not that it really mattered, I supposed, and as I went on talking I must have become less cautious for I found myself, rather to my dismay, insisting that *he* was much too nice for *her*.

'But, my dear, that's so often the way,' said William, 'one should never be surprised at it. All these delightful men married to such monsters, such fiends.'

'Oh, Mrs Napier isn't like that,' I protested, 'it's just that he is exceptionally nice.'

I suppose it must have been the Nuits St Georges or the spring day or the intimate atmosphere of the restaurant, but I heard myself, to my horror, murmuring something about Rocky

Napier being just the kind of person I should have liked for myself.

There was a marked silence after I said this, during which I looked round the restaurant with detachment, noticing a waiter concocting some dish over a flame at a side table, a man leaning across to touch the hand of the girl sitting opposite him, and I suddenly felt irritated with William for being so grey and fussy and Dora's brother whom I had known for years.

'But my dear Mildred, *you* mustn't marry,' he was saying indignantly. 'Life is disturbing enough as it is without these alarming suggestions. I always think of you as being so very balanced and sensible, such an excellent woman. I do hope you're *not* thinking of getting married?'

He stared across the table at me, his eyes and mouth round and serious with alarm. I began to laugh to break the unnatural tension which had arisen, and also at Dora's idea, which I believe she still cherished, that William and I might marry one day.

'Oh, no, of course not!' I said. 'I'm so sorry if I alarmed you. Why, I don't know anyone suitable, to begin with.'

'What about the vicar?' asked William suspiciously.

'Father Malory? Oh, he doesn't believe in marriage for the clergy, and in any case he isn't really the kind of person I should want to marry,' I assured him.

'Well, that's a relief,' said William. 'We, my dear Mildred, are the observers of life. Let other people get married by all means, the more the merrier.' He lifted the bottle, judged the amount left in it and refilled his own glass but not mine. 'Let Dora marry if she likes. She hasn't your talent for observation.'

I suppose I should have felt pleased at this little compliment but I was somehow irritated. In any case, it was not much of a compliment, making me out to be an unpleasant inhuman sort of person. Was that how I appeared to others? I wondered.

'What news have you of Dora?' I asked, to change the subject. 'I'm afraid I owe her a letter.'

'Oh, a lot of news.' He spread out his hands with an expansive gesture and leaned back in his chair. 'Much seems to happen in that little world. And yet I suppose a girls' school has as much happening in it as most worlds and the undercurrents are more deadly.'

'Oh? Anything in particular?'

William leaned forward and his small beady eyes gleamed with delight. '*Unpleasantness*,' he whispered dramatically.

'Oh, dear, what about?' I asked, but I was not surprised, for there seemed to be so much of it at Dora's schools. I had at times found myself wondering disloyally whether she did not perhaps invite it.

'Something about the girls wearing hats in chapel, or not wearing hats – it doesn't really matter which. Oh, the infinite variety and complication of that little world! The greater things, birth, death and copulation, are just passed by as if they were nothing.'

'Well, they don't really have things like that in a girls' school, at least not often,' I said, my thoughts going back to an occasion in my own schooldays when a mistress had died and her coffin had been placed in the chapel, 'and then only death.'

'Oh, not the other things!' said William, now in high good humour. 'But supposing they did!'

I stirred my coffee, feeling embarrassed, particularly as his voice had a penetrating quality.

'Of course Miss Protheroe is rather difficult to get on with,' I ventured. 'I've only met her once, but she seemed to me the kind of person I shouldn't like to have to work with myself.'

'But poor Dora is so irritating, too,' said William. 'I can never bear her for more than a weekend.'

We were standing outside on the pavement. After the warm rosy gloom of the restaurant, the fresh spring air was like another bottle of wine. There was a barrow full of spring flowers just opposite.

'Oh, look, mimosa!' I exclaimed, though not with any hope that William would buy me any. 'I must have some.'

'It always reminds me of cafés in seaside towns, all dried-up and rattling with the bottles of sauces on the table,' said William, standing by while I bought a bunch.

'Yes, I know the fluffiness doesn't last long, but it's so lovely while it does.'

'You seem unlike yourself today,' he said disapprovingly. 'I hope it wasn't the Nuits St Georges.'

'You know I'm not used to wine, particularly in the middle of the day,' I said, 'but it's rather pleasant to be unlike oneself occasionally.'

'I don't agree. They've moved me to a new office and I don't like it at all. Different pigeons come to the windows.'

'I've never been in your office,' I said boldly, 'may I come back with you and see it?'

'Oh, the prison, you mean, with its stone walls and iron bars, which the poet tells us do *not* a prison make. Yes, you may come if you like.'

We walked into Trafalgar Square and then into an anonymous-looking entrance in a back street somewhere beyond it. Grey-looking men like William, some even greyer, were hurrying in. He greeted one or two of them; they seemed to have double-barrelled names like Calverley-Hibbert and Radcliffe-Forde, but they did not look any the less grey for all that.

'Here we are!' William flung open a door with his name on it and I went in. Two elderly grey men were sitting at a table, one with a bag of sweets which he hastily put away into a drawer, the other with a card index which he naturally did not attempt to conceal. William did not acknowledge them in any way nor did they take any notice of him. He sat down at an enormous desk in the centre of the room, which had two telephones on it and a line of wire baskets, importantly labelled and stacked with files. I had no very clear idea of what it was that he did.

'This is a nice room,' I said, going to the window, 'and what a lovely desk you have.' I felt embarrassed at the presence of the grey men and did not quite know what to say. But suddenly a rattling sound, as if a trolley was being wheeled along the corridor, was heard and the two men leaped up, each carrying a china mug.

'Oh, excuse me,' said William, leaping up too and taking a china mug from a drawer in his desk, 'I think I hear the tea.'

He did not offer to get me any, nor did I feel I really wanted any as it was barely three o'clock. I wondered why the grey men, who were obviously of a lower grade or status than William, had not fetched his tea for him, but perhaps there was a rigid etiquette in these matters. Also, knowing William's fussiness, it was quite likely that he would insist on fetching his own tea. I began to wonder whether important-sounding people like Calverley-Hibbert and Radcliffe-Forde were also at this moment hurrying along corridors with mugs. Perhaps even the Minister himself was joining in the general scramble. I went on standing by the window and looked out at the view which was of another office building, perhaps the same Ministry, where there were rows of uncurtained windows and the activities of the rooms were exposed as if it was a doll's house. Grey men sat at desks, their hands moving among files; some sipped tea, one read a newspaper, another manipulated a typewriter with the uncertain touch of two fingers. A girl leaned from a window, another combed her hair, a third typed with expert speed. A young man embraced a girl in a rough playful way and she pulled his hair while the other occupants of the room looked on encouragingly ... I watched, fascinated, and was deep in contemplation when William and his underlings came back with their steaming mugs.

'Is that another Ministry across there?' I asked.

'Ah, yes, the Ministry of Desire,' said William solemnly.

I protested, laughing.

'They always look so far away, so not-of-this-world, those wonderful people,' he explained. 'But perhaps we seem like that to them. They may call us the Ministry of Desire.'

At that moment a clock struck a quarter past three. William jumped up, and picking up a paper bag from one of the wire trays, walked over to the window and flung it open. There was a whirring of wings and a crowd of pigeons swooped down on to the flat piece of roof outside the window. Some hopped up on to the sill and one even came into the room and perched on William's shoulder. He took two rolls from the paper bag and began to crumble them and throw the pieces among the birds.

One of the grey men looked up from his card-index and gave me a faint, as it were pitying, smile.

'Does this happen every afternoon?' I asked William.

'Oh, yes, and every morning too. I couldn't get through the day without my pigeons. I feel like one of those rather dreadful pictures of St Francis – I'm sure you and Dora had one at school – but it's a good feeling and one does so like to have that.'

I could not help smiling at the association of St Francis with a civil servant, but I had not known about William's fondness for pigeons and there was something unexpected and endearing about it. He seemed so completely absorbed in them, calling them by names, encouraging this one to come forward and telling that one not to be greedy, that I decided that he had forgotten all about me and it was time to go home.

'I really ought to be going now,' I said. 'I must be keeping you from your work,' I added, with no thought of irony until after I had said it.

William returned to his desk and opened a file. 'You must come and see my new flat,' he said, mentioning an address in Chelsea which seemed familiar.

I thanked him for my luncheon and walked away, carrying my bunch of mimosa down the bare corridors. Of course, I remembered as I waited for a bus, Everard Bone and his mother lived in that street, that was why the address had seemed familiar. What a good thing I had not said anything to William about Helena Napier and Everard Bone, though it was unlikely that he would know them. *My son is at a meeting of the Prehistoric Society . . .* I heard again Mrs Bone's querulous voice and smiled to myself.

When I reached the front door of my house I saw Rocky Napier approaching from the other side of the street.

'*Mimosa!*' he exclaimed. 'Why didn't *I* think of that?'

'I couldn't resist it,' I said. 'It makes one think . . .'

'Of Italy and the Riviera, of course.'

'I've never been there,' I reminded him; 'it's just that it seemed such a lovely day and I felt I wanted it.'

'Yes, that's a better reason.'

We walked upstairs together. As we came to his door some impulse made me unwrap the flowers. I saw that the bunch divided easily into two branches. 'Do have a piece,' I said, 'I should like you to.'

'How sweet of you and how like you,' he said easily. 'Have you got anything nice for tea? I haven't.'

'I don't think I have particularly,' I said, my thoughts going inside my cake tin with a harlequin on the lid and remembering only a small wedge of sandwich cake there.

'I know, let's be daring and go *out* to tea.'

I stood holding the mimosa. 'We must put this in water first.'

'Yes, put it in our kitchen.' He took it from me, filled a jug with water and put it on the draining board.

We went out again to a café he knew, a place I had never discovered, where they had good cakes. But it hardly seemed to matter about the cakes. Perhaps it was because I had had a large and rather late luncheon, but I didn't feel very hungry. He was so gay and amusing and he made me feel that I was gay and amusing too and some of the things I said were really quite witty.

It wasn't till afterwards that I remembered the Wren officers. By that time it was evening and I was back in my own kitchen, wondering what to have for supper. I suddenly realised, too, that we had left all the mimosa in the Napiers' kitchen. I could hardly go and ask him to give me back my

82

half of it. Anyway, Helena had come in and I could hear them laughing together. I shouldn't have gossiped to William in that naughty way, and in Lent, too. It served me right that I should have no mimosa to remind me of the spring day, but only a disturbed feeling which was most unlike me. There was a vase of catkins and twigs on the table in my sitting-room. 'Oh, the kind of women who bring dry twigs into the house and expect leaves to come on them!' Hadn't Rocky said something like that at tea?

CHAPTER NINE

Rocky returned my half of the mimosa next morning, when I was hurrying to go out to my work. It had lost its first fluffiness and looked like the café table decoration that William disliked. The spring weather had also gone and Rocky himself appeared in a dressing-gown with his hair ruffled. I felt too embarrassed to look at him and put my hand out through the half-open kitchen door and took the mimosa quickly, putting it in the vase with the twigs and catkins.

On the bus I began thinking that William had been right and I was annoyed to have to admit it. Mimosa did lose its first freshness too quickly to be worth buying and I must not allow myself to have feelings, but must only observe the effects of other people's.

I sat down at my table and began going grimly through a card-index of names and addresses. Edith Bankes-Tolliver, 118 Montgomery Square . . . that was quite near me. I wondered if she came to our church. Perhaps Julian would know her . . . I really ought to make a list of the distressed gentlewomen in our district and try to visit them. Most of them lived alone and it was quite likely that I might be able to do some shopping for them or read to them or even just sit and let them talk . . . I was deep in thoughts of the good works I was going to immerse myself in, when Mrs Bonner came into the room and reminded me that it was Wednesday and that we had arranged to go to the lunchtime service at St Ermin's. This meant that we had to hurry over our lunch – unlike yesterday's meal, it could not, I felt, be called luncheon – which we had at a self-service cafeteria near the church. Our trays rattled along on a moving belt at a terrifying speed, so that at the end of it all I found myself, bewildered and resentful, holding a tray full of things I would never have chosen had I had time to think about it, and without a saucer for my coffee. Mrs Bonner, who always came to such places, had done much better and began explaining to me where I had gone wrong.

'You get the saucer *after* you've taken a roll, if you have one. I generally don't as we are told not to waste bread, and *before* you get the hot dish,' she said, as we stood with our trays look-ing for two vacant places.

'Oh, that must be where I went wrong,' I said, looking down at the bullet-hard roll which I was sure I was going to waste. 'I think one ought to be allowed a trial run-through first, a sort of dress rehearsal.'

Mrs Bonner laughed heartily at the idea and at that moment saw two places at a table with two Indian gentlemen. 'I shouldn't go here if I were *alone*,' she whispered before we sat down, 'you never know, do you, but I think it's all right if you have somebody with you.'

Our companions certainly looked harmless enough and were evidently students of some kind, as they appeared to be discussing examination results. I listened fascinated to their staccato voices and the way they kept calling each other 'old boy'. They took no notice of us whatsoever and I do not think Mrs Bonner need have feared even if she had been alone.

We settled ourselves and our food at the table and I paused for a moment to draw breath before eating. The room was enormous, like something in a nightmare, one could hardly see from one end of it to the other, and as far as the eye could see was dotted with tables which were all full. In addition, a file of people moved in through a door at one end and formed a long line, fenced off from the main part of the room by a brass rail.

> 'Time like an ever-rolling stream
> Bears all its sons away . . .'

I said, more to myself than to Mrs Bonner. 'This place gives me a hopeless kind of feeling.'

'Oh, it's quite cheap and the food isn't bad if you don't come here too often,' she said, cheerfully down-to-earth as always. 'It's useful if you're in a hurry.'

'One wouldn't believe there could be so many people,' I said, 'and one must love them all.' These are our neighbours, I thought, looking round at the clerks and students and typists and elderly eccentrics, bent over their dishes and newspapers.

'Hurry up, dear,' said Mrs Bonner briskly, 'it's twenty past already.'

The Indians had left us by now so I ventured to tell her what I had been thinking.

She looked up from her chocolate trifle, rather shocked. 'Oh, I don't think the Commandment is meant to be taken as literally as that,' she said sensibly. 'We really ought to be

86

going, you know, or we shan't get a good seat. You know how crowded the church gets.'

We managed to find places rather near the back and Mrs Bonner expressed doubts as to whether we should be able to hear – the man last week had mumbled rather. Today the preacher was to be Archdeacon Hoccleve, a name that was unknown to me, and I guessed that he would be some old country clergyman who would certainly mumble. But I was completely wrong. He was an elderly man, certainly, but of a handsome and dignified appearance and his voice was strong and dramatic. His sermon too was equally unexpected. Hitherto the Lenten series had followed a more or less discernible course, but Archdeacon Hoccleve departed completely from the pattern by preaching about Judgement Day. It was altogether a most peculiar sermon, full of long quotations from the more obscure English poets, and although the subject may in itself have been a suitable one for Lent, its matter and the manner of its delivery occasioned dismay and bewilderment rather than any more suitable feelings. It was also much longer than the sermons usually were, so that some of the office workers, who no doubt had stringent lunch hours, could be seen creeping out before it was finished.

Mrs Bonner was disgusted. 'That talk about the *Dies Irae*,' she said, 'that's Roman Catholic, you know. It ought not to be allowed here. Not that he seemed very High in other ways, though. I couldn't make him out at all. Some of the things he said were really quite abusive.'

We were by now at the church door, moving slowly out. I had been so absorbed and astonished by the sermon that I had forgotten to look for Everard Bone and I now saw that he was standing almost beside me. I remembered my resolution to try to think well of him and to make some friendly advance if the opportunity should arise. I felt that there could never be a better one than the extraordinary sermon we had just heard.

'Good afternoon,' I said quietly; 'what did you think of the sermon?'

He looked down at me with a puzzled expression and then his rather austere features softened into a smile. 'Good afternoon,' he said. 'I'm afraid I was so busy trying to keep myself from laughing that I was hardly able to take it in. I had always thought that grown-up people should have no difficulty in keeping their composure, but I know differently now.'

We were standing by ourselves, for Mrs Bonner, seeing that I was talking to a man, had slipped tactfully away. But I knew that I should have to face her questionings, unspoken though they might be, at the office next day. For she was both inquisitive and romantic and could not bear that anyone under forty should remain unmarried.

'Yes, it was certainly most unexpected,' I said, liking him better for admitting to a human failing. 'How is your paper getting on?' I asked, trying to put an interested note into my voice.

'Oh, we are giving it in two or three weeks' time. I believe you wanted to come and hear it, but I shouldn't advise you to. It will be frightfully dull.'

'Oh, but I should like to hear it,' I said, remembering that Rocky and I had been going to observe the anthropologists.

'Well, Helena can get you an invitation,' he said. 'And now, if you'll excuse me, I really must hurry off. Perhaps I shall see you there.'

I felt that I had made a slight advance, that an infinitesimal amount of virtue had gone out of me, and although I did not really like him I did not feel as actively hostile to him as I had before. But how was it possible to compare him with Rocky? All the same, I told myself sternly, it would not do to go thinking about Rocky like this. Yesterday, with the unexpected spring weather and the wine at luncheon there had perhaps been some excuse; today there was none. The grey March day, the hurried unappetising meal and the alarming sermon made it more suitable that I should think of the stream of unattractive humanity in the cafeteria, the Judgment Day, even Everard Bone.

I decided to call in at the vicarage on my way home to see Winifred. It seemed a long time since I had had a talk with her and she would be interested to hear about the sermon.

I rang the bell and Mrs Jubb came to the door. Miss Malory was upstairs with Mrs Gray, helping her to get settled in. Perhaps I would like to go up to them?

I walked slowly upstairs, pausing on the first landing by the picture of the infant Samuel which hung in a dark corner and wondering if I should not turn back after all, for a talk with Winifred and Mrs Gray was not quite the same as the talk with Winifred which I had intended. But I decided that as Mrs Gray was coming to live at the vicarage I might just as well get to know her, so I went on and knocked at a door from behind which I heard voices.

'Oh, it's Miss Lathbury; how nice!' Mrs Gray herself opened the door. I looked beyond her into the room which Julian had been distempering not many weeks earlier. It was now attractively furnished and there was a coal fire burning in the grate. Winifred was crouching on the hearthrug, tacking up the hem of a curtain.

'Hasn't Allegra made this room nice, Mildred?' she said as I came in. 'You'd never recognise it as being the same place.'

'Well, Winifred has helped me so much,' said Mrs Gray. 'You know what a lot there is to do when you move.'

I agreed, noting to myself that they were now 'Allegra' and 'Winifred' to each other, and being surprised and, I was forced to admit, a little irritated. 'Moving is certainly a business,' I observed tritely, 'but you seem to have everything beautifully arranged.' I remembered that I had not helped Helena Napier with the hems of her curtains when she moved in. I had merely peered through the banisters at her furniture being taken in and had only offered to help when it seemed almost certain that there would be nothing for me to do. What a much nicer character Winifred was than I! And yet perhaps the circumstances were a little different. One could hardly offer to help complete strangers, especially when they were as independent as Helena Napier. 'Can't I help with the curtains?' I asked.

'Well, that would be most kind.' The words hardly seemed to be out of my mouth before Mrs Gray had picked up another pile of curtains which were to be shortened along the line of the pins. I was a little dismayed, as we often are when our offers of help are taken at their face value, and I set to work rather grimly, especially as Mrs Gray herself was not doing anything at all. She was sitting gracefully in an armchair, stroking back her hair which was arranged at the back of her head in a kind of Grecian knot. This style, together with her pale oval face and rather vague graceful air, made her appear like a heroine in an Edwardian novel. There was something slightly unreal about her.

'I'm afraid I'm not very good at sewing,' she said, as if in explanation of her idleness, 'but I can at least be making a cup of tea. I do hope you can stay, Miss Lathbury?'

'Thank you, I should like to.'

She went out of the room and I could hear her filling a kettle and collecting china. I also heard a step on the stairs and Julian's voice saying 'May I come up? I can hear the attractive rattle of tea things. I hope I'm not too late?'

He did not come straight into the room where we were, but stayed to talk to Mrs Gray in the kitchen. Winifred and I sat with our curtains, not speaking. I could feel that we were both wanting to talk about Mrs Gray, but that was naturally quite impossible at that moment.

'One of these curtains seems a little longer than the other,' I remarked in a loud, stilted tone. 'I wonder if they were hung up or just measured with a tape? You often find when you come to hang them that there's some inequality in the length.'

Julian came into the room carrying a tray with crockery, bread and butter, jam and a cake. Mrs Gray followed with the tea.

'Isn't it fun, just like a picnic,' said Winifred from her seat on the hearthrug.

'I really ought not to be eating your jam, Mrs Gray,' I protested in a way one did in those days. 'I like plain bread and butter just as well, really I do.'

'Oh, please have some of this,' she said. 'It isn't really my ration, it was a present from Father Greatorex.'

'What, does Greatorex make jam?' asked Julian. 'I never knew he had such accomplishments.'

'Oh, no,' Mrs Gray laughed; 'just imagine it, the poor old thing! This was made by his sister who lives in the country. It's really delicious.'

'How nice of him to give it to you,' I said, 'it's certainly lovely jam.'

'Oh, Allegra's the sort of person people *want* to give things to,' said Winifred enthusiastically. 'Mildred, doesn't this hearthrug look familiar to you?'

I glanced at it and then realised to my surprise that I had seen it somewhere before. In the vicarage, surely, perhaps in Julian's study?

'Yes, it's the one out of Julian's study,' said Winifred.

'Terribly kind of him, wasn't it?' said Mrs Gray. 'I hadn't got one suitable for this room and I just happened to be admiring it in Father Malory's study, quite *innocently* of course, when he gave it to me!'

'It looks much nicer in Mrs Gray's room than it did in my study,' said Julian, 'and anyway a rug isn't really necessary in a study.

I noted with interest that they were still 'Mrs Gray' and 'Father Malory' to each other. 'It certainly matches this carpet very well,' I ventured.

'Yes, but it matched Father Malory's carpet too,' said Mrs Gray. 'It was really very self-sacrificing of him to give it to me.'

Julian murmured a little in embarrassment.

'Of course,' went on Mrs Gray in a clear voice as if she were making a speech, 'I always feel that one *ought* to give men the opportunity for self-sacrifice; their natures are so much less noble than ours.'

'Oh, do you think so?' asked Winifred seriously. 'I have known some very fine men.'

Julian smiled indulgently, but said nothing. I felt it was not a very suitable remark for a clergyman's widow to have made, though it was certainly amusing in a rather cheap way.

'I really must be going now,' I said in a voice that may have sounded a little chilly.

'Oh, Mildred, you haven't finished your curtains,' said Winifred.

'No I'm sorry, I'm afraid I haven't.'

'I know, why don't you come to tea on Friday and finish them then?' suggested Mrs Gray, smiling rather sweetly.

'Thank you, that would be nice,' I said, very much taken aback. I had not really imagined that she would expect me to finish the curtains.

'Then you can see the rest of my little flat,' said Mrs Gray. 'It isn't really on show yet, but I hope to have got it tidy by then.'

'Shall I come down with you?' asked Julian.

'Oh, please don't bother. I'll let myself out,' I said. I hurried down the stairs, feeling that I had made an ungraceful exit. The three upstairs seemed so self-sufficient, as if they did not want me there. Was I annoyed because Mrs Gray seemed to be getting on so well with the Malorys? I asked myself. It surely could not be that I was jealous? No, I dismissed that disturbing thought from my mind as quickly as it came in. Today was obviously not a good day, that was it. It had not started well and it would not end well. But I could at least save something of it by going home and doing some washing.

'Hullo! You look like a wet week at Blackpool,' Sister Blatt's jolly voice boomed out of the dusk.

'Do I?' I said, forced to smile in spite of everything.

'Been to the vicarage?'

'Yes.'

'Oh, they're always with Mrs Gray now, those two,' said Sister Blatt bluntly. 'I wanted to see Father Malory about the Confirmation classes but he was helping *her* to put up curtain rods.'

'Well, the Malorys are such friendly helpful sort of people,' I said.

She snorted and I watched her hoist herself slowly on to her bicycle and move off to perform some good work. Then I went back to my flat and collected a great deal of washing to do. It was depressing the way the same old things turned up every week. Just the kind of underclothes a person like me might wear, I thought dejectedly, so there is no need to describe them.

CHAPTER TEN

At last the day came when Helena and Everard were to read their paper before the Learned Society. I had been afraid that she would forget her promise to invite me, but she came up to my flat the evening before and we arranged what time we should go. There was a tea party first to which guests could be taken.

'The new President will be in the Chair,' said Helena rather formally. 'He is such an old man that it's a wonder he hasn't been President before, but then there are a lot of the old ones. It will be our turn soon.'

I was a little preoccupied with what I should wear. I did not think it likely that a meeting of a Learned Society would be in any sense a fashionable gathering, but I was anxious not to disgrace the Napiers and had taken the bold step of buying a new hat to go with my brown winter coat even before I knew definitely that I was to go. Helena was very elegant in black. 'One mustn't *look* like a female anthropologist,' she explained.

'It wouldn't matter if you looked like some of those American girls,' said Rocky. 'They know how to dress.'

'Trust you to notice that,' she said rather sourly.

'I notice everything. Especially Mildred's charming new hat.'

I accepted the compliment as gracefully as I could, but I was sufficiently unused to having anybody make any comment on my appearance to find it embarrassing to have attention drawn to me in any way.

'Nothing is more becoming than a velvet hat,' Rocky went on, 'and the brown brings out the colour of your eyes which look like a good dark sherry.'

'Everard will meet us there,' said Helena rather impatiently. 'We shall have a few last minute things to discuss, so perhaps you would look after Mildred?' she added, turning to her husband. 'I think we had better take a taxi.'

The premises of the Learned Society were not very far from St Ermin's and I pointed it out to Helena on the way.

'Why, isn't it a ruin?' she asked. 'Fancy having services in a ruin! I should feel there was something particularly holy about that.'

I explained that one aisle was undamaged and that we had the services there, but I suppose she must have been nervous at the idea of the paper, for she did not seem to be listening and a minute or two afterwards the taxi drew up outside a good solid-looking Victorian house, with the brass plate of the Learned Society on its door.

In the hall Helena signed a book for us and we went upstairs to the library where the tea party was to be held. Everard Bone, looking elegant and rather cross, was standing by the door.

'I thought you were never coming,' he said to Helena, and then nodded 'good afternoon' to Rocky and me in a cursory way.

'I think we had better retire to a corner and observe the Learned Society,' said Rocky, guiding me over to where a table was spread with cups and saucers and plates of food.

'What a lot of strange-looking people,' I whispered.

'Nobody seems to be eating yet,' Rocky observed, 'but I think we had better station ourselves near the food. I dare say these types are little better than primitive peoples when it comes to eating.'

'My dear sir, I fear we are even worse,' said an elderly man with a large head, who was standing near us. 'The so-called primitive peoples have an elaborate order and precedence in eating but I'm afraid that when we get started it's every man for himself.'

'The survival of the fittest?' Rocky suggested.

'Yes, perhaps that is it. I hope we shall remember our manners sufficiently to offer refreshment to the ladies first,' continued the old man, with a little bow in my direction. 'Ah, here is our excellent Miss Clovis with the teapot.' He turned away and busied himself with cups and saucers.

'Do you think he is going to bring some to us?' I asked Rocky.

'Well, after what he has just said I should think he will surely bring you a cup of tea.'

But we were wrong, for he quickly helped himself to tea, collected an assortment of sandwiches and cakes on a plate and retired to the opposite corner of the room. We watched other elderly and middle-aged men doing the same, though one was held back by an imperious woman's voice calling 'Now, Herbert, no milk for Miss Jellink, remember!'

Rocky and I joined in a general scramble and took our spoils to a convenient bookcase where we could put our cups down on a shelf.

'These are quite obviously the books that nobody reads,' said Rocky, studying their titles. 'But it's a comfort to know that they are here if you ever should want to read them. I'm sure I should find them more entertaining than the more up-to-date ones. *Wild Beasts and their Ways*; *Five Years with the Congo Cannibals*; *With Camera and Pen in Northern Nigeria*; *Sunshine and Storm in Rhodesia*. I wish people still wrote books with titles like that. Nowadays I believe it simply isn't done to show a photograph of "The Author with his Pygmy Friends" – we have become to depressingly scientific.'

'You might write a book about your adventures in Italy,' I suggested. 'It might well have such a title.'

We amused ourselves by discussing the variations on this theme and while we were in the middle of our fantasies Everard and Helena came up to us and began to point out some of the more eminent persons present. The President was a tall mild-looking old man with a white wispy beard, in which some crumbly fragments of meringue had lodged themselves. In his younger days he had apparently written some rather startling pamphlets about the nature of the universe.

'I believe his father turned him out of the house,' said Everard. 'You see, he was a Methodist Minister and when he found out that his son was a militant atheist I suppose it became awkward.'

'That old man an atheist!' I exclaimed, unable to believe that anyone who looked so mild and benevolent should be what always sounded such a very wicked and startling thing. 'But he looks so unlike that. More like a bishop, really.'

'Or an old-fashioned picture of God,' suggested Rocky. 'I like to imagine the scene in the Victorian household, the father's wrath and the mother's tears, those dreadful scenes at the breakfast table. And yet, what does it all matter now? In a few years' time they will all be together in Heaven.'

'Oh, *darling*,' said Helena impatiently, 'how ridiculous you are. Afterwards I'll introduce you to some of the really worthwhile people here. Apfelbaum, Tyrell Todd, and Steinartz from Yale – the new generation.'

'They sound delightful,' said Rocky gravely.

'I think we should be going in,' said Everard. 'The President seems to be moving.'

We now followed them into a room adjoining the library where a number of people were already sitting. I noticed that the front rows were basket chairs and that one or two elderly men and women had settled themselves comfortably. One old man wore a purple muffler wound round his neck; an old woman took a piece of multicoloured knitting from a raffia bag and began to work on it.

Rocky and I took our seats somewhere in the middle of the room on the harder chairs. The younger people sat here, girls with flowing hair and scarlet nails and youths with hair almost as flowing and corduroy trousers. I noticed one or two Americans, serious-looking young men with rimless glasses and open notebooks, and a group of Africans, talking in a strange language. There was a buzz of unintelligible conversation all around us.

'What an interesting-looking lot of people,' I said, 'quite unlike anything I'm used to.'

'You can understand people saying that it takes all sorts to make a world,' said Rocky. 'One wonders if quite so many sorts are necessary.'

'It must be wonderful to have an interest in some learned

subject,' I said. 'This seems to be a thing that old and young can enjoy equally.'

Rocky laughed. 'I don't think Helena or Everard would approve of that attitude. You make it sound like a game of golf. And remember, we aren't here to enjoy ourselves. The paper will be long and the chairs hard. I think our ordeal is about to begin.'

The President had now risen to his feet and was introducing Helena and Everard in a vague little speech. It almost sounded as if he thought they were husband and wife, but he smiled so nicely through his wispy beard that nobody could possibly have taken offence. Everard and Helena sat to one side of him, while a stocky red-haired young man, who had been pointed out to us as the Secretary, took notes.

'And now I will leave our young friends to tell their own tale,' said the President. 'Their paper is entitled . . .' he fumbled with a pair of gold-rimmed spectacles and then read in a clear deliberate voice some words which conveyed so little to me at the time that I am afraid I have now forgotten them. Doubtless the title is recorded somewhere in the archives or minutes of the Learned Society.

I looked hopefully towards the lantern which stood at the back of the room, but it did not seem as if there were going to be any slides. The Americans' pencils were poised over their notebooks, the elderly lady put down her knitting for a moment. Helena Napier stood up and began to speak. I can only say that she 'began to speak' for I very soon lost the thread of what she was saying and found myself looking round the room, studying my surroundings and companions.

The room was very high with a Lincrusta ceiling and an elaborate mantelpiece of brawn-like marble. Long windows opened on to a balcony and through them I could just see the tender green of a newly unfolded tree in the square gardens. It seemed strange that we should all be sitting indoors on such a lovely day. But I must not look out of the window; this was a great occasion and I was a privileged person. It was certainly a pity that my lack of higher education made it impossible for me to concentrate on anything more difficult than a fairly straightforward sermon or committee meeting. Helena's voice sounded so clear and competent that I was sure that what she was saying was of great value. Rocky must be very proud of her. I noticed the Americans writing furiously in their books. It was a pity I had not thought of reading up the subject a little; that would have been far more to the point than buying a new hat. It was humiliating to realise that everybody in the room but me understood and was able to take an intelligent interest in what Helena was saying. I fixed my eyes on her with a fresh determination to concentrate, but then my attention was distracted by the old lady with her knitting. I saw that the knitting drooped slackly from her hands and that her head was bowed forward on her breast. Then I saw it suddenly jerk up. She had been asleep. This revelation gave me some comfort and I began looking round the room again, this time at the gold-lettered boards with the names of those who had won a particular medal or had been benefactors of the society in some way. I read down the list, fascinated. 1904 – Herbert Franklin Crisp, 1905 – Egfried Stummelbaum, 1906 – Edward Ellis Darwin Rumble, 1907 – Ethel Victoria Thorneycroft-Nollard . . . A woman, in 1907! What had she done to win this medal? What must she have been like? I imagined her in a long skirt, striding through the jungle, fearlessly questioning natives who had never before seen a white woman. A kind of

Mary Kingsley, but perhaps even more remarkable in that she was an anthropologist, the kind of thing a woman would not naturally be, especially in 1907. Perhaps she was among the elderly people in the basket chairs, she might even be the one knitting and dozing . . . I was so absorbed in my speculations that I did not notice that Helena had stopped speaking, until I was aware of Everard Bone standing up in her place and saying, as far as I could judge, very much the same sort of thing that Helena had already said. He spoke exceptionally well, hardly consulting his notes at all, and once or twice a ripple of laughter ran through the audience as if he had made a joke. I took this opportunity of studying him dispassionately, wondering what it was that made Helena's eyes sparkle when his name was mentioned. He was certainly very clever and handsome, too, in his own way, but there was no warmth or charm about his personality. I began imagining him as a clergyman and decided that he would make a good one. His rather forbidding manner would be useful to him. I realised that one might love him secretly with no hope of encouragement, which can be very enjoyable for the young or inexperienced.

When Everard had finished, the President, who looked as if he too had been dozing, got up and made a kindly speech. 'And now, I am sure there are many points you are eager to discuss,' he went on, 'who is – ah – going to start the ball rolling?'

There was the usual embarrassed silence, nobody liking to be first. Some chairs scraped on the floor and a woman sitting along our row pushed past us and went out. She was carrying a string-bag, containing a newspaper-wrapped bundle from which a fish's tail protruded. Helena smiled nervously. Everard took off his horn-rimmed spectacles and covered his eyes with his hand.

'Ah, Dr Apfelbaum – first in the field,' said the President in a relieved voice and everybody sat back in their chairs and looked up expectantly. How dreadful it would have been, I thought, if *nobody* had wanted to ask a question.

Dr Apfelbaum was a stocky man of Teutonic appearance. What he said was quite unintelligible to me, both from its content and because of his very marked foreign accent, but Everard dealt with him very competently. Now that the ball was rolling, other speakers followed in quick succession. In fact, they were jumping up and down like jacks-in-the-boxes, hardly waiting for each other to finish. It seemed that they had all 'done' some particular tribe or area and could furnish parallels or contradictions from their own experience.

'I shall just let it *flow* over me,' said Rocky, but this was not always possible. There was, at one point, a sharp exchange between Dr Apfelbaum and a stout dark-haired woman, and an apparently irrelevant question from the old man in the purple muffler provoked hearty laughter.

'*No* ceremonial devouring of human flesh?' he repeated in a disappointed tone, and sat down, shaking his head and muttering.

At last the meeting appeared to be at an end. Helena took Rocky away and began to introduce him to various people. I stood rather awkwardly by the door, wondering whether I ought to go home now or whether it would seem discourteous not to thank Helena and Everard for inviting me. The people round me seemed to have settled down into little groups, many of which were carrying on learned discussions.

'Well, what did you think of it? I'm afraid you must have been very bored?'

Everard Bone had broken away from a group of Americans

and was standing by my side. I was grateful to him for rescuing me though I could think of no conversation beyond a polite murmur and was quite sure that he was wanting to get back to discussing his paper with people who were able to.

'I think I must be going home now,' I said. 'Thank you very much for asking me.'

'Oh, I expect we shall be going somewhere for dinner,' he said vaguely. 'You may as well come too.'

'Well, I haven't really anything to eat at home,' I began, but then stopped as I realised that a dreary revelation of the state of one's larder was hardly the way to respond to an invitation to dinner. 'I should like to join you if I may.'

'I wish they'd hurry up,' said Everard, looking over to where Helena and Rocky were talking to a group of people.

'They are just like everybody else, really,' I said, half to myself. 'That old woman knitting, she went to sleep.'

'That was the President's wife,' said Everard, 'she always does.'

'Did she work with him in the field?' I asked.

'Good Heavens, no! She knows nothing at all about anthropology.'

'Didn't she even do the index or the proofreading for one of his books? You know what it often says in a preface or dedication – "To my wife, who undertook the arduous duty of proofreading" or making the index.'

'She may have done that. After all, it's what wives are for.' He suddenly smiled and I remembered my Lenten resolution to try to like him. It was getting a little easier but I felt that at any moment I might have a setback.

'God, how I want a drink!' said Helena in her characteristic way. She and Rocky had now joined us.

'I hope God is listening,' said Rocky, 'because I do too. I was very much afraid that those people were going to join us for dinner.'

'I think you were rude to them,' said Helena crossly, 'otherwise they might have done and we could have had some interesting conversation for a change.'

'Are there any of the conveniences of civilisation in this place?' asked Rocky.

'Yes, of course there are. Everard will show you. Perhaps you would like to come with me, Mildred?' said Helena.

I followed her upstairs and into a room which had 'Ladies' printed on a card on the door. The first thing that caught my eye inside was a rolled-up Union Jack. This seemed a little out of place, as did the portraits of native chiefs which were stacked against the walls under the washbasins.

'There isn't nearly enough storage space here, as you may have gathered,' explained Helena. 'This room is the repository for any junk that can't go anywhere else.'

'It seems in character with the rest of the place,' I remarked.

'So does the fact that there is neither soap nor towel,' said Helena. 'We are at our most primitive here, but after all it is only the basic needs that have to be supplied.'

'Well, that's the main thing,' I said feebly.

'At least we don't have a brooding old woman who expects you to drop sixpence into a saucer,' said Helena. 'I always think those women must see real drama, when you realise what scenes are enacted in ladies' cloakrooms.'

'Yes, I suppose things do go on there,' I agreed. I remembered girlhood dances where one had stayed there too long, though never long enough to last out the dance for which one hadn't a partner. I didn't suppose Helena had ever known that, and yet it was in its way quite a deep experience.

'It used to be worse, somehow, during the war,' said Helena. 'I remember once – oh, it was so depressing – there was just a dim blue bulb that made everything look ghastly and I was never going to see him any more. When I came out he was going to tell me that it was all over – you know the kind of thing, tears and whisky and then going out into that awful darkness.'

As I did not know I could only go on tidying my hair in a sympathetic silence. Helena came to the mirror and began doing something to her eyelashes with a little brush. 'Everard seems to like you,' she remarked carelessly.

'Oh, I'm sure he doesn't. I can never think of anything to say to him.'

'You think Rocky is much more attractive, don't you?'

'Well, yes, I do think he is nicer,' I said confusedly, for I was not used to discussing people in such terms. And yet I supposed that if I was honest with myself I should have to admit that 'attractive' was a better word than 'nice', and expressed my feeling about Rocky more accurately. But it was wrong to talk like this, and I wished Helena would stop or that I had gone home and left the three of them to have dinner together. 'I suppose we'd better not keep them waiting too long,' I said, in an attempt to stop the conversation from going any further.

'Oh, it won't do them any harm, but I could certainly do with a drink,' said Helena. 'Come along.'

I followed her downstairs, feeling like a dog or some inferior class of person.

The men were standing waiting for us in the hall. Whatever conversation they may have been having appeared to be at an end now, and they hurried us out rather unceremoniously leaving us to walk a little way behind them. I suppose they were too hungry and tired of waiting to think anything of it, but it did not seem a very good beginning to the evening.

Eventually we reached a restaurant and were shown to a table. Some drinks were ordered and one was handed to me. It was something very strong, made with gin, I think. I sipped cautiously while Rocky and Everard argued over the wine list. They were nearly as fussy as William, though in a different way, and I began to think that it would really be much easier if we just had water, though I lacked the courage to suggest it.

When the first course came, it turned out to be spaghetti of a particularly long and rubbery kind. Rocky showed me how to twist it round my fork but I found it very difficult to manage and it made conversation quite impossible. Perhaps long spaghetti is the kind of thing that ought to be eaten quite alone with nobody to watch one's struggles. Surely many a romance must have been nipped in the bud by sitting opposite somebody eating spaghetti?

After that ordeal some meat was brought and the wine with it, and conversation started again. Rocky began to ask frivolous questions about the paper.

'What was that about a man being expected to sleep with an unmarried sister-in-law who is visiting his house?' he asked.

'That's called a joking relationship,' said Everard precisely.

'Not exactly what one would call a joke,' said Rocky, 'though it could be fun. It would depend on the sister-in-law, of course. Does he *have* to sleep with her?'

'Oh, Rocky, you don't understand,' said Helena impatiently. It was obvious that she and Everard did not appreciate jokes about their subject.

'I wonder if the study of societies where polygamy is a commonplace encourages immorality?' asked Rocky seriously, turning to Everard. 'Would you say that it did?'

'There is no reason why it should,' said Everard.

'Do anthropologists tend to have many wives at the same time?' he went on. 'Have you found that?'

'They would naturally tend to conceal such things,' said Everard with a half smile, 'and one could hardly ask them.'

'Oh, they are drearily monogamous,' said Helena, 'and very virtuous in other ways too. Much better than many of these so-called good people who go to church.' She turned a half-amused, half-spiteful glance towards me.

'Well, Mildred, what do you say to that?' asked Rocky.

'Churchgoers are used to being accused of things,' I said. 'I have never found out what exactly it is that we do or are supposed to do.'

'We are whited sepulchres,' said Everard. 'We don't practise what we preach. Isn't that it, Helena?'

'One expects you to behave better than other people,' said Helena, 'and of course you don't.'

'Why should we? We are only humans, aren't we, Miss Lathbury?'

It seemed now as if we had changed sides. Before, Helena and Everard had been ranged against Rocky and me – now Everard was my partner. I have never been very good at games; people never chose me at school when it came to picking sides. But Everard had no choice. This state of affairs continued through dinner and afterwards when we went out into the street. Everard and I walked together, almost as if he had arranged it that way, but it cannot have been for the pleasure of my company, as our conversation was very poor.

'Do you live near here?' I asked, knowing that he did not.

'No, I live in Chelsea. I suppose one would hardly call it near.'

'No, but it isn't as far away as if you lived in Hendon or Putney.'

'That would be further, certainly.'

We walked a few steps in silence. I could hear Rocky and Helena having an argument in low angry tones.

'Do you live in a house or a flat?' I asked in a loud desperate voice.

'I did live in my mother's house after I came out of the Army, but I've just moved into a flat of my own, quite near.'

'You were lucky to find one.'

'Yes, I know the person who owns the house and one of the tenants happened to be leaving.' He stood by a bus stop. 'I think I can get a bus from here.'

Helena and Rocky had caught us up and we stood in a little group by the bus stop. Goodnights and thanks were exchanged.

'Will you ring me up?' said Helena to Everard.

'I shall probably be away for a few days,' he said vaguely.

At a meeting of the Prehistoric Society? I wondered.

'Aren't you coming to the next meeting?' Helena persisted. 'Tyrell Todd is reading a paper on pygmies.'

'Oh, pygmies – well, I don't know.'

At that moment Everard's bus came and he got on to it without looking back.

Rocky found a taxi and we drove most of the way in silence, or rather Helena was silent while Rocky and I discussed the evening or as much of it as could be discussed.

'You and Everard seemed to be having an interesting conversation,' said Helena at last. 'Was he declaring himself or something?' Her tone was rather light and cruel as if it were the most impossible thing in the world.

'He was telling me about his new flat,' I said lamely.

'Actually he might do very well for Mildred,' said Rocky. 'Had we thought of that? Obviously, we must find her a good husband.'

'The driver seems to be going past our house,' I said. 'Did you tell him the number?'

'Oh, this will do.' Rocky tapped on the glass and we got out. We were rather far from our own door, and just as we were walking past the parish hall, Teddy Lemon and a group of lads came out, laughing and talking in their rough voices. My heart warmed towards them, so good and simple with their uncomplicated lives. If only I had come straight home after the paper. This was Julian's boys' club night and I could have been there serving in the canteen – much more in my line than the sort of evening I had just spent.

CHAPTER ELEVEN

Love was rather a terrible thing, I decided next morning, remembering the undercurrents of the evening before. Not perhaps my cup of tea. It would be best not to see too much of the Napiers and their disturbing kind of life, but to meet only people like Julian and Winifred Malory and Dora Caldicote, from whom I had had a letter that morning. She hinted vaguely at 'unpleasantness' at school, perhaps the affair William had told me about, and asked if she might come and stay with me for a part of her Easter holiday. So I busied myself getting the little spare room ready, arranging daffodils in a bowl on the mantelpiece and putting out the rather useless little embroidered guest towels. The room looked pretty and comfortable like an illustration in one of the women's magazines. I knew it would not look like that for long after Dora's arrival and was a little sad when I went to talk to her over her unpacking and saw the familiar bulging canvas bag and her hairnet lying on the mantelpiece.

'Why, Mildred,' she exclaimed, 'what have you done to yourself? You look different.'

No compliments, of course; Dora was too old and honest a friend ever to flatter me, but she had the power of making me feel rather foolish, especially as I had not realised that she might find any difference in my appearance since the last time we met. I suppose I had taken to using a little more make-up, my hair was more carefully arranged, my clothes a little less drab. I was hardly honest enough to admit even to myself that meeting the Napiers had made this difference and I certainly did not admit it to Dora.

'You must be trying to bring William up to scratch,' she said, 'is that it?'

I laughed gratefully.

'There's not much you can do when you're over thirty,' she went on complacently. 'You get too set in your ways, really. Besides, marriage isn't everything.'

'No, it certainly isn't,' I agreed, 'and there's nobody I want to marry that I can think of. Not even William.'

'I don't know anyone either, at the moment,' said Dora.

We lapsed into a comfortable silence. It was a kind of fiction that we had always kept up, this not knowing anyone at the moment that we wanted to marry, as if there had been in the past and would be in the future.

'How's school?' I asked.

'Oh, Protheroe and I aren't on speaking terms,' said Dora vigorously. She was a small, stocky person with red hair, not at all like her brother, and could look very fierce at times.

'I'm sorry to hear that,' I said. 'But I should imagine Miss Protheroe is rather difficult to get on with.'

'Difficult! It's a wonder that woman keeps any of her staff.'

'What happened?'

'Oh, well, I let my form go into chapel without hats one

morning, and you know how she is about that sort of thing. Of course I've no use for any of this nonsense . . .' I let Dora go on but did not really listen, for I knew her views on Miss Protheroe and on organised religion of any kind. We had often argued about it in the past. I wondered that she should waste so much energy fighting over a little matter like wearing hats in chapel, but then I told myself that, after all, life was like that for most of us – the small unpleasantnesses rather than the great tragedies; the little useless longings rather than the great renunciations and dramatic love affairs of history or fiction.

'What would you like to do this afternoon?' I asked. 'Shall we go shopping?'

Dora's face brightened. 'Oh, yes, that would be nice.'

Later, as we were trying on dresses in the inexpensive department of a large store, I forgot all about the Napiers and the complications of knowing them. I was back in those happier days when the company of women friends had seemed enough.

'Oh, dear, this is too tight on the hips,' said Dora, her ruffled head and flushed face emerging through the neck of a brown woollen dress.

'I'm not sure that it's your colour,' I said doubtfully. 'I've come to the conclusion that we should avoid brown. It does the wrong kind of things to people over thirty, unless they're *very* smart. When my brown coat is worn out I shall get a black or a navy one.'

'Now you're talking like a fashion magazine,' said Dora, struggling with the zip-fastener. 'I've always had a brown wool dress for every day.'

Yes, and look at you, I thought, with one of those sudden

flashes of unkindness that attack us all sometimes. 'Why not try this green?' I suggested. 'It would suit you.'

'Good Heavens, whatever would people at school say if I appeared in a dress that colour?' Dora exclaimed. 'I shouldn't know myself. No, I'll just ask for the brown in a larger size. It's just what I want.'

They had the dress in a larger size which was now a little too large, but Dora seemed perfectly satisfied and bought it. 'I don't know what's the matter with you, Mildred,' she complained. 'You never used to bother much about clothes.'

'Where shall we have tea?' I asked, changing the subject because I felt myself unable to give a satisfactory explanation.

'Oh, the Corner House!' said Dora enthusiastically. 'You know how I enjoy that.'

We made our way to one of these great institutions and found ourselves in an almost noble room with marble pillars and white and gold decorations. The orchestra was playing *Si mes vers avaient des ailes* and I was back in imagination in some Edwardian drawing-room. How had they been able to bear those songs? I wondered. Sometimes we could hardly bear them now, although we might laugh at them, the nostalgia was too much. I felt suddenly desolate in Dora's company.

She was studying the menu with a satisfied expression on her face. 'Scrambled eggs,' she read, 'but of course they wouldn't be real. Curried whale, goodness, you wouldn't feel like having that for tea, would you? I had an argument about it the other day with Protheroe – you know how strictly she keeps Lent and all that sort of nonsense – well, there she was eating whale meat thinking it was fish!'

'Well, isn't it?'

'No, of course it isn't. The whale is a *mammal*,' said Dora in a loud truculent tone. 'So you see it can hardly count as fish.'

The waitress was standing over us to take our order. 'Just tea and a cake for me,' I murmured quickly, but Dora took her time and ordered various sandwiches.

'Was there unpleasantness about the whale?' I asked unkindly.

'Oh, no. I think Protheroe was rather upset though. I couldn't help feeling it was one up to me – paid her back for all that fuss about wearing hats in chapel.'

The orchestra started to play a rumba and I to pour out the tea. Dora opened a sandwich and looked inside. 'Paste,' she declared. 'I tell you what, Mildred, how would it be if we went down to the Old Girls' Reunion on Saturday? You know they're dedicating the window in memory of Miss Ridout? Had you thought of going?'

'Oh, is it this Saturday? I had a notice about it, of course, but hadn't realised it was so soon. It would be a nice expedition,' I ventured. 'The spring flowers would be out.'

We discussed the expedition further as we rode along Piccadilly on the top of a bus. The sun was out and there were still people sitting on chairs in the park.

'It looks odd to see a clergyman holding somebody's hand in public,' said Dora chattily. 'I don't know why, but it does.'

'Where?' I asked.

'Look – there,' she said, pointing out a couple lolling in deckchairs.

'Oh, but it *can't* be!' I exclaimed, but there was no doubt that the clergyman was Julian Malory and that the hand he was holding was Allegra Gray's.

'How do you mean it can't be?' said Dora looking again. 'He

certainly was holding her hand. Why, isn't it Julian Malory? What a joke! Who's he with?'

'She's a widow, a Mrs Gray, who's come to live in the flat at the vicarage.'

'Oh, I see. Well, I suppose there's nothing wrong in that?'

'No, of course there isn't,' I said rather sharply. It was just thoroughly unsuitable, sitting there for everyone to see, not even on the hard iron chairs but lolling in deckchairs. 'Fancy going into the park to hold hands, though, it seems rather an odd thing to do.'

'Well, I don't suppose they went there expressly for that purpose,' said Dora stubbornly. 'They probably went for a walk and decided to sit down and then somehow it came about. After all, holding hands is quite a natural affectionate gesture.'

'How do *you* know?' I heard myself say.

'Mildred! What *is* the matter with you? Are *you* in love with the vicar or what?' she said, so loudly that the people in front of us nudged each other and sniggered.

'No, of course not,' I said in a low angry tone, 'but it seems so unsuitable, the whole thing. Winifred and everything, oh, I can't explain now.'

'Well, I don't see what you're making such a fuss about,' said Dora, maddeningly calm. 'It's a lovely day and she's very attractive and a widow and he's not married, so it's all right. I see quite a little romance blowing up.'

By the time we had got off the bus we were arguing quite openly. It was foolish and pointless but somehow we could not stop. I saw us in twenty or thirty years' time, perhaps living together, bickering about silly trifles. It was a depressing picture.

'After all a clergyman is a man and entitled to human feelings,' Dora went on.

It was obvious to me now that she was in a kind of mood to disagree automatically with everything I said, for usually she maintained that clergymen didn't count as men and therefore couldn't be expected to have human feelings.

'Julian isn't the marrying sort,' I persisted. 'Anyway, Mrs Gray wouldn't be at all suitable for him.'

'Oh, I think you've had your eye on him for yourself all this time,' said Dora in an irritating jocular tone. '*That's* why you've been smartening yourself up.'

It was useless to deny it, once she had got the idea into her head. I was grateful to see the grey bulk of Sister Blatt looming before us as we reached the church.

'Hullo,' she said as we came up to her. 'What on earth's happened to Father Malory?' she asked. 'Evensong's in five minutes and there's no sign of him. Miss Malory said he was going to a meeting at S.P.G. House this afternoon. It must have been a very long one.' She laughed. 'You don't think he's had a sudden call to the Mission Field, do you?'

'Surely he would have come back here first and let us know?' I said.

'Oh, well, I dare say Father Greatorex will turn up,' said Sister Blatt cheerfully and went into church.

Dora giggled. '*We* could tell her where Father Malory is, couldn't we, Mildred? I think we should blackmail him.'

We went into the house. Dora decided to do some washing before supper and within half an hour the kitchen was festooned with lines of depressing-looking underwear – fawn locknit knickers and petticoats of the same material. It was even drearier than mine.

At supper we talked about our old school, William, and matters of general interest. Julian Malory was not mentioned again. I was in the kitchen making some tea when there was a knock at the door and Rocky's head peeped round.

'Helena has gone to hear a paper about pygmies,' he said, 'and I'm all alone. May I come in?'

'Yes, do,' I said, in a confused way, embarrassed by the washing hanging up.

'My friend Dora Caldicote is here,' I said, as he threaded his way through the lines of dripping garments.

'Oh, what fun!' he said lightly. 'Are you going to give me some coffee?'

'Well, we were having tea,' I said, feeling a little ashamed, both of the tea and of myself for feeling ashamed of it, 'but I can easily make you some coffee.'

'No, indeed you won't. I love tea.'

'You are Mildred's old school chum,' he said to Dora in a teasing way. 'I've heard all about you.'

Dora flushed and smiled. Oh, the awkward Wren officers, I thought, seeing them standing on the balcony at the Admiral's villa. How they must have blossomed under that charm!

Rocky was standing by the window. 'There's your vicar,' he said. 'Would there be a service now?'

'Is he alone?' asked Dora.

'Yes, very much so, and wearing rather a becoming cloak. I always think I should look rather well in one of those.'

'We saw him holding somebody's hand in the park this afternoon and Mildred was rather upset,' said Dora gaily. 'Poor man, *I* didn't see why he shouldn't.'

'Oh, but we can't have that,' said Rocky. 'I always look on him as Mildred's property. But never mind,' he turned towards me, 'I don't suppose his hand would be very pleasant to hold. We'll find somebody better for you.'

'He was supposed to be in church taking Evensong,' said Dora, who would not leave the subject.

'Oh, the poor man, I can imagine nothing more depressing on a fine weekday evening. Wondering if anybody will come or getting tired of seeing just the same faithful few. Why don't we go out and have a drink?' he asked in a bored way.

'Not after drinking tea, thank you. I don't think I should feel like it,' I said.

'Dear Mildred, you must learn to feel like drinking at *any* time. I shall make myself responsible for your education.'

So of course we did go. Dora had cider and got rather giggly with Rocky, telling him stories about our schooldays which I found embarrassing. I, in my wish to be different and not to be thought a schoolmarm, had said I would have beer, which turned out to be flat and bitter, with a taste such as I imagine washing-up water might have.

'Mildred is sad about her vicar,' said Rocky. 'We'll find her an anthropologist.'

'I don't want anyone,' I said, afraid that I was sounding childish and sulky but quite unable to do anything about it.

'If Everard Bone were here we might persuade him to hold your hand,' he went on teasingly. 'How would you like that?'

For a moment I almost did wish that Everard Bone could be with us. He was quiet and sensible and a churchgoer. We should make dull stilted conversation with no hidden meanings to it. He would accept the story of Julian and Mrs Gray in the park without teasing me about it; he might even understand that it was a worrying business altogether. For it was. If Julian were to marry Mrs Gray what was to happen to Winifred? I was quite sure now that he did intend to marry her and could not imagine why I had not seen it all along. Clergymen did not go holding people's hands in public places unless their intentions were honourable, I told myself, hoping that I might perhaps be wrong, for clergymen were, as Dora had pointed out, human beings, and might be supposed to share the weaknesses of normal men. I worried over the problem in bed that night and wondered if I ought to do anything. I suddenly remembered some of the 'Answers to Correspondents' in the *Church Times*, which were so obscure that they might very well have dealt with a problem like this. 'I saw our vicar holding the hand of a widow in the park – what should I do?' The question sounded almost frivolous put like that; what kind of an answer could I expect? 'Consult your Bishop immediately'? Or, 'We feel this is none of your business'?

CHAPTER TWELVE

By the time Saturday came things seemed better. It was a sunny day and Dora and I were to go to our old school for the dedication of the window in memory of Miss Ridout, who had been headmistress in our time. In the train we read the school magazine, taking a secret pleasure in belittling those of the Old Girls who had done well and rejoicing over those who had failed to fulfil their early promise.

"'Evelyn Brandon is still teaching Classics at St Mark's, Felixstowe,'" Dora read in a satisfied tone. 'And she was so *brilliant*. All those prizes she won at Girton – everyone thought she would go far.'

'Yes,' I agreed, 'and yet in a sense we all go far, don't we? I mean far from those days when we were considered brilliant or otherwise.'

'Oh, I don't think you and I have altered much.'

'Well, we haven't got shingled hair and waists round the behind still. Isn't it depressing, really, to think that we remember those fashions? It seems very unromantic to have been young then.'

'But, Mildred, we were only twelve or thirteen then. Look, here's a bit about you – "M. Lathbury is still working part-time at the Society for the Care of Aged Gentlewomen",' she read. 'That doesn't sound much better than Evelyn Brandon.'

'Yes, of course, that is what I do,' I agreed, but somehow it seemed so inadequate; it described such a very little part of my life. 'Of course,' I went on, 'some people do write more details about themselves, don't they, so that one gets more of a picture of their lives.'

'Oh, yes. Here's a bit about Maisie Winterbotham: do you remember her, red hair and glasses? She married a missionary or something. "M. Arrowsmith (Winterbotham) writes from Calabar, Nigeria, that her husband is opening a new mission station on the Imo River, 'My third child (Jeremy Paul) was born out here, so that what with Christopher and Fiona still at the toddling stage I really have my hands full. Luckily I have a wonderful African nurse for them. I ran into Miss Caunce in Lagos, but came on here immediately.'"' Dora giggled. 'The Caunce would be enough to make anyone leave a place immediately. Oh, look, we're nearly there!'

My heart sank as I recognised familiar landmarks. I could almost imagine myself a schoolgirl again, arriving at the station on a wet September evening for the autumn term and smelling the antiseptic smell of the newly scrubbed cloak-rooms.

'Oh, look, there's Helen Eggleton and Mavis Bush . . .' Dora was leaning out of the window as the train drew into the platform. It seemed as if most of the Old Girls had chosen the same train for there was quite a crowd of us getting out of it. Now the printed news in the magazine seemed to come alive. 'M. Bush is doing Moral Welfare work in Pimlico . . . H. B.

Eggleton is senior Domestic Science mistress at St Monica's, Herne Hill . . .' Now one saw them and they were very much as one had remembered them. There were older women too, some of whom might have been grandmothers, and younger ones whose rather too smart clothes indicated that they had left school only very recently. The staff were comfortingly the same. Miss Lightfoot, Miss Gregg, Miss Davis . . . it seemed that they had not aged at all, but there were one or two new mistresses, younger than we were, mere girls.

Tea was served in the hall before the dedication service and there was an opportunity for conversation, or rather exchange of news, for it could hardly be called conversation, consisting as it did of phrases like 'What's so-and-so doing now? Are you still teaching? Fancy old Hurst getting married!'

After tea we moved rather soberly in the direction of the chapel to inspect the new window before the ceremony. The chapel had been built in 1925 and was in a rather cold modern style with white walls, uncomfortable light oak chairs and rather a lot of saxe blue in carpets and hangings. Here Dora and I had been confirmed at the age of fifteen and here we had knelt, uncomfortably, expecting something that never quite came. Certainly I myself had no very inspiring memories of school religion. Only agonised gigglings over certain lines in hymns and psalms and later a watchfulness to reprove those same gigglings in the younger girls. I supposed that Dora and I, who had both been fat as schoolgirls, could now stand side by side singing

Frail children of dust,
And feeble as frail,

without a tremor or the ghost of a smile. It was rather sad, really.

The window to be dedicated was by a modern stained-glass artist and in keeping with the rest of the chapel. It showed the figure of a saint with the name OLIVE STURGIS RIDOUT in Gothic lettering, her dates and a Latin inscription. We stood in front of it in a reverent silence, which was unbroken save for an occasional admiring comment. After a few minutes we took our places for the service which was to be conducted by the school chaplain. In our day he had been a tall good-looking middle-aged man, a canon of the town's cathedral, with whom all of us were more or less secretly or openly in love. Then his visits had been eagerly looked forward to, but now, perhaps wisely, things appeared to be different, for the chaplain was a fussy little man, bald and wearing pince-nez. He conducted a suitable form of service and gave a short address, extolling the virtues of Miss Ridout, the Sturge, we had called her, after her middle name. Suddenly I was moved and felt the tears pricking at the back of my eyes. The Sturge had been a good woman and very kind to me; she had had a keen sense of the ridiculous too, which I had not appreciated until I had grown up. I imagined her now smiling down on us from some kind of Heaven, perhaps a little sardonically.

Going back in the train Dora and I were both in an elegiac mood and started reminiscing. We no longer belittled our successful contemporaries or rejoiced over our unsuccessful ones. For after all, what had *we* done? We had not made particularly brilliant careers for ourselves, and, most important of all, we had neither of us married. That was really it. It was the ring on the left hand that people at the Old Girls' Reunion looked for. Often, in fact nearly always, it was an uninteresting ring, sometimes no more than the plain gold band or the very smallest and dimmest of diamonds. Perhaps the husband was also of this variety, but as he was not seen at this female gathering he could only be imagined, and somehow I do not think we ever imagined the husbands to be quite so uninteresting as they probably were,

'Fancy anyone marrying old Hurst!' said Dora, as if reading my thoughts. 'I wonder what on earth her husband can be like?'

'How can we ever know? A little dim man going bald but very kind and good-tempered? An elderly clergyman, perhaps a widower? Or even somebody distinguished and handsome? It might be any of those.'

We fell into a melancholy silence. It was dark now and the train went slowly. Every time I looked out of the window we seemed to be passing a churchyard.

Within the churchyard side by side
Are many long low graves,

I thought, but once we passed a large cemetery and there was something less comfortable about the acres of tombstones, relieved occasionally by a white marble figure whose outstretched arms or wings looked almost menacing in the dim light.

I turned the pages of the school magazine and found something sympathetic to my mood, an obituary notice of an Old Girl who had been at the school from 1896 to 1901. Dorothy Gertrude Pybus, 'D.G. or Pye to her friends', with her eager face, her love of practical jokes, her splendid work at St Crispin's, and then the poem of an embarrassing badness, a confused thing about mists and mountain tops rather in the style of 'Excelsior' . . . all these details and obscure personal references moved me deeply so that I hardly knew whether to laugh or cry. Dora and I were obviously not old enough yet, but there might come a time when one of us might write an obituary for the other, though I hoped that neither of us would be rash enough to attempt a poem.

There was a young woman in the carriage with us, but we did not realise she had come from the school until Dora drifted into conversation with her. She told us that she had left school at the beginning of the war and had afterwards served in the Wrens.

'I was awfully lucky and got sent to Italy,' she babbled. 'Marvellous luck – I was there over a year.'

'Did you know Rockingham Napier?' I asked idly. 'He was in an Admiral's villa somewhere, I believe.'

'Did I know Rocky – the most glamorous Flags in the Med.? Why, *everyone* knew him!'

I looked at her with a new interest. She had not seemed to be the kind of person who could have had any interesting experiences, one wouldn't have given her a second glance, but now I saw her on the terrace of the Admiral's villa in that little group.

'You had white uniforms,' I ventured.

'Oh, goodness, yes! And they never fitted properly until they had shrunk with washing or been altered. Mine were like sacks on me at first. We were invited to cocktails at the Admiral's villa the day after we arrived and Rocky Napier was awfully kind to us. You see, it was his job to arrange the Admiral's social life and be nice to people.'

'I'm sure he did it well,' I murmured.

'Oh, yes,' she said gaily. 'People used to fall in love with him but it only lasted about a month or two, usually. After that one saw what a shallow kind of person he really was. He used to take people up for a week or two and then drop them. We Wren officers used to call ourselves the Playthings – sometimes we were taken off our shelf and dusted and looked at, but then we were always put back again. Of course, he had an Italian girlfriend, so you see . . .'

'Yes, of course . . .' An Italian girlfriend, yes, that was to be expected. I wondered if Helena had known or minded, and then decided that it was probably naive of me to look at it like that.

'Men are very strange,' said Dora complacently. 'You never know what they'll be up to.'

'No,' I agreed, for that seemed a comfortable way of putting it. 'Of course all men aren't like that,' said the Wren officer. 'There were some very nice Army officers out there too.'

'And didn't they have Italian girlfriends?'

'Oh, no. They used to show you photographs of their wives and children.'

I looked at her suspiciously but she appeared to be quite serious.

The train drew into the station and we prepared to get out.

'By the way, I hope Rocky Napier isn't a bosom friend of yours or a relation? Perhaps I ought not to have said what I did.'

'Oh, not a bosom friend,' I said. 'He and his wife live in the same house as I do and he always seems very pleasant.' After all, what did it matter what this depressing woman thought of him? She had only seen him in falsely glamorous surroundings.

The train drew up at a platform and we went our separate ways.

'Well, there you are,' said Dora in a satisfied tone. 'I thought as much. I wasn't a bit surprised to hear that about him. We've had a lucky escape, if you ask me.'

A lucky escape? I thought sadly. But would we have escaped, any of us, if we had been given the opportunity to do otherwise?

'Perhaps it's better to be unhappy than not to feel anything at all,' I said.

> 'Oh Love they wrong thee much
> That say thy sweet is bitter . . .'

Dora looked at me in astonishment. 'I think I'd just like to go into the Ladies,' she said, 'before we get the bus home.'

I followed her meekly although I did not really want to go myself. It was a sobering kind of place to be in and a glance at my face in the dusty ill-lit mirror was enough to discourage anybody's romantic thoughts.

CHAPTER THIRTEEN

The next few weeks passed uneventfully. Rocky was as charming as ever, but I was careful to say to myself 'Italian girlfriend' or 'rather a shallow sort of person' whenever I saw him, so that I might stop myself from thinking too well of him. He and Helena had managed to acquire some kind of a country cottage and were now spending quite a lot of time there. He told me that he had started to paint again but I could not make anything of the specimens of his work that he showed me. I did not see Everard Bone at all and soon forgot all about him and my efforts to like him. Dora went back to school with her brown woollen dress and I settled down to my gentlewomen in the mornings and the routine of home and church for the rest of the day. It seemed that the spring had unsettled us all but now that summer had come we were our more sober selves again. I did not see Julian Malory and Allegra Gray holding hands anywhere, although it was obvious that she was very friendly with both Julian and Winifred, and Winifred continued to be enthusiastic about her.

'Allegra's going to help me about my summer clothes,'

she said. 'She has such good taste. Don't you think so, Mildred?'

I agreed that she always looked very nice.

'Yes, and she's even smartening Julian up. Haven't you noticed? She'll probably start on Father Greatorex next.'

'Are you all getting on well together in the house?' I asked. 'You don't find that you have lost any of your independence having somebody living above you?'

'Oh, no, it's really like having Allegra living with us. We're in and out of each other's rooms all the time.'

It was a Saturday morning and we had assembled in the choir vestry before decorating the church for Whit Sunday. It was the usual gathering, Winifred, Sister Blatt, Miss Enders, Miss Statham and one or two others. The only man present, apart from the clergy, was Jim Storry, a feeble-minded youth who made himself useful in harmless little ways and would sometimes arrange the wire frames on the windowsills for us or fill jam jars with water.

The vestry was a gloomy untidy place, containing two rows of chairs, a grand piano and a cupboard full of discarded copies of *Hymns Ancient and Modern* – we used the *English Hymnal*, of course – vases, bowls and brasses in need of cleaning.

'Well, well, here we all are,' said Julian in a rather more clerical tone than usual. 'It's very good of you all to come along and help and I'm especially grateful to all those who have brought flowers. Lady Farmer,' he mentioned the only titled member remaining in our congregation, 'has most kindly sent these magnificent lilies from her country home.'

There was a pause.

'Is he going to say a prayer?' whispered Sister Blatt to me, and as nobody broke the silence I bent my head suitably and waited. But the words Julian spoke were not a prayer but a gay greeting to Allegra Gray, who came in through the door at that moment.

'Ah, here you are, now we can start.'

'Well, really, were we just waiting for *her*?' mumbled Sister Blatt. 'We've been decorating for years – long before Mrs Gray came.'

'Well, she is a newcomer, perhaps Father Malory thought it more polite to wait for her. I dare say he will help her.'

'Father Malory help with the decorating! Those men never do anything. I expect they'll slink off and have a cup of coffee once the work starts.'

We went into the church and began sorting out the flowers and deciding what should be used where. Winifred, as the vicar's sister, had usurped the privilege of a wife and always did the altar, but I must confess that it was not always very well done. I had graduated from a very humble window that nobody ever noticed to helping Sister Blatt with the screen, and we began laboriously fixing old potted-meat jars into place with wires so that they could be filled with flowers. Lady Farmer's lilies were of course to go on the altar. There was a good deal of chatter, and I was reminded of Trollope's description of Lily Dale and Grace Crawley, who were both accustomed to churches and 'almost as irreverent as though they were two curates'. For a time all went peacefully, each helper was busy with her particular corner, while Julian and Father Greatorex wandered round giving encouragement, though no particular help, to all.

'That's it!' said Julian as I placed a cluster of pinks into one of the potted-meat jars. 'Splendid!'

I did not feel that there was anything particularly splendid about what I was doing and Sister Blatt and I exchanged smiles as he passed on to Miss Statham and Miss Enders at the pulpit. It was at this point that I heard Winifred and Mrs Gray, who were both doing the altar, having what sounded like an argument.

'But we always have lilies on the altar,' I heard Winifred say.

'Oh, Winifred, why are you always so conventional!' came Mrs Gray's voice rather sharply. 'Just because you've always had lilies on the altar it doesn't mean that you can never have anything else. I think these peonies and delphiniums would look much more striking. Then we can have the lilies in a great jar on the floor, at the side here. Don't you think that would look splendid?'

I could not hear Winifred's reply but it was obvious that the flowers were going to be arranged in the way Mrs Gray had suggested.

'Of course she's been a vicar's wife,' said Sister Blatt, 'so I suppose she's used to ordering people about and having her own way with the decorations.'

'I suppose it's really a question of whether a vicar's sister should take precedence over a vicar's widow,' I said. 'I don't imagine that books of etiquette deal with such refinements. But I didn't realise Mrs Gray's husband had been a vicar – I thought he was just a curate and then an Army chaplain.'

'Oh, yes, he had a parish before he became a chaplain. They say he was a very good preacher, too, very slangy and modern. But I *have* heard,' Sister Blatt lowered her voice as if about to tell me something disgraceful, 'that he had *leanings* . . .'

'Leanings?' I echoed.

'Yes, the Oxford Group movement. He had tendencies that way, I believe.'

'Oh, dear, then perhaps . . .'

'You mean that it was just as well that he was taken, poor man?' said Sister Blatt, finishing my sentence for me.

'Do you think Mrs Gray will marry again?' I asked craftily, wondering if Sister Blatt had seen or heard anything.

'Well, who, that's the point, isn't it? She's an attractive woman, I suppose, but there aren't really any eligible men round here, are there?'

'What about the clergy?'

'You mean Father Greatorex?' asked Sister Blatt in astonishment.

'He did give her a pot of jam.'

'Well, well, that's certainly news to me.'

'And Father Malory gave her a hearthrug,' I went on, unable to stop myself.

'Oh, that moth-eaten old thing out of his study? I shouldn't think that means anything. Besides, Father Malory wouldn't marry,' said Sister Blatt positively.

'I don't know. We have no reason for thinking that he wouldn't. Anyway, widows nearly always do marry again.'

'Oh, they have the knack of catching a man. Having done it once I suppose they can do it again. I suppose there's nothing in it when you know how.'

'Like mending a fuse,' I suggested, though I had not previously taken this simple view of seeking and finding a life partner.

It was just as well that we were interrupted here by Miss Statham, asking if we had any greenery to spare, for our conversation had not been at all suitable for church and I really felt a little ashamed.

The church looked as beautiful as its Victorian interior

would allow when we had finished decorating. The altar was striking and unusual and the lilies stood out very well, so that even if Lady Farmer had been present, which she was not, she would not have thought that they had been overlooked.

The next morning we were all singing *Hail Thee Festival Day*, as the procession wound round the church, and the smell of incense and flowers mingled pleasantly with the sunshine and birdsong outside. The Napiers were away and I was feeling peaceful and happy, as I had felt before they came and disturbed my life. As I walked out of the church Mrs Gray came up to me. We were both wearing new hats for Whitsuntide, but I felt that hers with its trimming of fruit was smarter and more unusual than mine with its conventional posy of flowers.

'Oh, dear, that *is* a difficult hymn,' she said, 'the one we had for the procession.'

'But so beautiful,' I said, 'and well worth singing even if one falters a little in the verse part sometimes.'

'I was wondering if you'd have lunch with me one day,' said Mrs Gray suddenly and surprisingly.

'Lunch?' I asked as if I had never heard of the meal, for I was wondering whatever could have induced her to want to have lunch with me. 'Thank you, I should like to very much.'

'Of course tomorrow is Whit Monday, so perhaps we had better say Tuesday or Wednesday – if you're free, that is?'

'Oh, I'm always free,' I said unguardedly. 'Tuesday would suit me very well. Where shall I meet you?'

She named a restaurant in Soho which I had often seen from the outside. 'Would that be convenient for you? At one-fifteen, say?'

I went back to my flat puzzling a little about this friendly overture. I was sure that she did not really like me, or at best thought of me as a dim sort of person whom one neither liked nor disliked, and I did not feel that I really cared for her very much either. Still, this was no doubt an interesting basis for social intercourse and we might even become friends. The people I was going to become friendly with! It made me laugh to think of them and I began playing with the idea of bringing them together. Everard Bone and Allegra Gray – perhaps they might marry? It would at least take her away from Julian, unless he was really determined to have her. Did the clergy display the same determination in these matters as other men? I wondered. I supposed that they did. And who would win if it came to a fight – Julian or Everard Bone?

On Whit Monday I decided to tidy out some drawers and cupboards and possibly begin making a summer dress. I always did these tidyings on Easter and Whit Mondays, but somehow not at any other time. It seemed to be connected with fine weather rather than the great Festivals of the Church – a pagan rather than a Christian rite.

I started with the pigeonholes of my desk, but I did not get very far because I came upon a bundle of old letters and photographs which set me dreaming and remembering. My mother in a large hat, sitting under the cedar tree on the rectory lawn – I would be too young to remember the exact occasion but I knew the life, even to the shadowy curate who could be seen hovering in the background, his features a little blurred. Then there was one of Dora and me at Oxford, on the river with William and a friend. Presumably the friend, a willowy young man of a type that does not look as if it would marry, had been intended for Dora, as William was regarded as my property. But what had happened that afternoon? I could not even remember the occasion now.

I opened a drawer and came upon a large and solemn-looking studio portrait (in sepia) of the young man with whom I had once imagined myself to be in love, Bernard Hatherley, a bank clerk who occasionally read the Lessons and who used to be included with the curates in Sunday evening supper parties. The face reminded me a little of Everard Bone, except that the features were less striking. It seemed incredible to remember now how often at nineteen I had pressed my cheek against the cold glass, and I found the recollection embarrassing, turning from it quickly and from the remembrance of myself hurrying past his lodgings in the dusk, hoping yet fearing that I might see his face at the window, his hand drawing aside the lace curtain of his first-floor sitting-room. 'Loch Lomond', Victoria Parade . . . I could still remember the name of the house and street. He had given me the photograph one Christmas and I had given him an anthology of poetry, which seemed an unfair exchange, my gift being so much more revealing than his. It had all seemed rather romantic, hearing him read the Lessons at Evensong, seeing him by chance in the town or through the open door of the bank, and then the long country walks on Saturday afternoons and the talks about life and about himself. I did not remember that we had ever talked about me. Eventually he had gone on a holiday to Torquay and things were not the same after that. I had suffered, or I supposed that I had, for he had not broken the news of another attachment very gracefully. Perhaps high-principled young men were more cruel in these matters because less experienced. I am sure that Rocky would have done it much more kindly.

I got up stiffly, for I had been crouching uncomfortably on the floor. I bundled the letters and photographs back and decided that it would be more profitable to make tea and cut out my dress. Tidying was over now until next Easter or Whitsuntide.

CHAPTER FOURTEEN

I dressed rather carefully in preparation for my lunch with Mrs Gray and my appearance called forth comments from Mrs Bonner, who assumed that I was going to have lunch with 'that good-looking man you spoke to after one of the Lent services'. She was disappointed when I was honest enough to admit that my companion was to be nobody more exciting than another woman.

'I did hope it was that young man,' she said. 'I took a liking to him – what I saw, that is.'

'Oh, he's not at all the kind of person I like,' I said quickly. 'And he doesn't like me either, which does make a difference, you know.'

Mrs Bonner nodded mysteriously over her card index. She was a great reader of fiction and I could imagine what she was thinking.

I was punctual at the restaurant and I had been waiting nearly ten minutes before Mrs Gray arrived.

'I'm so sorry,' she smiled, and I heard myself murmuring politely that I had arrived too early, as if it were really my fault that she was late.

'Where do you usually have lunch?' she asked. 'Or perhaps you go home to lunch as you only work in the mornings?'

'Yes, I do sometimes – otherwise I go to Lyons or somewhere like that.'

'Oh, dear, Lyons – I don't think I could! *Far* too many people.' She shuddered and began looking at the menu. 'I think we should like a drink, don't you? Shall we have some sherry?'

We drank our sherry and made rather stilted conversation about parish matters. When the food came Mrs Gray ate very little, pushing it round her plate with her fork and then leaving it, which made me feel brutish, for I was hungry and had eaten everything.

'I'm like the young ladies in *Crome Yellow*,' she said, 'although it isn't so easy nowadays to go home and eat an enormous meal secretly. What was it they had? A huge ham, I know, but I don't remember the other things.'

I did not really know what she was talking about and could only ask if she would like to order something else.

'Oh, no, I'm afraid I have a very small appetite naturally. And then things haven't been too easy, you know.' She looked at me with a penetrating gaze that seemed to invite confidences.

It made me feel stiff and awkward as if I wanted to withdraw into my shell. But I felt that I had to say something, though I could produce nothing better than 'No, I suppose they haven't.'

At that moment the waiter came with some fruit salad.

'I don't suppose you have had an altogether easy life, either.' Mrs Gray continued.

'Oh, well,' I found myself saying in a brisk robust tone, 'who has, if it comes to that?' It began to seem a little absurd, two women in their early thirties, eating a good meal on a fine summer day and discussing the easiness or otherwise of their lives.

'I haven't been married, so perhaps that's one source of happiness or unhappiness removed straight away.'

Mrs Gray smiled. 'Ah, yes, it isn't always an unmixed blessing.'

'One sees so many broken marriages,' I began and then had to be honest with myself and add up the number of which I had a personal knowledge. I could not think of a single one, unless I counted the Napiers' rather unstable arrangement, and I hoped that Mrs Gray would not take me up on the point.

'Yes, I suppose you would see a good deal of that sort of thing in your work,' she agreed.

'In my work?' I asked, puzzled. 'But I work for the Care of Aged Gentlewomen.'

'Oh,' she smiled, 'I had an idea it was fallen women or something like that, though I suppose even a gentlewoman can fall. But now I come to think of it, Julian did tell me where you worked.'

She said the name casually but it was obvious that she had been waiting to bring it into the conversation. I imagined them talking about me and wondered what they had said.

'Julian has asked me to marry him,' she went on quickly. 'I wanted you to be the first to know.'

'Oh, but I think I *did* know, I mean I guessed,' I said rather quickly and brightly. 'I'm so glad.'

'You're glad? Oh, what a relief!' She laughed and lit another cigarette.

'Well, it seems a very good thing for both of you and I wish you every happiness,' I mumbled, not feeling capable of explaining any further a gladness I did not really feel.

'That really is sweet of you. I was so afraid . . . oh, but I know you're not that kind of person.'

'What were you afraid of?' I asked.

'Oh, that you'd disapprove . . .'

'A clergyman's widow?' I smiled. 'How could I possibly disapprove?'

She smiled too. It seemed wrong that we should be smiling about her being a clergyman's widow.

'You and Julian will be admirably suited to each other,' I said more seriously.

'I think you're marvellous,' she said. 'And you really don't mind?'

'Mind?' I said, laughing, but then I stopped laughing because I suddenly realised what it was that she was trying to say. She was trying to tell me how glad and relieved she was that I didn't mind too much when I must surely have wanted to marry Julian myself.

'Oh, no, of course I don't mind,' I said. 'We have always been good friends, but there's never been any question of anything else, anything more than friendship.'

'Julian thought perhaps . . .' She hesitated.

'He thought that I loved him?' I exclaimed, in rather too loud a voice, I am afraid, for I noticed a woman at a nearby table making an amused comment to her companion. 'But what made him think that?'

'Oh, well, I suppose there would have been nothing extraordinary in it if you had,' said Mrs Gray, slightly on the defensive.

'You mean it would be quite the usual thing? Yes, I suppose it might very well have been.'

How stupid I had been not to see it like that, for it had not occurred to me that anyone might think I was in love with Julian. But there it was, the old obvious situation, presentable unmarried clergyman and woman interested in good works – had everyone seen it like that? Julian himself? Winifred? Sister Blatt? Mr Mallett and Mr Conybeare? Of course, I thought, trying to be completely honest with myself, there had been a time when I first met him when I had wondered whether there might ever be anything between us, but I had so soon realised that it was impossible that I had never given it another thought.

'Oh, I hope you weren't worrying about that,' I said in a hearty sort of way to cover my confusion.

'No, not *worrying* exactly. I'm afraid people in love are rather selfish and perhaps don't consider other people's feelings as much as they ought.'

'Certainly not when they fall in love with other people's husbands and wives,' I said.

Mrs Gray laughed. 'There you are,' she said, 'one *does* see these broken marriages.'

'Winifred will be delighted at your news,' I said.

'Oh, yes, dear Winifred,' Mrs Gray sighed. 'There's a bit of a problem there.'

'A problem? How?'

'Well, where is she going to live when we're married, poor soul?'

'Oh, I'm sure Julian would want her to stay at the vicarage. They are devoted to each other. She could have the flat you've been living in,' I suggested, becoming practical.

'Poor dear, she *is* rather irritating, though. But I know you're very fond of her.'

Fond of her? Yes, of course I was, but I could see only too well that she might be a very irritating person to live with.

'That's why I was wondering,' Mrs Gray began and then hesitated. 'No, perhaps I couldn't ask it, really.'

'You mean you think that she might live with me?' I blurted out.

'Yes, don't you think it would be a splendid idea? You get on well, and she's so fond of you. Besides, you haven't any other ties, have you?'

The room seemed suddenly very hot and I saw Mrs Gray's face rather too close to mine, her eyes wide open and penetrating, her teeth small and pointed, her skin a smooth apricot colour.

'I don't think I could do that,' I said, gathering up my bag and gloves, for I felt trapped and longed to get away.

'Oh, do think about it, Mildred. There's a dear. I know you are one.'

'No, I'm not,' I said ungraciously, for nobody really likes to be called a dear. There is something so very faint and dull about it.

The waiter was hovering near us with a bill, which Mrs Gray picked up quickly from the table. I fumbled in my purse and handed her some silver, but she closed my hand firmly on it and I was forced to put it back.

'The very least I can do is to pay for your lunch,' she said.

'Does Julian know this? About Winifred, I mean?' I asked.

'Heavens, no. I think it's much better to keep men in the dark about one's plans, don't you?'

'Yes, I suppose it is,' I said uncertainly, feeling myself at a disadvantage in never having been in the position to keep a man in the dark about anything.

'I'm sure you and Winifred would get on *frightfully* well together,' said Mrs Gray persuasively.

'She could live with Father Greatorex,' I suggested frivolously.

'Poor dears; I can just imagine them together. I wonder if there *could* be anything in that, or would it be quite impossible? What do women *do* if they don't marry,' she mused, as if she had no idea what it could be, having been married once herself and about to marry again.

'Oh, they stay at home with an aged parent and do the flowers, or they used to, but now perhaps they have jobs and careers and live in bed-sitting-rooms or hostels. And then of course they become indispensable in the parish and some of them even go into religious communities.'

'Oh, dear, you make it sound rather dreary.' Mrs Gray looked almost guilty. 'I suppose you have to get back to your work now?' she suggested, as if there were some connection, as indeed there may well have been, between me and dreariness.

'Yes,' I lied, 'I have to go back there for a while. Thank you very much for my lunch.'

'Oh, it was a pleasure. We must do it again some time.'

I walked away in the direction of my office and, when I had seen Mrs Gray get on to a bus, went into a shop. I had a feeling that I must escape and longed to be lost in a crowd of busy women shopping, which was why I followed blindly the crowd that surged in through the swinging doors of a large store. Some were hurrying, making for this or that department or counter, but others like myself seemed bewildered and aimless, pushed and buffeted as we stood not know-ing which way to turn.

I strolled through a grove of dress materials and found myself at a counter piled with jars of face cream and lipsticks. I suddenly remembered Allegra Gray's smooth apricot-coloured face rather too close to mine and wondered what it was that she used to get such a striking effect. There was a mirror on the counter and I caught sight of my own face, colourless and worried-looking, the eyes large and rather frightened, the lips too pale. I did not feel that I could ever acquire a smooth apricot complexion but I could at least buy a new lipstick, I thought, consulting the shade-card. The colours had such peculiar names but at last I chose one that seemed right and began to turn over a pile of lipsticks in a bowl in an effort to find it. But the colour I had chosen was either very elusive or not there at all, and the girl behind the counter, who had been watching my scrabblings in a disin-terested way, said at last, 'What shade was it you wanted, dear?'

I was a little annoyed at being called 'dear', though it was perhaps more friendly than 'madam', suggesting as it did that I lacked the years and poise to merit the more dignified title.

'It's called Hawaiian Fire,' I mumbled, feeling rather foolish, for it had not occurred to me that I should have to say it out loud.

'Oh, Hawaiian Fire. It's rather an orange red, dear,' she said doubtfully, scrutinising my face. 'I shouldn't have thought it was quite your colour. Still, I think I've got one here.' She took a box from behind the counter and began to look in it.

'Oh, it doesn't matter really,' I said quickly. 'Perhaps another colour would be better. What would you recommend?'

'Well, dear, I don't know, really.' She looked at me blankly, as if no shade could really do anything for me. 'Jungle Red is very popular – or Sea Coral, that's a pretty shade, quite pale, you know.'

'Thank you, but I think I will have Hawaiian Fire,' I said obstinately, savouring the ludicrous words and the full depths of my shame.

I hurried away and found myself on an escalator. Hawaiian Fire, indeed! Nothing more unsuitable could possibly be imagined. I began to smile and only just stopped myself from laughing out loud by suddenly remembering Mrs Gray and the engagement and the worry about poor Winifred. This made me proceed very soberly, floor by floor, stepping on and off the escalators until I reached the top floor where the Ladies' Room was.

Inside it was a sobering sight indeed and one to put us all in mind of the futility of material things and of our own mortality. *All flesh is but as grass . . .* I thought, watching the women working at their faces with savage concentration, opening their mouths wide, biting and licking their lips, stabbing at their noses and chins with powder-puffs. Some, who had abandoned the struggle to keep up, sat in chairs, their bodies slumped down, the hands resting on their parcels. One woman lay on her couch, her hat and shoes off, her eyes closed. I tiptoed past her with my penny in my hand.

Later I went into the restaurant to have tea, where the women, with an occasional man looking strangely out of place, seemed braced up, their faces newly done, their spirits revived by tea. Many had the satisfaction of having done a good day's shopping and would have something to gloat over when they got home. I had only my Hawaiian Fire and something not very interesting for supper.

CHAPTER FIFTEEN

On my way home, I was just passing the vicarage when Julian
Malory came out.

'Congratulations,' I said, 'I've just heard your news.'

'Thank you, Mildred, I wanted you to be among the first to
know.'

I felt that the 'among' spoilt it a little and imagined a crowd
of us, all excellent women connected with the church, hearing the news.

'I had lunch with Mrs Gray,' I explained.

'Ah, yes.' He paused and then said, 'I thought it would be
better, easier, more suitable, that is, if you heard the news from
her.'

'Oh, why?'

'Well, for one thing I thought it would be nice if you got to
know each other better, become friends, you know.'

'Yes, men do seem to like the women they know to become
friends,' I remarked, but then it occurred to me that of course it
is usually their old and new loves whom they wish to force into
friendship. I even remembered Bernard Hatherley, the lay reader

bank clerk, saying about the girl he had met on holiday in Torquay, 'You would like her so much – I hope you'll become friends.' But as I had been at home in my village and she had been in Torquay the acquaintance had never prospered.

'Well, yes, naturally one likes everybody one is fond of to like each other,' said Julian rather feebly.

'Yes, of course,' I agreed, feeling that I could hardly do otherwise. 'I expect Winifred is very pleased, isn't she?'

'Oh, yes, although she did once say that she hoped – I wonder if I can say what she hoped?' Julian looked embarrassed, as if he had said more than he meant to.

'You mean . . .' I did not quite like to go any further.

'Ah, Mildred, you understand. Dear Mildred, it would have been a fine thing if it could have been.'

I pondered on the obscurity of this sentence and gazed into my basket, which contained a packet of soap powder, a piece of cod, a pound of peas, a small wholemeal loaf and the Hawaiian Fire lipstick.

'It's so splendid of you to understand like this. I know it must have been a shock to you, though I dare say you weren't entirely unprepared. Still, it must have been a shock, a blow almost, I might say,' he laboured on, heavy and humourless, not at all like his usual self. Did love always make men like this? I wondered.

'I was never in love with you, if that's what you mean,' I said, thinking it was time to be blunt. 'I never expected that you would marry *me*.'

'Dear Mildred,' he smiled, 'you are not the kind of person to expect things as your right even though they may be.'

The bell began to ring for Evensong. I saw Miss Enders and Miss Statham hurrying into church.

'I'm sure you'll be very happy,' I said, my consciousness of the urgent bell and hurrying figures making me feel that the conversation should come to an end.

But Julian did not appear in any hurry to go.

'Thank you, Mildred, it means a great deal to me, your good wishes, I should say. Allegra is a very sweet person and she has had a hard life.'

I murmured that yes, I suppose she had.

'The fatherless and widow,' said Julian in what seemed a rather fatuous way.

'Is she fatherless too?'

'Yes, she is an orphan,' he said solemnly.

'Well, of course, a lot of people over thirty are orphans. I am myself,' I said briskly. 'In fact I was an orphan in my twenties. But I *hope* I shan't ever be a widow. I'd better hurry up if I'm going to be even that.'

'And I had better hurry into Evensong,' said Julian, for the bell had now stopped. 'Are you coming or do you feel it would upset you?'

'Upset me?' I saw that it was no use trying to convince Julian that I was not heartbroken at the news of his engagement. 'No, I don't think it will upset me.' Perhaps the consciousness that I was already an orphan and not likely to be a widow was enough cause for melancholy, I thought, as I put my basket down on the pew beside me.

We were the usual little weekday congregation, though Mrs Gray was not with us. It seemed almost as if the service might be a kind of consolation for the rejected ones, although I did not imagine that Miss Enders or Miss Statham or Sister Blatt had ever been in the running.

After the service I went home and cooked my fish. Cod

seemed a suitable dish for a rejected one and I ate it humbly
without any kind of sauce or relish. I began trying to imagine
what it would have been like if Julian had wanted to marry me
and was absorbed in these speculations when there was a
knock at the door and Rocky came in.

'I'm all alone,' he said, 'and hoping that you will offer me
some coffee.'

'Yes, of course,' I said, 'do come in and talk to me.'

'Helena has gone to a memorial service, or rather, the
equivalent of one.'

'Can there be such a thing?'

'I gather so. You remember the President of the Learned
Society where they read their paper? Well, he died suddenly
last week and this is in commemoration of him.'

'Oh, dear, how sad.' I was really sorry to think that the
benevolent-looking old man with crumbs in his beard was no
more.

'He dropped down dead in the library – the kind of way
everybody says they'd like to go.'

'But so suddenly, with no time for amendment of life . . .' I
said. 'What form will the service take?'

'Oh, I gather it's a sort of solemn meeting. Fellow anthropologists and others will read out tributes to him. One feels
that they ought to sing Rationalist hymns as he was so strong
in the movement.'

'But do they have hymns?'

'I think they may very well have done in the early days.
Most of them had a conventional Victorian childhood and
probably felt the need for something to replace the Sunday
services they were rejecting.'

'Poor old man,' I murmured. And of course the old lady

knitting and dozing in the basket chair would now be a widow, I thought, which led me on to remember Julian's engagement. 'I've heard a piece of news today,' I said. 'Julian Malory is to marry Mrs Gray.'

'The fascinating widow whose hand he was holding in the park?' asked Rocky. 'Poor Mildred, this is a sad day for you.'

'Oh, don't be ridiculous!' I said indignantly. 'I didn't care for him at all in that way. I never expected that he would marry me.'

'But you may have hoped?' said Rocky looking at me. 'It would be a very natural thing, after all, and I should think you would make him a much better wife than that widow.'

'She is a clergyman's widow,' I reminded him.

'Oh, then she is used to loving and losing clergymen,' said Rocky lightly.

'Widows always do marry again,' I said thoughtfully, 'or they very often do. It must be strange to replace somebody like that, though I suppose one doesn't actually replace them, I mean, not in the way you buy a new teapot when the old one is broken.'

'No, my dear, hardly in that way.'

'It must be a different kind of love, neither weaker nor stronger than the first, perhaps not to be compared at all.'

'Mildred, the coffee has loosened your tongue,' said Rocky. 'I've never heard you talk so profoundly. But surely you've been in love more than once, haven't you?'

'I don't know,' I said, conscious of my lack of experience and ashamed to bring out the feeble memory of Bernard Hatherley reading the Lessons at Evensong and myself hurrying past his lodgings in the twilight.

'Once you get into the habit of falling in love you will find that it happens quite often and means less and less,' said Rocky lightly. He went over to my bookcase and took out a volume of Matthew Arnold which had belonged to my father.

> 'Yes! *In the sea of life enisled,*
> *With echoing straits between us thrown,*
> *Dotting the shoreless watery wild,*
> *We mortal millions live* ALONE,'

he read. 'How I hate his habit of emphasising words with italics! Anyway, there it is.'

'What a sad poem,' I said. 'I don't know it.'

'Oh, there's a lot more.'

'Father used to be so fond of Matthew Arnold,' I said, rather hoping that Rocky would not read aloud any more; I found it embarrassing, not quite knowing where to look, 'and I love *Thyrsis* and *The Scholar Gipsy*.'

'Ah, yes,' Rocky shut the book and flung it down on the floor. 'Long tramps over the warm green-muffled Cumnor hills. How one longs for that world. I can imagine your father striding along with a friend. But I don't think they'd have taken much notice of the poem I read to you. Healthy undergraduates would have no time for such morbid nonsense.'

'No, perhaps not. And then, of course, my father was a theological student.'

Rocky sighed and began pacing round the room. I suppose it was a compliment to me that he made no effort to hide his moods, but I did not really know how to deal with him.

'The other day I met somebody who knew you,' I said brightly, 'or rather who had known you in Italy. She was a Wren officer.'

'What was her name?' he asked with a faint show of interest.

'Oh, I don't know. She was tall with greyish eyes and brown hair, not pretty but quite a pleasant face.'

'Oh, Mildred,' he looked at me seriously, 'there were so *many*. I couldn't possibly recognise her from that description – "not pretty but quite a pleasant face" – most Englishwomen look like that, you know.'

I realised that it was probably how I looked myself and was sad to think that after a year or two he might not remember me either.

'I think she rather liked you,' I said tentatively. 'She may even have been a little in love with you.'

'But, Mildred, there again,' said Rocky gently, 'there were so *many*. I know I can be honest with you.'

'Poor things,' I said lightly. 'Did you throw them any scraps of comfort? They may have been unhappy.'

'Oh, I'm sure they were,' he said earnestly, 'but that was hardly my fault. I was nice to them at the Admiral's cocktail parties, naturally, that was part of my duty. I'm afraid women take their pleasures very sadly. Few of them know how to run light-hearted flirtations – the nice ones, that is. They cling on to these little bits of romance that may have happened years ago. *Semper Fidelis*, you know.'

I burst out laughing. 'Why, that's our old school motto! Dora and I used to have it embroidered on our blazers.'

'How charming! But of course it has a kind of school flavour about it. Or it might be the title of a Victorian painting of a huge dog of the Landseer variety. But it's very suitable for a girls' school when you consider how faithful nice women tend to be. I can just see you all, running out on to the asphalt

154

playground at break after hot milk or cocoa in the winter or lemonade in the summer.'

'We didn't have an asphalt playground. Still, I suppose *Semper Fidelis* would remind one of that rather than of a past love,' I said. 'I suppose it was too much to expect that you would remember that girl.'

The conversation seemed to come to an end here. Rocky stood by the door and thanked me for the coffee. 'And your company too,' he added. 'You really must come and see our cottage now that the weather is nice. It needs a woman's hand there and Helena isn't really interested. Perhaps I should never have married her.'

I stood awkwardly, not knowing what to say, I, who had always prided myself on being able to make suitable conversation on all occasions. Somehow no platitude came, the moment passed and Rocky went down to his own flat.

CHAPTER SIXTEEN

One evening a few days later I was coming out of my office at six o'clock when I noticed Everard Bone, standing and looking in a nearby shop window. I was thinking of hurrying past him as I was not very well dressed that day – I had had a 'lapse' and was hatless and stockingless in an old cotton dress and a cardigan. Mrs Bonner would have been horrified at the idea of meeting a man in such an outfit. One should always start the day suitably dressed for anything, she had often told me. Any emergency might arise. Somebody – by which she meant a man – might suddenly ring up and ask you out to lunch. Although I agreed with her in theory I found it difficult to remember this every morning as I dressed, especially in the Summer.

'Mildred – at last!' He turned round and faced me, but his voice betrayed the irritation of one who has been waiting for a long time rather than any pleasure at the sight of me. 'I thought you were never coming out. Don't people usually work till five?'

'I don't usually work in the afternoons at all,' I said, 'but

156

some of our staff are away on holiday and I'm helping out. I hope you haven't been waiting here on other evenings?'

'No; I found out that you were working this afternoon.'

'Really? But how?'

'Oh, there are ways of finding out things,' he answered shortly.

'But you could have telephoned me and saved yourself this trouble,' I said, wondering why he should want to see me and whether I ought to feel flattered.

'Let's go and have a drink, shall we?' he asked.

I looked down at myself doubtfully, but he seemed impatient to be off, so I followed a step behind him, my string bag with its loaf of bread and biography of Cardinal Newman dangling at my side. I had certainly not expected to have any engagement that evening. We passed ruined St Ermin's and I saw the grey-haired lady who played the harmonium hurrying out, also with a string bag. I wondered if she too had a biography of Cardinal Newman – I could see that she had a loaf and a large book that might well have been a biography.

'Omar Khayyam,' I murmured to myself, 'only it was a book of verse, wasn't it?' And Everard Bone wasn't very suitable for the 'Thou' and although we were going to have a drink it probably wouldn't be wine. So it was not really like Omar Khayyam at all.

'Let's go in here, shall we?' he said, stopping at a public house near St Ermin's, but he was already opening the door before I could say whether I wanted to or not.

I am not used to going into public houses, so I entered rather timidly, expecting a noisy, smoky atmosphere and a great gust of laughter. But either it was too early or the house was too near the church, for all that I saw and heard was two elderly women sitting in a corner together talking in low voices and drinking stout, and a young man, whom I recognised as the curate of St Ermin's without his clerical collar, having what seemed to be an earnest conversation with the woman behind the bar. I could not call her a barmaid, for she was elderly and of a prim appearance. I felt that she probably cleaned the brasses in St Ermin's when she wasn't polishing the handles of the beer pumps.

'Good Heavens,' murmured Everard, 'isn't it quiet? I suppose it's early.'

'Yes, I expect most people hurry away from this district at this time.'

'Well, we needn't stay long. What would you like to drink?'

'Beer,' I said uncertainly.

'What kind of beer?'

'Oh, bitter, I think,' I said, hoping that it wasn't the kind that tasted like washing-up water, but not being certain.

When it came I found that it was and I was a little annoyed to see that Everard himself had a small glowing drink that looked much more attractive than mine. He shouldn't have asked me what I wanted just like that, I thought resentfully; he should have suggested various things, as Rocky would certainly have done.

I took a sip of my bitter drink and looked round the room. Being so near St Ermin's gave it an almost ecclesiastical air, especially as there was much mahogany, and I was fanciful enough to imagine that I even detected a faint smell of incense. A few more people had come in now and were drinking very quietly and soberly, almost sadly, sitting on a black horsehair bench or at one of the little tables. I stared into the fireless grate, filled now with teazles and pampas grass, and wondered why I should be sitting here with Everard Bone. He was silent too, which did not help matters, and the other people in the bar were so quiet that it was difficult to think of having a private conversation, assuming that we had anything private to talk about, which seemed unlikely.

'I'm reading a biography of Cardinal Newman,' I began, feeling that I could hardly have chosen a more unsuitable topic of conversation for a convivial evening's drinking.

'That must be very interesting,' he said, finishing his drink.

'Yes, it is really,' I faltered. 'One has great sympathy for him, I think.'

'Rome, yes, I suppose so. One can see its attraction.'

'Oh, that wasn't what I really meant,' I said, with really very little idea of what I had meant. 'More as a person . . .' my sentence trailed off miserably and there was now complete silence in the room.

Everard stood up holding his glass. 'You don't seem to like that drink,' he said, suddenly becoming less withdrawn. 'What do you really like?'

'What you had looked nice.'

'I rather doubt if you would like it. I'll get you something like gin and orange or lime – they're quite harmless.'

I felt somewhat humiliated but was glad when he came back from the bar with a gin and orange for me, and after I had taken a sip or two I felt quite cheerful.

'Why did you say you wanted bitter when you obviously don't like it?' Everard asked.

'I don't know, really, I thought it was the kind of thing people did drink. I'm not really used to drinking much myself.'

'Well, you stay as you are. It isn't the kind of thing one wants to get used to,' he said, in what I thought was r~'

priggish way. 'You're better off reading about Cardinal Newman.'

I laughed. 'When I was at school we were sometimes allowed to choose hymns, but Miss Ridout would never let us have *Lead, kindly light* – she thought it was morbid and unsuitable for schoolgirls. Of course we loved it.'

'Yes, I can imagine that. Women are quite impossible to understand sometimes.'

I pondered over this remark for a while, asking myself what it could be going to lead up to, and then wondered why I had been so stupid as not to realise that he wanted to say something about Helena Napier. It was not for the pleasure of my company that Everard Bone had asked me out this evening – or rather not even asked me and given me the chance of appearing better dressed and without my string bag, but had waylaid me in the street.

'I suppose each sex finds the other difficult to understand,' I said, doing the best I could. 'But perhaps one shouldn't expect to know too much about other people.'

'One can't always help knowing,' said Everard. 'Some things are so obvious and stand out even to the most imperceptive.'

I reflected that we could not go on indefinitely in this cryptic way, it was altogether too much of a strain. I took a rather large sip of my drink and said boldly, 'I feel perhaps that women show their feelings for men without realising it sometimes.'

'Have you noticed that too?'

'Why, yes,' I said, rather at a loss. 'It's often a difficult thing to conceal.'

'But it ought to be concealed,' he said irritably, 'especially

160

when the whole thing is quite impossible and the feeling isn't returned in the same way. If they are really going to separate, the whole thing may become most awkward and unpleasant.'

'What *are* you talking about?' I asked, startled.

'Oh, you must know that I mean the Napiers. Helena has been behaving in a most foolish and indiscreet way.'

'I'm afraid I haven't seen much of her lately,' I said, as if I could somehow have prevented her.

'She came to my flat the other night after ten o'clock, *alone*, and stayed for nearly three hours talking, although I did everything I could to get her to go.'

I felt I could hardly ask what methods he had employed.

'Of course I had to go out with her eventually to find her a taxi – you will agree that I could hardly have done less than that,' Everard continued. 'By that time it was nearly one o'clock and naturally I didn't expect to see many people about, let alone anyone who knew both of us.'

'And did you?' I asked, feeling that the story was really getting quite exciting.

'Yes, it could hardly have been more unfortunate. We were just coming out of the house when who should walk by but Apfelbaum and Tyrell Todd – the last two people I should have expected or chosen to see.'

'Oh, Tyrell Todd's the man who gave the paper on pygmies, isn't he?' I asked, in an honest effort to place him. 'And Apfelbaum kept asking questions after your paper.'

Everard looked annoyed at this irrelevant interruption, so I said soothingly, 'I don't see why you should worry about seeing them. I am sure they would think nothing of it. Anthropologists must see such very odd behaviour in primitive societies that they probably think anything we do here is very tame.'

'Don't you believe it. Tyrell Todd revels in petty gossip.'

I stopped myself from making the facetious observation that possibly it was his work among the pygmies that had made him small-minded and petty, and went on to ask reassuring questions.

'But what were *they* doing together so late? It may well have been something disgraceful. Did they speak to you?'

'No, they just said "Good evening" or words to that effect. I think we were all a little surprised.'

'Four anthropologists meeting unexpectedly in a London square at one o'clock in the morning,' I said. 'There does seem to be something a little surprising about that.'

'You make everything into a joke,' said Everard resentfully, but with the suspicion of a smile.

'Well, I think the whole things sounds slightly ridiculous. If you can see it like that perhaps you won't worry about it.'

'But Helena is so indiscreet and from what I've seen of Rockingham I shouldn't imagine he would be likely to behave in a very sensible way, either.'

'No,' I murmured, 'I don't think you would exactly call him sensible.'

'On the other hand, it is unlikely that he would want a divorce,' said Everard thoughtfully.

'Oh, no,' I exclaimed, shocked out of the pleasant haze into which the drink had lulled me, 'and I suppose you would not want to marry Helena even if she were free. I mean, divorce would be against your principles.'

'Naturally,' he said stiffly. 'And I don't love her, anyway.'

'Oh, poor Helena. I think she may love you,' I said rashly.

'I'm sure she does,' said Everard in what seemed to be a satisfied tone. 'She has told me so.'

'Oh, no! Not without encouragement! Do women declare themselves like that?'

'Oh, yes. It is not so very unusual.'

'But what did you tell her?'

'I told her that it was quite impossible that I should love her.'

'You must have been rather startled,' I said. 'Unless you had expected it, and perhaps you had if it can happen. But it must have been like having something like a white rabbit thrust into your arms and not knowing what to do with it.'

'A white rabbit? What do you mean?'

'Oh, if you don't see I can't explain,' I said. I gathered my string bag to me. 'I think I had better be going home now.'

'Oh, please don't go,' said Everard. 'I feel you are the only person who can help. You could perhaps say something to Helena.'

'*I* say something? But she wouldn't listen to me.'

We stood up and went out together.

'I'm sorry,' said Everard. 'Why should you be brought into it, really? I just thought you might be able to drop a hint.'

'But men ought to be able to manage their own affairs,' I said. 'After all most of them don't seem to mind speaking frankly and making people unhappy. I don't see why you should.'

We walked on in silence.

'I should be very distressed if I thought I had purposely made anybody unhappy,' said Everard at last.

There seemed to be nothing more to say. I was to tell Helena that Everard Bone did not love her. I might just as well go home and do it straight away.

We came to St Ermin's. 'I wonder if anybody is making coffee on a Primus in the ruins?' I asked idly.

'Do people do that?'

'Oh, yes, that little woman who plays the harmonium.'

'Yes, she looks as if she might.'

We had suddenly forgotten about Helena Napier and were talking quite easily about other things.

'I promised to go and have dinner with my mother tonight,' said Everard. 'Perhaps you would like to come too?'

I decided that I might as well put off telling Helena that Everard did not love her for an hour or two at least, so we got into a taxi and drove to a dark red forbidding-looking house in a street of similar houses.

'My mother is a little eccentric,' he said as we got out of the taxi. 'I just thought I should warn you.'

'I don't suppose I shall find her any more odd than many people I have met,' I said, feeling that it was not perhaps a good beginning to the evening. 'I'm sorry I'm not more suitably dressed. If I had known ... only, things do seem to happen so unexpectedly.'

'You seem to be very nicely dressed,' said Everard without looking. 'And my mother never notices what anybody is wearing.'

An old bent maidservant opened the door and we went in. There was a good deal of dark furniture in the hall and a faintly exotic smell, almost like incense. The walls were covered with animals' heads and their sad or fierce eyes looked down on us.

'Perhaps you would care to wash your hands, miss?' said the maid in a hushed voice. She led me upstairs and into a bathroom, with much marble and mahogany and a stained-glass window. I began to think that it was perhaps suitable that I was carrying a biography of Cardinal Newman in my string bag, and as I washed my hands and tidied my hair I found myself thinking about the Oxford Movement and the architecture associated with it. But then I was seized with a feeling of alarm, waiting outside the bathroom door on a dark landing, then creeping down the stairs and wondering where I should go when I got to the bottom. I was surprised to see that Everard was standing in the hall waiting for me, turning over a heap of old visiting cards that lay in a brass bowl on an antique chest.

'Mother will be in the drawing-room,' he said, opening a door.

I found myself in a room with two women, one of whom was standing by the fireplace while the other was sitting on the edge of a chair with her hands folded in her lap.

'This is my mother,' said Everard, leading me towards the standing woman, who was tall with a long nose like his own, 'and this is – er . . .' he glanced at the nondescript woman sitting on the edge of her chair who might really have been anybody or nobody, and then back to his mother,

'It's Miss Jessop, dear,' she said.

'Oh, yes, of course.'

Miss Jessop! I remembered my telephone conversation with Mrs Bone and looked at the nondescript woman with new interest. *If it's Miss Jessop, I can only hope you're ringing up to apologise* . . . She did not look like the kind of person who could possibly do anything for which an apology might be demanded. What *had* she done? I supposed I should never know. Presumably all was now well between her and Mrs Bone.

We all murmured politely at each other and Mrs Bone did not seem to be at all eccentric. I was beginning to think that

Everard had misjudged his mother when she suddenly said in a clear voice, 'Miss Jessop and I are very much interested in the suppression of woodworm in furniture.'

'I should think it's very important,' I said. 'I know a lot of our furniture at home got the worm in it. There didn't seem to be anything we could do about it.'

'Oh, but there is a preparation on the market now which is very effective,' said Mrs Bone, clasping her hands together almost in rapture. 'It has been used with excellent results in many famous buildings.' She began to enumerate various Oxford and Cambridge colleges and well-known churches and cathedrals. 'It has even been used in Westminster Cathedral,' she declared.

'Not Westminster Cathedral, surely, Mother,' said Everard. 'The wood isn't old enough.'

'Westminster Abbey, perhaps,' I suggested.

'Oh, well, it was something to do with Westminster,' said Mrs Bone. 'Wasn't it, Miss Jessop?' She turned towards her with a rather menacing look.

Miss Jessop seemed to agree.

'I think we had better have some sherry,' said Everard, going out of the room.

I thought I had better revive the conversation which had lapsed, so I commented on the animals' heads in the hall, saying what fine specimens they were.

'My husband shot them in India and Africa,' said Mrs Bone, 'but however many you shoot there still seem to be more.'

'Oh, yes, it would be a terrible thing if they became extinct,' I said. 'I suppose they keep the rarer animals in game reserves now.'

'It's not the animals so much as the birds,' said Mrs Bone fiercely. 'You will hardly believe this, Miss – er – but I was sitting in the window this afternoon and as it was a fine day I had it open at the bottom, when I felt something drop into my lap. And do you know what it was?' She turned and peered at me intently.

I said that I had no idea.

'Unpleasantness,' she said, almost triumphantly so that I was reminded of William Caldicote. Then lowering her voice she explained, 'From a bird, you see. It had *done* something when I was actually sitting in my own drawing-room.'

'How annoying,' I said, feeling mesmerised and unable even to laugh.

'And that's not the worst,' she went on, rummaging in a small desk which stood open and seemed to be full of old newspapers. 'Read this.' She handed me a cutting headed OWL BITES WOMAN, from which I read that an owl had flown in through a cottage window one evening and bitten a woman on the chin. 'And this,' she went on, handing me another cutting which told how a swan had knocked a girl off her bicycle. 'What do you think of *that*?'

'Oh, I suppose they were just accidents,' I said.

'*Accidents!* Even Miss Jessop agrees that they are rather more than *accidents*, don't you, Miss Jessop?'

Miss Jessop made a quavering sound which might have been 'Yes' or 'No' but it was not allowed to develop into speech, for Mrs Bone broke in by telling Everard that Miss Jessop wouldn't want any sherry.

'The Dominion of the Birds,' she went on. 'I very much fear it may come to that.'

Everard looked at me a little anxiously but I managed to

keep up the conversation until Mrs Bone declared that it was dinner time. 'You had better be going home, now, Miss Jessop,' she said. 'We are going to have our dinner.'

Miss Jessop stood up and put on her gloves. Then, with a little nod which seemed to include all of us, she went quietly out of the room.

'I eat as many birds as possible,' said Mrs Bone when we were sitting down to roast chicken. 'I have them sent from Harrods or Fortnum's, and sometimes I go and look at them in the cold meats department. They do them up very prettily with aspic jelly and decorations. At least we can eat our enemies. Everard, dear, which was that tribe in Africa which were cannibals?'

'There are several thousand tribes in Africa, Mother,' said Everard patiently, 'and many of them have been and probably still are cannibals.'

'But surely the British Administration have stamped it out?' I asked.

'Certainly they have attempted to,' said Everard. 'And the missionaries have also done a lot to educate the people.'

'Yes, I suppose that would make them see that it was wrong,' I said feebly, wondering whether anthropologists really approved of these old customs being stamped out.

'Missionaries have done a lot of harm,' said Mrs Bone firmly. 'The natives have their own religions which are very ancient, much more ancient than ours. We have no business to try to make them change.'

'My mother is not a Christian,' said Everard, perhaps unnecessarily.

'The Jesuits got at my son, you know, Miss – er—' said Mrs Bone, turning to me. 'They will stop at nothing, those Jesuits.

You would hardly believe the things that go on in their semi-naries. I can lend you some very informative pamphlets if you are interested.'

I was by now in a state of considerable confusion and wished that Everard would make some attempt to lead the conversation into normal channels, though I realised that this would probably be quite impossible. It occurred to me that I had been bearing the full burden of the evening, and at half past nine I began to feel both tired and resentful and decided that I would go home.

'You seem to have made a favourable impression,' he said, as I stuffed some pamphlets about woodworms and Jesuits into my string bag with Cardinal Newman and the loaf. 'Most people are quite incapable of carrying on a conversation with my mother. I admired the way you did it.'

'Oh, but I'm used to coping with people,' I said. 'Being a clergyman's daughter is a good training.' It was only people like the Napiers who were beyond my experience. 'It is splendid that your mother should have so many interests in her life,' I said. 'So often elderly people think only of themselves and their illnesses.' Birds, worms and Jesuits . . . it might almost have been a poem, but I could not remember that anybody had ever written it.

'Yes, her life is quite busy, I suppose, but she is getting rather difficult now.'

'Who is Miss Jessop?' I asked.

'Oh, I don't know; just some woman who comes to see my mother sometimes,' said Everard vaguely. 'She is quite often there.'

'But does she never speak?'

'Oh, I don't know. It would be such a help if you could say

something to Helena. You remember what we were talking about earlier in the evening.'

It seemed to have been a very long evening, but I did remember and the memory depressed me.

'A sensible person, with no axe to grind,' Everard was saying, almost to himself.

I accepted this description of myself without comment. 'But what could I say?' I protested. 'The occasion may not arise and even if it did I still shouldn't know.'

'Oh, surely, words would come,' said Everard impatiently. 'You said you were used to coping with people.'

I did not attempt to explain that my training had not fitted me for this kind of a situation. But I saw myself, having no axe to grind, calling in on the Napiers as I went up to my flat and making the attempt. But Rocky would be there, so of course it wouldn't do. And when I passed their door their voices seemed to be raised as if they were having an argument. I am afraid it was impossible not to hear some of the things they were saying, but I cannot bring myself to record them here. I think I hurried up to my kitchen and made a cup of tea and then went to bed trying to take my mind off the situation by thinking about Miss Jessop and her curious relationship with Mrs Bone. I wondered if I should ever hear her speak or know why an apology had been demanded from her.

CHAPTER SEVENTEEN

The next day I worked until lunchtime and came home at about half past one. This was the only time when the offices on the ground floor of the house where I lived seemed to show any signs of life. Typewriters were clacking, telephones ringing, and a man was dictating a letter, weighing each word, or so it appeared, though the words that came to my ears through the open door seemed to be hardly worth such ponderous consideration.

Above this it was very quiet, so I guessed that the Napiers must be out, but when I passed their kitchen I could hear the gas hissing and there was a smell of something burning. I knocked on the half-open door but there was no answer, so I went in. I found one of the gas rings full on and on it a saucepan of potatoes which had boiled dry and were now sticking to the bottom in a brownish mass. I dealt with them quickly but the saucepan was in a very bad state. I ran some water into it so that it could soak. I noticed with distaste and disapproval that the breakfast things and what appeared to be dishes and glasses from an even earlier date were not washed up. The table by the window was also crowded; there were two bottles of milk, each half full, an empty gin bottle, a dish of butter melting in the sun, and a plate full of cigarette stubs. I felt very spinsterish indeed as I stood there, holding the burnt saucepan in my hand.

'The potatoes – I forgot them.' Rocky was standing behind me in the doorway.

'Yes, you did,' I said rather sharply. 'The gas was full on and they boiled dry. I'm afraid the saucepan's ruined.'

'Oh, the saucepan,' Rocky said, passing his hand over his brow with a gesture of weariness that seemed to me rather theatrical. 'There have been other things to think about besides saucepans.'

'Oh. Is anything the matter?' I asked, moving towards him, still holding the saucepan in my hand.

'Yes, I suppose so. Helena has left me.' He went into the sitting-room and sank into an armchair. I stood helplessly by him, trying to think of something to say or do, but he took no notice of my faltering words of sympathy. I looked round the room and saw that another saucepan had evidently been put down on a polished walnut table, where it had burnt an unsightly mark.

'That was the last straw, the table,' he said. 'She put a hot saucepan down on the table. Such a trivial thing, I suppose you might think, but typical of her lack of consideration. And all the washing-up left for days sometimes until Mrs Morris came . . .' He rambled on, cataloguing her faults while I sat by him not liking to interrupt. At last I was conscious of a feeling something like hunger stirring in me, for it was now about two o'clock, and I began to wonder whether Rocky had had any lunch.

'Lunch? I haven't thought about it,' he said. 'Perhaps one doesn't on these occasions.'

'I'm sure you should eat something,' I said. 'Why don't you come up to my flat, which is tidier than this, and I will clear up these things afterwards.'

He followed me apathetically and began to tell me what had happened. It appeared that they had had a quarrel when he was getting lunch and that Helena had run out of the house, saying that she was never coming back.

'I went after her,' Rocky said, 'but she must have got into a taxi, because there was no sign of her. So eventually I just came back here.'

'But surely she will have to come back? Did she take anything with her, any luggage?'

'I don't know. I shouldn't think so.'

'But where could she have gone?' I persisted, feeling that somebody ought to be practical.

'To Everard Bone, I suppose,' said Rocky indifferently.

'No, surely not!' I exclaimed. That must not happen. The irrelevant and unworthy thought crossed my mind that he would think I had failed in my duty and I should be blamed. But I had really had very little time in which to tell Helena that Everard did not love her; I had been meaning to say something at the first opportunity. And yet, in a way, I could not help feeling that it would serve him right if she did arrive on his doorstep and cause him embarrassment. 'If she *has* gone to him,' I said, 'she will have arrived by now. I will ring up his flat and find out.'

I was a little taken aback when Everard himself answered me, though I don't know who else I had expected, and could only stammer out the news and ask if Helena had come to him.

'No, she certainly has not,' he said, his voice full of alarm. 'In any case, I am leaving for Derbyshire immediately.'

'Derbyshire?' I repeated stupidly. It seemed such an unlikely place.

'Yes, the Prehistoric Society is holding a conference there,' he said quickly.

'You will be able to hide in a cave,' I said, giggling in the nervous way one does sometimes at a moment of crisis. I composed myself before going back to Rocky, who was still reclining in a chair.

'She isn't with Everard Bone,' I said, 'so perhaps she will be back soon, unless there are any friends of hers I could ring up for you?'

'Oh, no, don't bother. One can't go ringing up people all over London.'

'Well, I may as well get lunch,' I said. 'I'm afraid it will be something very simple, but you must eat.'

Rocky followed me into my kitchen and stood under the line of washing, which I noticed with irritation had become too dry to be ironed comfortably. He began pulling down the garments and making jokes about them, but I felt that this was not the time for coyness or embarrassment, so I took no notice of him.

I washed a lettuce and dressed it with a little of my hoarded olive oil and some salt. I also had a Camembert cheese, a fresh loaf and a bowl of greengages for dessert. It seemed an idyllic sort of meal that ought to have been eaten in the open air, with a bottle of wine and what is known as 'good' conversation. I thought it unlikely that I should be able to provide either the conversation or the wine, but I remembered that I had a bottle of brandy which I kept, according to old-fashioned custom, for 'emergencies' and I decided to bring it in with the coffee. I could see my mother, her lips slightly pursed, saying, 'For medicinal purposes only, of course . . .' But now respectable elderly women do not need to excuse themselves for buying brandy or even gin, though it is quite likely that some still do and perhaps one may hope that they always will.

Rocky began to eat with a show of appetite, but the conversation he made was not 'good' conversation;

'She couldn't even *wash* a lettuce properly,' he said, 'let alone prepare a salad like this.'

I did not know what answer to make and we continued to eat in silence on my part. The brandy seemed to rouse him a little further, though to no great heights, but what he said was pleasing to me personally.

'Mildred, you really are the most wonderful person,' he said, turning his gaze on me. 'I don't know *what* I should do without you.'

You do very well without me, I thought, with a flash of impatience, and will continue to do well.

'To think that you should have come in just at this moment, this awful crisis, and given me a delicious lunch.' He closed his eyes and lay back in his chair. 'I really couldn't have borne to have got lunch myself.'

'Oh, it was nothing,' I said, feeling that no other answer could be given. 'Anybody else would have done the same.' And perhaps even a less attractive man than Rocky would have a devoted woman to prepare a meal for him on the day his wife left him. A mother, a sister, an aunt, even . . . I remembered an advertisement I had once seen in the *Church Times* – 'Organist and aunt require unfurnished accommodation; East Sheen or Barnes preferred'. Rather fishy, I had thought it, probably not his aunt at all, though surely the kind of people who expressed a preference for East Sheen or Barnes could hardly be anything but highly respectable?

'What are you smiling at?'

I started guiltily, for I had temporarily forgotten the dreadful thing that had happened. 'I'm sorry,' I said. 'I didn't realise I was smiling.'

'You are almost cheering me up,' said Rocky resentfully. 'I suppose everyone must have a friend to comfort them at times like this.'

'Not everybody,' I said, thinking of the many rejected ones who lived in lonely bed-sitting-rooms with nobody to talk to them or prepare meals for them. I told Rocky of my thought.

'They could always wash stockings or something,' he said callously. 'Assuming, of course, that they are women, and it's usually women who live in bed-sitting-rooms.'

'And are rejected,' I added.

'Well, yes, it all hangs together somehow, doesn't it? Of course my position is hardly the same. You mustn't think that I have been rejected.'

We sat there almost bickering until the church clock struck a quarter to four.

'Tea,' said Rocky, 'I think I should like some tea now.'

'Yes, of course,' I said, going meekly to the kitchen. I was just filling the kettle when my bell rang. 'Oh, dear, who can that be?' I asked.

'Perhaps Helena has also come to you for comfort,' said Rocky. 'I think it would be more suitable if you answered the door, just in case, you know.'

He continued to loll in the armchair, so there was nothing for me to do but hurry downstairs, feeling rather flustered and irritated. I'm afraid my dismay must have shown in my face when I opened the front door and found Julian Malory standing there, for his expression altered and he hesitated before coming in.

'I was just going to make some tea,' I said, as we walked upstairs, 'so you're just in time.'

'Ah, tea,' he said. 'I had hoped to be in time for that.'

I did not tell him that Rocky Napier was with me and the expressions of the two men when they saw each other was something that made me smile, Rocky frowning and sulky and Julian puzzled and dismayed. Rocky rose rather ungraciously and offered Julian his armchair, though in a half-hearted manner. Julian accepted it. Rocky then flung himself down on the sofa. At this point I hurried out to see if the kettle was boiling and by the time I had come back with the tea the two men were engaged in some sort of a conversation about Italy. Julian was asking about the church of Santa Chiara in Naples and quoting a poem about Palm Sunday, but Rocky said that the church had been destroyed by bombs and the poem always depressed him anyway.

I began to pour out tea. As so often happens at a moment of crisis, there was something wrong with it. It seemed much too weak and flowed in what a poet might call an amber stream from the imperfectly cleaned spout of the silver teapot. Mrs Morris had been neglecting her duty and I should have to 'speak' to her.

'Ah, what a treat, China tea!' Julian exclaimed.

I have often wondered whether it is really a good thing to be honest by nature and upbringing; certainly it is not a good thing socially, for I feel sure that the tea party would have been more successful had I not explained that the tea was really Indian which I had unfortunately made too weak. Thus, instead of feeling that I had provided a treat for them the two men seemed resentful and embarrassed, almost as if I had done it on purpose. I stirred the pot despairingly and offered to go and make some more, but neither of them would hear of it. Rocky was polite but impatient and Julian polite but disappointed, almost grieved.

It seemed to me that both men appeared at their worst that afternoon, as if they had the effect of bringing out the worst in each other, unless it was that I had never before had the opportunity of observing each of them dispassionately. Rocky seemed shallow and charming in an obvious and false way, and his sprawling on the sofa seemed to me both affected and impolite. Julian, on the other hand, appeared to have no charm at all, not even of an obvious kind. By the side of Rocky he seemed pompous and clerical, almost like a stage clergyman, his voice taking on an unctuous quality which it did not usually possess. 'She worships at St Mary's . . . The other morning, after I had said Mass . . .' even his conversation seemed stilted and unnatural. This had the effect of making Rocky flippant, so that although Julian made an effort to respond to his little jokes about the best quality incense and glamorous acolytes, there was a kind of hostility between them, and I felt almost as if I were the cause of it. It was unusual, certainly, for me to be alone with two men even when each of them was the property of some other woman, but I could not make anything of the opportunity.

I fussed over the weak tea, regretted that I had not bought another cake or some tomatoes or a cucumber to make sandwiches, wished passionately that I had been a more brilliant conversationalist. As it was, Rocky had now lapsed into silence and Julian was looking around him with frightened, suspicious glances. What was the matter with him? I wondered. There was surely nothing compromising or embarrassing about the situation? And then I saw what it was that was upsetting him – the brandy bottle was still on the mantelpiece, looking very large and shocking among my small ornaments and the picture postcards of Exmoor and North Wales, where Mrs Bonner and another woman from my office respectively were spending their holidays. I supposed that on all the occasions when Julian had visited me before he had never seen a brandy bottle on the mantelpiece.

'Have you made any plans for your wedding?' I asked, anxious to make light conversation.

'Oh, yes, we are hoping to be married quite soon,' said Julian gratefully. 'And we do want all the congregation of St Mary's and all our friends to come to the wedding.'

'I suppose you mean what are known as "regular communicants"?' asked Rocky. 'Mildred may have told you that I can't do with religion before breakfast. Would those who have just been to Evensong be eligible? They might surely count as friends?'

'Oh, anybody, really, all well-wishers, of course,' said Julian in an embarrassed but jocular manner. 'We want everybody to rejoice with us.'

'I should certainly like to do that,' said Rocky. 'You see, I *do* wish you well, and as my wife has just left me the very least I can do is to hope that yours will not do the same.'

Julian dropped half of the slice of cake he was holding on to the floor and stooped quickly to pick up the fragments.

I took off the lid of the teapot and peered into its depths, but without hope. I supposed that the shock he had suffered should be enough to excuse Rocky's curious behaviour but it made me feel rather uneasy.

'My dear fellow,' Julian began in a confused way, 'I really am most awfully distressed . . . but surely you must be mistaken? Some misunderstanding, perhaps, or a quarrel . . . Why, I saw Mrs Napier only this morning.'

'Oh, these things happen quickly when they do happen,' said Rocky, who now seemed to be almost enjoying himself. 'After all, somebody must have seen her for the last time – perhaps it was you.'

'This is *most* distressing news – there must be something we can do.' Julian was now pacing about the room, frowning.

I began piling cups and saucers on to a tray. I suppose it was cowardly of me, but I felt that I wanted to be alone, and what better place to choose than the sink, where neither of the men would follow me?

I started in my own kitchen where the lunch and tea things were quickly washed and dried, but then I moved down to the Napiers' with the idea of making some order out of the confusion there. No sink has ever been built high enough for a reasonably tall person and my back was soon aching with the effort of washing up, especially as yesterday's greasy dishes needed a lot of scrubbing to get them clean. My thoughts went round and round and it occurred to me that if I ever wrote a novel it would be of the 'stream of conscious-ness' type and deal with an hour in the life of a woman at the sink. I felt resentful and bitter towards Helena and Rocky and even towards Julian, though I had to admit that nobody had compelled me to wash these dishes or to tidy this kitchen. It was the fussy spinster in me, the Martha, who could not comfortably sit and make conversation when she knew that yesterday's unwashed dishes were still in the sink. Martha's back must have ached too, I thought grimly, noticing that the plate rack needed scrubbing and the tea-cloths boiling.

At last everything was done except for the saucepan with the burnt potatoes. I looked hopelessly around for something to scrape it with.

'Clean glasses?' came Rocky's voice from outside the door. 'Are there any?'

'Yes, in the cupboard,' I said. 'I've just washed them.'

'There *was* some gin,' said Rocky, delving among a cluster of bottles in a corner. 'I suppose we could drink your brandy?'

'Oh, yes, do.'

'Ah, this is better.' He held up a straw-covered flask of wine. 'The vicar and I are really getting on rather well. I like him. It's a pity you didn't marry him, Mildred, you'd have made a pleasant pair. Come and have a drink with us when you've finished that saucepan. We're upstairs in your room.'

I sat down on a chair in the Napiers' kitchen, ready to feel tired and resentful, but suddenly something came to the rescue and I began to see the funny side of it. Then the telephone rang. It was Helena.

'Oh, thank goodness, it's you, Mildred,' she said. 'I couldn't bear it to be Rocky after all the things he said. Listen, I'm staying with Miss Clovis.'

'Miss Who?'

'Miss Clovis – you remember her, surely? She works at the Learned Society.'

'Oh, of course.' Our excellent Miss Clovis with the tea. Did she also give sanctuary to runaway wives?

'She has offered to collect some of my things. I was wondering if you could pack a suitcase for me and meet her at Victoria Station under the clock?'

I agreed to do this, mainly because it seemed simpler to agree. I was to pack a few necessities and slip out of the house without letting Rocky know what I was doing, though I could tell him later that Helena was with Miss Clovis.

It was not very easy to find the things Helena had asked for; all the drawers in the bedroom were so untidy that it was difficult to know what was supposed to be where, but at last I had packed the case and was waiting at the appointed place at Victoria, feeling rather foolish, as if I were about to elope with somebody myself.

It was the rush hour and droves of people hurried by me to catch their trains. Men in bowler hats, with dispatch cases so flat and neat it seemed impossible that they could contain anything at all, and neatly rolled umbrellas, ran with undignified haste and jostled against me. Some carried little bundles or parcels, offerings to their wives perhaps or a surprise for supper. I imagined them piling into the green trains, opening their evening papers, doing the crossword, not speaking to each other . . .

'Miss Lathbury?' A crisp voice interrupted my fantasies and the stocky figure of Miss Clovis was standing at my side.

'Yes. I've brought the things Mrs Napier asked for.'

'Splendid!' She took the case from me with a firm gesture.

'I hope she's all right?' I asked.

'Oh, perfectly – now that she's got away from that brute of a husband.'

I wanted to protest but hardly knew what to say. I was surprised that such a person as Miss Clovis appeared to be should express herself so conventionally.

'She will be quite safe with me,' she went on chattily. 'I have a cosy little flat on top of the Society's premises, you know.'

Pictures of savage chiefs and a rolled-up flag in the lavatory, I thought, but perhaps she would have a bathroom of her own.

'I do hope that Mrs Napier will soon return to her husband,' I said firmly. 'He is very upset.'

'You think the separation may be only temporary?' said Miss Clovis, looking disappointed. '*I* hadn't gathered that at all. He will go to the country where I believe he has a cottage and she will return to the flat. That's what I understood.'

'Oh, I see. Well, I hope they will meet again and talk it over before doing anything so drastic.' I could not admit to Miss Clovis that apart from anything else I did not want Rocky to go away.

'Well, I must be going,' said Miss Clovis. 'Thank you for bringing the things. I will let you know if there are any developments. I believe Mr Bone is in Derbyshire?'

'Oh, surely this has nothing to do with him?' I exclaimed in alarm. 'I'm certain he wouldn't want to be concerned in it.'

'For the sake of anthropology,' declared Miss Clovis, grasping her umbrella and brandishing it as if it were a weapon or a banner. 'There is a great bond between those who have worked together *in the field* – their work on matrilineal groupings, most valuable, a real contribution . . .' She lowered her voice confidentially. 'There was that affair of Dr Medlicott and Miss Etty – I don't know if you heard about it – I always feel that I brought them together. His wife didn't like it at first. Still, there you are.' She nodded briskly and was off.

I stood for a moment in a kind of daze and then made my way slowly home. I was just approaching Grantchester Square when I saw two men going into the public house at the end of it. They were Rocky Napier and Julian Malory. Well, let them go, I thought. It was somehow a comfort to know that they had made friends over a glass of wine. A comfort for them, though not for me, I decided, unable to face the thought of returning to the flat to wash their empty glasses which they had no doubt left in my sitting-room. It would be better to call in at the vicarage and see Winifred.

I had just rung the bell when it occurred to me that Allegra Gray would probably be there and I should have turned back had not Winifred herself opened the door almost immediately.

'Oh, Mildred, how nice! You hardly ever come to see us now,' she complained. 'Since Allegra and Julian became engaged, things haven't been the same, somehow. But she's gone to supper with a friend in Kensington tonight and Julian's out somewhere, so I'm all alone. You look upset, dear. Has anything happened?'

'I almost wish the Napiers hadn't come to live in my house,' I said. 'Things were much simpler before they came.'

Winifred did not ask any questions but under the influence of a cup of tea her tongue was loosened. We began talking about 'old times' as they now seemed to be. 'Oh, Mildred,' she blurted out, 'sometimes I wish Allegra hadn't come to live here, either!'

CHAPTER EIGHTEEN

Rocky behaved rather dramatically the next day, packing suitcases and going round his flat marking various articles of furniture and small objects which were to be sent after him to his cottage in the country. When I came home after lunch I found him almost ready to go.

He came up to me with a list in his hand.

'We may as well get it quite clear,' he said. 'I shall want to have my own things with me and you can hardly be expected to know exactly which they are.'

'*I?*' I exclaimed in surprise.

'Oh, yes, I imagine you will be here, won't you? I have asked the remover's men to come on Saturday morning so that you will be able to supervise them.'

'Yes, of course,' I said weakly. 'I suppose they couldn't be expected to do it alone. About what time will they be coming?'

'Oh, I told them to come really early, about eight o'clock. Then Helena can come back on Sunday or Monday if she wants to. You might ring up Miss Clovis and tell her so' – I had of course told him where Helena was – 'and then everything will be as it was.'

I wanted to protest, not so much about the furniture-removing and the part I was to play in it, as about his idea that everything could then be as it had been before. But no words came. I wondered if he would suggest that we had tea together before he went, but he did not say anything and somehow I did not feel inclined to offer to make any. I suppose I did not want him to remember me as the kind of person who was always making cups of tea at moments of crisis.

'Goodbye, Mildred; we'll meet again, of course,' he said casually. 'You must come and stay at my cottage one week-end.'

'I should like to,' I began, wondering even as I said it if it would be quite proper. But obviously no such thought had occurred or would ever occur to Rocky. 'You *will* remember which pieces of furniture are to come, won't you?' were his last words to me.

After he had gone I stood looking out of the window until his taxi was out of sight.

The effects of shock and grief are too well known to need description and I stood at the window for a long time. At last I did make a cup of tea but I could not eat anything. There seemed to be a great weight inside me and after sitting down for a while I thought I would go into the church and try to find a little consolation there.

I opened the door rather timidly and went in. I was relieved to see that there was nobody else there and I sat down hopelessly and waited, I did not know for what. I did not feel that I could organise my thoughts but I hoped that if I sat there quietly I might draw some comfort from the atmosphere.

Centuries of devotion leave their mark in a place, I knew, but then I remembered that it was barely seventy years since St Mary's had been built; it seemed so bright and new and there were no canopied tombs of great families, no weeping cherubs, no urns, no worn inscriptions on the floor. Instead I could only read the brass tablets to past vicars and benefactors or contemplate the ugly stained glass of the east window. And yet, I thought after a while, wasn't the atmosphere of good Victorian piety as comforting as any other? Ought I not be as much consoled by the thought of our first vicar, Father Busby – Henry Bertram Busby and Maud Elizabeth, his wife – as by any seventeenth-century divine? I was half unconscious of my surroundings now and started when I heard a voice calling my name.

'Miss Lathbury! Miss Lathbury!'

I looked up almost guiltily as if I had been doing something disgraceful and saw Miss Statham creeping towards me. She held a polishing-cloth and a tin of Brasso in her hand.

'You were sitting so still, I thought perhaps you'd had a turn.'

'A turn?' I repeated stupidly.

'Yes, been taken ill, you know. I said to myself as I came out of the vestry, "Why, there's Miss Lathbury sitting there. I wonder what *she's* doing? It isn't her week for the brasses and it's too early for Evensong." Then I thought you must be ill.'

'No, I'm all right, thank you,' I said smiling at Miss Statham's reasons for my presence in church. 'I was just thinking something over.'

'Thinking something over? Oh, dear . . .' she let out a stifled giggle and then clapped her hand over her mouth fearfully. 'I'm sorry, Miss Lathbury, I didn't mean to laugh really.

Only it seemed a bit funny to be sitting here on a nice after-noon thinking things over. Wouldn't you like to come home with me and have a cup of tea?'

I refused as graciously as I could and Miss Statham went off to do her brasses. My little meditation in the church was at an end; obviously I could not go on with it now. Had the church been older and darker and smaller, had it perhaps been a *Roman* Catholic church, I thought wickedly . . . But it was no use regretting it; the fault lay in myself. Nevertheless, I did feel a little calmer and better able to face furniture removals and whatever else might be in store for me.

When I got home Mrs Morris was cleaning my sitting-room. It was really her day for the Napiers, but she had finished their work sooner than usual and expressed surprise at the tidiness of the kitchen.

'Only the breakfast washing-up to do and a few odd plates,' she said. 'Usually it's all the meals from the day before and *glasses* – you'd think they lived on wine.'

I explained that I had done some washing up the previous afternoon. 'Mrs Napier is away,' I said delicately, 'so she wasn't able to do it.'

'And she wouldn't do it even if she was here,' said Mrs Morris emphatically. '*He's* always the one to do things in the house. The next thing is we'll have the vicar washing up. Just wait till he's married and you'll soon see.'

'You don't think that men should help with the house-work?' I asked.

She gave me a look but said nothing for a moment. 'Not a clergyman, Miss Lathbury,' she said at last, shaking her head.

'You think they have enough burdens to bear without that?'

'I don't know about *burdens*,' she said doubtfully, 'but that

Mrs Gray will lead him a dance, I don't mind telling you. A widow! What happened to her first? That's what *I'd* like to know!' She opened the window and shook the mop vigorously out of it.

'Oh, I think he was killed in the war,' I said.

Mrs Morris shook her head again.

'You told me, Miss Lathbury, that the vicar wasn't a marrying man,' she said accusingly.

'Well, I had always thought he wasn't,' I admitted. 'But we're sometimes mistaken, aren't we?'

'A pretty face,' said Mrs Morris; 'well, she has got that. But what's his poor sister going to do? What about poor Miss Winifred? Hasn't she made a home for him for all these years? Given up the best years of her life to making him comfortable?'

I could think of no ready answers to her challenging question, especially when I remembered with some uneasiness what Winifred had hinted at the other evening. Not that she had exactly *said* anything against Allegra Gray, but she seemed less enthusiastic than she had been.

'I wouldn't put it quite like that, Mrs Morris,' I said at last. 'I think Miss Malory has liked to make a home for her brother. After all, it was the natural thing for her to do, as I suppose it would be for most women.'

'*You* haven't made a home for a man, Miss Lathbury,' Mrs Morris went on, her tone full of reproach so that I felt as if I had in some way failed in my duty.

'Well, no,' I admitted, 'though after my mother died I kept house for my father for a short time. But then he died too and I've been by myself ever since, except when Miss Caldicote was here.'

'It's not natural for a woman to live alone, without a husband.'

'No, perhaps not, but many women do and some have no choice in the matter.'

'No choice!' Mrs Morris's scornful laugh rang out. 'You want to think of yourself a bit more, Miss Lathbury, if you don't mind me saying so. You've done too much for Father Malory and so has Miss Winifred and in the end you both get left, if you'll excuse me putting it plainly.'

'Yes, I suppose you're right,' I said, smiling, for really she *was* right. It was not the excellent women who got married but people like Allegra Gray, who was no good at sewing, and Helena Napier, who left all the washing up. 'I can't change now. I'm afraid it's too late.' I felt it would not sound very convincing if I said that I hadn't really wanted to marry Julian Malory. I was obviously regarded in the parish as the chief of the rejected ones and I must fill the position with as much dignity as I could.

'You're not bad-looking,' said Mrs Morris quickly and then looked shocked, as if she had gone too far. She bent down, unhooked the bag from the Hoover and shook out a great mound of dust on to a newspaper. 'Things happen, even at the last minute,' she said mysteriously. 'Not that you'd want to marry a man who'd been divorced. Too much of this old divorce, there is,' she muttered, going out into the kitchen with the bundle of dust. I heard her say that there was a drop of milk in the jug that would do for my tea.

She left me feeling a little shaken, almost as if I really had failed in some kind of duty and must take immediate action to make up for it. I must go to Julian and not do things for him and then he might reject Allegra and marry me. As for Rocky, in his cottage surrounded by nettles, perhaps it did not matter how much I did for him since he could never be regarded as a possible husband. Too much of this old divorce. But then I smiled at myself for the heavy seriousness of my thoughts. Had the Wren officers had their dreams too? I wondered. Had they imagined Rocky wifeless and turning to them for comfort or had they always known they were just playthings, taken down from their shelves only when he wanted an evening's diversion? I could not flatter myself that I had done even that for him.

I also had a limp suede-bound volume of Christina Rossetti's poems among my bedside books.

> Better by far you should forget and smile,
> Than that you should remember and be sad . . .

It was easy enough to read those lines and to be glad at his smiling but harder to tell myself that there would never be any question of anything else. It would simply not occur to him to be sad.

It must not be poetry that I read that night, but a devotional or even a cookery book. Perhaps the last was best for my mood, and I chose an old one of recipes and miscellaneous household hints. I read about the care of aspidistras and how to wash lace and black woollen stockings, and I learned that a package or envelope sealed with white of egg cannot be steamed open. Though what use that knowledge would ever be to me I could not imagine.

CHAPTER NINETEEN

It seemed odd to be able to enter the Napiers' flat freely and to treat their possessions almost as if they had been my own. Rocky's list made it quite clear what was to be moved – the big desk, the Chippendale chairs, the gate-legged table and then the smaller objects, paperweights and snowstorms and some china. Even the books were to be sorted out, leaving only Helena's forbidding-looking anthropological works and a few paper-backed novels. The rooms would be bare and characterless when these things were gone, but even now they looked impersonal and depressing. I wondered if I ought to attempt to tidy the desk, whose pigeonholes were stuffed with papers, and I did make an effort, conscious all the time that I might come across something which was none of my business. I dare say I hoped that I might but my curiosity was not gratified. There were no love letters, no diaries, no photographs, even. The pigeonholes contained only bills and Helena's anthropological notes. The love letters from the Wren officers had no doubt been crumpled up and thrown into the wastepaper basket after a perfunctory reading. But perhaps they had been wise enough not to tell their love. It seemed to me that the natural inclination of women to assume a Patience-on-a-monument attitude was a kind of strength, though judging by what Everard Bone had told me they sometimes gave away their advantage by declaring themselves.

I took care to be up before eight o'clock on the Saturday morning, but it was after half past nine when the remover's men arrived. There were three of them, two cheerful and strong-looking, and the third, perhaps as befitted his position as foreman, wizened and melancholy and apparently incapable of carrying anything at all.

He shook his head when he saw the big desk.

'We'll never get that round the corner of the stairs,' he declared.

I pointed out that it could be taken to pieces, but he had his moment of triumph when the bottom half of the desk was pulled away from the wall and a fine powdering of sawdust was revealed on the carpet.

'Worm,' he said. 'I knew it as soon as I set eyes on it.'

'Oh, dear,' I said feebly, feeling that it might almost be my fault. 'I wonder if Mr. Napier knows about that.'

'I shouldn't think he does. You never know what goes on at the back, unless you're an expert. I've been handling furniture for over forty years, of course.'

'I suppose there's nothing we can do about it now?' I asked, thinking of Everard Bone's mother but feeling that it would hardly be any use to telephone her now. I should have to mention it to Rocky in a letter.

'Hundreds of them,' said the foreman, tapping the little holes with his finger and watching the fine dust pour out. 'We shall be lucky if it doesn't fall to pieces. It rots the whole piece, madam. It's probably riddled with them.'

'Amazing how those little insects get in, boring all those neat little holes,' I commented fatuously.

'Ah,' he smiled for the first time, 'that's just what they *don't* do, madam. It's surprising the number of people that think that. The holes are made when the beetles come *out* – that's what it is.'

'Oh, really? That's interesting,' I murmured.

'Slowly, now,' he called, as the two strong men lifted the base of the desk as easily as if it had been made of cardboard. I was relieved to see that it did not fall to pieces, but the episode had disturbed me. It was disconcerting to think that worms or beetles could eat their way secretly through one's furniture. *Something is rotten in the state of Denmark . . . Men have died and worms have eaten them, but not for love . . .* 'Perhaps you would like a cup of tea?' I suggested.

This proved to be a good idea and the rest of the things were taken away smoothly and without incident. The foreman was able to carry a cushion downstairs but otherwise took little part in the proceedings. After I had seen the van go away I went upstairs to my flat to eat a melancholy lunch. A dried-up scrap of cheese, a few lettuce leaves for which I could not be bothered to make any dressing, a tomato and a piece of bread and butter, followed by a cup of coffee made with coffee essence. A real *woman's* meal, I thought, with no suggestion of brandy after-wards, even though there was still a drop left in the bottle. Alcohol would have made it even more of a mockery.

I had just finished when the telephone bell rang. It was Miss Clovis, asking if I would care to take tea with her and Mrs Napier.

'No doubt you will have something to report?' she asked eagerly.

'Oh, yes, the furniture has just gone.'

'What, all of it?' she asked in alarm.

'Oh, no, just Mr Napier's own things. The flat is quite habitable now for Mrs Napier whenever she likes to come back.'

A snorting noise came down the telephone.

'That man! I think it's the limit. Anyway, Miss Lathbury, I shall expect you about four o'clock.'

I was a little apprehensive at entering the premises of the Learned Society alone and felt quite nervous as I pushed open the heavy door, whose dark carvings might have been the work of some primitive sculptor. On the stairs I met an old bearded man, and I thought for a moment that it was the old President, until I remembered that he was dead. He stood aside courteously for me to pass and said, beaming and nodding, 'Ah, miss, er – hard at work, I see'

'Oh, yes,' I beamed and nodded back at him.

'It would be pretty hot in New Guinea now, eh?' he chuckled as I mounted the flight of stairs above him.

'Yes, it certainly would be,' I called out, confident that this was a safe answer to make.

'Oh, good. I was just going to make tea.' Miss Clovis emerged from a door with a kettle in her hand. 'Do go on into the sitting-room – it's the door in front of you.'

I went into the room indicated, but then drew back, thinking that I had entered a library or store-room by mistake, for the floor was littered with books which seemed to have overflowed from the tall shelves which lined three of the walls. There were also several dark wooden images, some with fierce and alarming expressions. In the middle of the books and images sat Helena Napier, wearing a crumpled cotton dress and apparently busy sorting a mass of notes in typescript and sprawling handwriting.

We greeted each other stiffly, for I could not help feeling self-conscious at being, as it were, the last person to see her husband, and she may have had something of the same feeling.

'You look busy,' I began.

'Has he taken the furniture?' she asked bluntly.

'Oh, yes; it went this morning.'

Miss Clovis came in with a teapot which she put down on a low table on which a rough attempt at laying tea had been made, with three odd cups and saucers, a loaf of bread, a pot of jam and a slab of margarine still in its paper. Helena must feel quite at home here, I thought spitefully.

'Dig in,' said Miss Clovis. 'I've got a cake somewhere, left over from the Society's last tea party.' She produced a tin from behind one of the images. I wondered whether there had been a tea party since the one I had been to in the spring, for the cake, when it was put out, looked weeks or even months old. Fortunately, however, it was a shop cake made of substitute ingredients and I had learned from my own experience that such cakes would keep almost indefinitely.

'I met such a nice old man on the stairs,' I said. 'He had a grey beard and looked very much like the old President, the one who died.'

'Oh, that would be old Hornibrook – New Guinea, 1905,' said Helena shortly.

'How sad that was, the old President dying,' I said.

'Oh, well, in the midst of life we are in death,' said Miss Clovis casually, cutting a thick slab of bread.

'Yes, of course, he went so suddenly.'

'Suddenly with meat in his mouth,' said Miss Clovis.

'Oh, surely . . .'

'Ah, I can see you aren't an antiquarian, Miss Lathbury,' said Miss Clovis triumphantly, 'or you would know your Anthony à Wood better. *In the beginning of this month I was told that Henry Marten died last summer, suddenly with meat in his mouth, at Chepstow in Monmouthshire,*' she quoted. 'But that's the way they go. The President was standing in the library and was just reaching up to take *Dynamics of Clanship among the Tallensi* out of a shelf, when he fell.'

'What a splendid title for a book,' I remarked. 'Perhaps not a book for an *old* man to read, though. Who is to be the new President?'

'Tyrell Todd,' said Helena. 'You may remember him at our do.'

'Oh, yes, he talked about pygmies.'

'He is a young man,' said Miss Clovis. 'New brooms sweep clean, or so they say.'

The conversation now turned into an exchange of views about various personalities whose names meant nothing to me. I am afraid Miss Clovis brought out little titbits of scandal about them and she and Helena seemed to be enjoying themselves very much. I began to wonder why I had been asked to tea as they made so little attempt to entertain me.

At last there was a pause and I made a remark about the books and images, asking if they belonged to Miss Clovis.

'Good Heavens, no,' said Miss Clovis. 'The late President's widow gave them. She could hardly wait to get them out of the house. I suppose they were just so much junk to her.'

'Oh, yes; I think I remember her.' The old woman nodding

in her chair and falling asleep over her knitting. How she must have disliked those images, nasty malevolent-looking things, some with dusty unhygienic raffia manes. Perhaps they had even come between her and the man she had married. I wondered if she had had to have them in her drawing-room, though even if they had been relegated to his study they must have been a continual worry to her, especially at spring-cleaning time. 'I suppose you are glad to have his relics,' I said. 'Will his wife's name go up on the board among the list of benefactors?'

'I suppose it will have to,' said Miss Clovis, 'though I doubt if she will ever have the pleasure of seeing it there. I'm sure she won't attend any of our meetings now that her husband is dead.'

'I wonder if she feels a great sense of freedom,' I said, more to myself than my companions. 'Perhaps she never really understood the papers and wasn't interested, and now she need never come again. Or perhaps she feels lost without the discipline of sitting through them and will find nothing to take its place.'

'Well, she certainly hasn't got your churchgoing and good works,' said Helena quite genially.

'Oh, did he take even that from her?' I asked, shocked by the idea that she could now have been the backbone of some parish, one of the invaluable helpers of some overworked vicar, had not her husband made her an unbeliever. 'Oh, the wicked things men do, leaving her nothing for her old age, not even anthropology!'

'You put yourself too much in other people's places,' said Helena. 'I believe she is quite happy pottering about her garden and reading novels. To be free and independent, that's the thing.'

'But surely you don't want that when you're old?' I protested. 'Would you know what to do with freedom and independence if it came so late in life?'

'Well, all I can say is that I'm thankful *I* never got myself tied up with any man,' said Miss Clovis.

Helena looked at her doubtfully, perhaps wondering, as I was, whether Miss Clovis had ever had the opportunity of entering into this bondage.

'You will do better work without your husband,' said Miss Clovis. 'You will now be able to devote your whole life to the study of matrilineal kin-groups.'

I could not help pitying Helena, condemned to something that sounded so uninteresting, and she may have pitied herself a little as she said bitterly, 'You should have said higher things. Isn't that what one usually devotes one's life to? Come along, Mildred, it's time we were going now.'

I thanked Miss Clovis, who seemed unwilling to let Helena go, and we went down the stairs with Helena's suitcase and a small evil-looking image, which was given to me to carry. I felt awkward when people in the bus started to stare and giggle and I had to sit with it in my lap, trying vainly to cover it with my gloves and handbag.

As we approached the house Julian Malory came towards us. I had imagined that the sight of Helena would frighten him away, but he stood his ground.

'I am sorry to hear of this trouble between you and your husband, Mrs Napier,' he said. 'I think you should go back to him and talk things over.'

We were all – even Julian, I think – so taken aback at his boldness that for a moment nobody said anything. I myself was full of admiration for him, for I had not expected that he would speak so frankly. I had imagined he would make some trivial social remark and that our encounter would end with remarks about the weather.

'Well, he has gone into the country,' said Helena, without her usual self-possession. 'And there are difficulties, you know.'

'There are always difficulties in human relationships,' said Julian. 'You won't think I am trying to interfere, I hope, but I do think you should see him. And if there is anything I can do for you, please let me know.'

Helena thanked him in an embarrassed way and we went into the house. I felt almost as if I ought to apologise for Julian's boldness, as if he and all the clergymen were my personal responsibility, and perhaps they were when I was up against unbelievers. I could not help feeling glad that he had spoken.

'I suppose he felt he ought to say something,' said Helena in a detached way. 'It must be a bore having to go about doing good, saying a word here and there. I didn't realise they ever *did* anything like that, though.'

'Oh, yes, Julian certainly has the courage of his convictions,' I said. 'I believe he and Rocky had a drink together the other night. I saw them going into the pub at the end of the square.'

'Really, Mildred, the things you see happening! Is there anything that escapes you?'

'Well, I couldn't help seeing them. I just happened to be passing. I expect they had a talk and Rocky would feel more at ease talking to a man than he would to me. I suppose there must be times when men band together against women and women against men. You and Miss Clovis against Julian and Rocky, and I like the umpire in a tennis match.'

Helena laughed, but when we reached her sitting-room she exclaimed angrily, 'But my chairs have gone! Really, this is too bad. And the desk too! Mildred, why did you let them go?'

'I'm sorry,' I said meekly. 'Rocky gave me a list of the furniture that was to go and I just followed his instructions.'

'Oh, you were always on his side!' she burst out. 'Anyway, those chairs were a wedding present to both of us. He had no right to take them.'

'Yes, it is difficult, when something is given as a wedding present,' I said. But how could people foresee the separation of a happy pair and always give presents that could if necessary be easily divided? Surely that was too cynical a view for even the most embittered giver to take of marriage?

Helena darted here and there in the flat, missing objects which she claimed as hers. 'Mildred, you'll have to write to him,' she declared, sitting down in the one armchair that was left.

'I write to him? Wouldn't it be better if you did?'

'Oh, I certainly couldn't do it myself. You know him and he might take more notice of a letter from you. Otherwise I might ask Esther Clovis to do it, or even Everard.'

'Oh, I don't think you should ask *him*,' I burst out, suddenly remembering that I had never had the opportunity of telling Helena, as he had bidden me to, that he did not love her. But it hardly seemed to matter now. 'Anyway,' I went on, 'he's at a conference of the Prehistoric Society in Derbyshire, so it wouldn't be much use.'

'Oh, *that*,' said Helena impatiently. 'I can't think why he bothers with archaeology. All this dabbling won't get him anywhere.'

'I shouldn't have thought he dabbled,' I said. 'He gives me the impression of being a very definite kind of person.'

'How do you mean?' asked Helena suspiciously.

'Well, he knows what he wants or doesn't want,' I floundered. 'I should think he has – er – very high principles.'

'Oh, he doesn't believe in divorce, if that's what you mean,' said Helena in a light tone. 'And naturally he imagined that if I quarrelled with Rocky I should go rushing to him. That's why he went to Derbyshire, of course.'

I was a little taken aback at her summing-up of the position and must have shown it in my face, for she laughed and said, 'Oh, yes, men are very simple and obvious in some ways, you know. They generally react in the way one would expect and it is often rather a cowardly way. I should think Everard was most alarmed when he heard that Rocky and I weren't getting on very well. He doesn't really care twopence about prehistory, you know. He always uses the society as an excuse, just because I don't happen to be a member myself.'

This seemed to me rather a waste of a subscription and there was something altogether comic about the thought of a man hiding from a woman behind a cloak of prehistory.

'I met his mother,' I said, hoping to change the subject. 'She seems rather odd.'

'Yes, she is odd, but then people's mothers usually are, don't you think?' said Helena. 'I suppose there's really no reason why Everard and I should ever meet again, except at the Society. It would be more dramatic, really, if we didn't for about ten years, and then we should be like the pair in that sonnet that people always think of when they part from somebody,

Be it not seen in either of our brows,
That we one jot of former love retain.'

'I dare say you wouldn't still love a person after ten years,' I suggested, 'so you wouldn't retain one jot of former love, anyway, and that would spoil the excitement of the meeting.'

'Yes, one would have nothing to conceal and would probably wonder how one could ever have felt anything at all. It would be better if I forgot all about Everard, I suppose, since he obviously doesn't intend to have anything more to do with me.'

'Yes, of course, it would. But forgetting isn't very easy,' I said doubtfully.

'I suppose you have perhaps had to forget somebody too?' asked Helena, equally doubtful.

'Oh, yes,' I said cheerfully, thinking of Bernard Hatherley, but unwilling to bring such a poor thing out into the open after so many years. 'I suppose everybody does at some time in their lives.'

'I was wondering if you were rather fond of Rocky,' said Helena, with what seemed to me unsuitable frankness. 'People do fall in love with him, you know.'

'Oh, you mean the Wren officers?' I said, with an attempt at laughter.

'Yes, they certainly did, but that was only to be expected. Rocky looked so fine in his uniform and was kind to them at parties and danced with them all in turn. But you have seen him much more as he really is. And I know he likes you very much. He has said so several times.'

This was very little consolation to me and the whole subject of the conversation was a most uncomfortable one, I felt.

'Perhaps I had better get down to writing that letter about the furniture,' I said firmly. 'If you could give me a list of things you want sent back, I might start it tonight.'

'Oh, yes,' Helena stood up, 'that would be a great help. I wonder if your vicar would take me out for a drink? He did say that I was to let him know if there was anything he could do for me, didn't he?'

'I'm not sure that was quite the kind of thing he meant,' I said, 'though if he takes Rocky to have a drink I don't see why he shouldn't take you. But I rather think tonight is his boys' club night.'

CHAPTER TWENTY

A list of furniture is not a good beginning to a letter, though I dare say a clever person with a fantastic turn of mind could transform even a laundry list into a poem.

I sat for a long time at my desk, unable to put pen to paper, idly turning the pages of a notebook in which I kept accounts and made shopping lists. How fascinating they would have been, had they been medieval shopping lists! I thought. But perhaps there was matter for poetry in them, with their many uncertainties and question marks. 'Rations, green veg., soap flakes, stamps,' seemed reasonable enough and easily explained, but why 'red ribbon?' What could I have wanted red ribbon for? Some daring idea for retrimming an old hat, perhaps; if so it had been stillborn, for I knew that I had never bought any and that it was unlikely anyway that I should wear a hat trimmed with red ribbon. As for 'egg poacher?' – that was an unfulfilled dream or ambition to buy one of those utensils that produce a neat artificial-looking poached egg. But I had never bought it and it seemed likely that on the rare occasions when I had a fresh egg to poach I should continue to delve for it in the bubbling water where the white separated from the yolk and waved about like a sea anemone. Sometimes I had noted down places or shops to visit. I came across the name of a well-known Roman Catholic bookshop, also with a question mark. I do not think I had ever bought anything there, but I remembered going into it at Christmas, when the basement, with its brightly coloured plaster figures, seemed to offer a peaceful refuge from the shopping crowds.

I went on turning the pages until I was reduced to studying old gas and electricity bills, but I knew that I could not brood over such trivia indefinitely and at last, after several false starts, I managed to produce some kind of a letter, beginning 'Dear Rocky,' stating the facts and giving the list of furniture and ending 'I hope you are settling down well, Yours ever, Mildred.' The ending had cost me more anxious thought than was justified by the result, but I believed that 'yours ever' was the correct way to finish a friendly letter to a person for whom one was supposed to have no particular feelings. I dare say there would have been no harm in sending my love, but I could not bring myself to do this.

Rocky's answer, when it came, was characteristic and had obviously cost him no anxious thought at all.

'Dearest M.,' he wrote, 'Helena is quite wrong about all this and the things I have taken are definitely MINE. As for the *Blue Casserole*, I admit that she bought it, but only to replace one of mine which Everard Bone broke. so let's have no more of this nonsense.

'I hope you are well and that the church is flourishing, also Father Malory – ought I to write Fr.? All those

Sundays after Trinity must be tedious but I suppose there will come an end some time!

'You must come and see me some time and (if fine) I will give you lunch in my wild garden with an amusing wine.

'In haste and with lots of love,

'R.'

I brooded over this letter with pleasure and sadness, but after I had learned its contents nearly by heart the chief impression that remained was one of surprise. I could not imagine Everard Bone breaking a casserole! It was a silly trivial thing, but every time I thought of it I smiled, sometimes when I was by myself in a street or in a bus.

As I had expected, Helena received the letter with indignation and decided that she would have no further communication with her husband but would go home and stay with her mother in Devonshire. I had not expected that she would behave in this conventional way and somehow liked her better for it. So it seemed that my part in the unhappy affair was at an end, and I could only hope that something would occur to make them come to their senses. I began to think that if I went to see Rocky I might be able to bring them together again; I saw myself playing a rather noble part, stepping into the background when they were reunited and going quietly away to make a cup of tea or do some washing or ironing. But although Rocky had said that I must go and see him some time, he had not suggested any definite date and I did not like to invite myself.

It was the middle of August now, a difficult time in the church. There were, as Rocky had pointed out, all those

Sundays after Trinity; even the highest church could not escape them and it was sometimes difficult to remember whether we were at Trinity eight, nine or ten. Then too, Julian Malory was away, leaving Father Greatorex in charge, and we were like a rudderless ship. There was no sermon on Sunday mornings and little things seemed to go wrong – sparks came out of the censer and alarmed some of the older members of the congregation; one of the little acolytes tripped over his too-long cassock and fell down the steps, causing the others to dissolve into giggles. One Sunday Teddy Lemon went to Margate for the weekend, and Mr Conybeare, looking like an angry bird, was called up out of the congregation to act as Master of Ceremonies. It was the organist's holiday too, and although Sister Blatt made a valiant attempt to take his place those peculiarly unnerving noises that only a church organ can produce would keep bursting out.

Julian and Winifred had gone on holiday with Allegra Gray to a farm in Somerset. I could not help feeling that they were an ill-assorted trio, but perhaps Julian had not thought it quite proper to go on a holiday alone with his fiancée and there was always the problem of what to do with Winifred. I could have offered to go somewhere with her myself had I not been pledged to go away with Dora Caldicote in September, as I did every year. I began to look forward to my holiday as never before. I felt that I needed to get away from all the problems – mostly other people's – with which I had been worried in the last few months. If I could look at them from a distance they might solve themselves. Helena would forget about the furniture, Allegra Gray would turn out to be the perfect wife for Julian, Winifred would marry or enter a religious community. Even the woodworms in the back of Rocky's desk would be destroyed and their ravages arrested by the application of that remedy Mrs Bone had been talking about.

One day towards the end of August I was coming out of my office at one o'clock when I saw Everard Bone standing looking in a shop window some distance away. My immediate reaction was one of irritation. What was he doing? If he wanted to see me, why couldn't he telephone and arrange a meeting in a normal way? I remembered the last time we had met, I in my old cotton dress and no stockings, with Cardinal Newman and a loaf in my string bag. Today I was at least wearing a respectable dress and had no domestic shopping with me. I had planned to hurry home and finish a dress I was making for my holiday, so, imagining that he had not seen me, I turned and walked briskly in the opposite direction. I heard the sound of somebody running after me but I did not look round. Then my name was called and I had to stop and feign surprise.

'Oh, it's you,' I said ungraciously.

'Yes, I've been waiting for you. I hoped you would have lunch with me.'

'Why didn't you write or telephone, then?'

'Well, it didn't occur to me till this morning. I've been away, you see. A little archaeological tour in the Dordogne.'

'Have you been hiding in a cave?' I asked.

'I have been in some caves, certainly,' he replied. 'But I don't know why you should think I have been hiding.'

'Oh, it doesn't matter,' I said, feeling rather ashamed. 'I was only making a kind of joke. I thought anthropology was your subject anyway.'

'Yes, but it all links up, you know. Archaeology seems to fit in better with a holiday.'

'There are stone circles in Brittany, aren't there?' I began, trying to show an intelligent interest. 'And then of course there's always Stonehenge.' I remembered that my father had been interested in Stonehenge, and I seemed to see us all sitting round the dinner-table, my mother and father, a curate – I could not remember which curate – and a canon and his wife. We were having a conversation about Stonehenge and suddenly all of the lights had gone out. The curate had let out a cry of alarm but the canon's voice went on without a tremor – I could hear it now – just as if nothing had happened. My mother got up and fussed with candles and the canon went on explaining his theory of how the great stones had been carried to Salisbury Plain. It was an impressive performance and had been rewarded, or so it seemed to me, by a bishopric not long afterwards. Thinking about it after all these years, I smiled.

'Yes, there's always Stonehenge,' said Everard rather stiffly.

We walked on in silence until we came to an area where there were restaurants.

'You haven't said in so many words that you will have lunch with me,' said Everard, 'but as we seem to be going in the right direction I assume that you will.'

'Oh, well, I suppose so,' I said indifferently and then realised that I was not behaving very well. It seemed too late to apologise and I felt resentful towards him for bringing out the worst in me, but I made some attempt. 'You must think me very impolite,' I said, 'but the worst side of me seems to be coming out today. It does seem to have been coming out more lately.'

'I expect you are upset at all this happening,' he said.

'Yes, I suppose I might make that excuse. It is upsetting when things happen to friends.'

We went into a restaurant and were shown to a table. It was not until we were sitting down that I realised that it was the restaurant where I had had lunch with William Caldicote in the spring.

'What exactly *has* happened?' he asked casually.

'Rocky is in the country and Helena has gone home to her mother in Devonshire.'

'Oh, that is a relief,' he said, taking up the menu and ordering lunch with rather less fuss than William did.

'I don't really know that one should have expected anything else. Women who quarrel with their husbands usually do go home to their mothers, if they have mothers.'

'I certainly gave her no encouragement,' said Everard, almost in a satisfied tone.

'Oh, I'm sure you didn't,' I said, contemplating my hors d'œuvre. 'I can't imagine you doing such a thing.'

'Of course,' he went on, with a note of warning in his tone, 'I shall probably marry eventually.'

'Yes, men usually do,' I murmured.

'The difficulty is finding a suitable person.'

'Perhaps one shouldn't try to find people deliberately like that,' I suggested. 'I mean, not set out to look for somebody to marry as if you were going to buy a saucepan or a casserole.'

'You think it should just be left to chance? But then the person might be most unsuitable.'

The idea of choosing a husband or wife as one would a casserole had reminded me of Rocky's letter and his allegation that Everard had broken one of his casseroles. I suppose a smile must have come on to my face, for he said, 'You seem to find it amusing, the idea of marrying somebody suitable.'

'I wasn't really smiling at that. It was just that I couldn't imagine you breaking a casserole.'

'Oh, that,' he said rather irritably. 'Helena had put it in the oven to warm and when I took hold of it it was so hot that I dropped it.'

'Yes, I could imagine it happening in that way, with a perfectly reasonably explanation. It was a pity you didn't use the oven cloth,' I suggested.

'But it had only been in the oven a few minutes. Besides, I don't think there was an oven cloth.'

'I always have mine hanging on a nail by the side of the cooker.'

'Well, you're a sensible person. It's just the kind of thing you would have.'

Oh, dear, one was to be for ever cast down, I thought, brooding over the piece of fish on my plate. If I had been flattered by Everard's invitation to lunch I was now put in my place as the kind of person who would have an oven cloth hanging on a nail by the side of the cooker.

'Would you have married Helena if she had not been married already?' I asked boldly.

'Certainly not,' he declared. 'She is not at all the kind of person I should choose for my wife.'

'What would she be like, that Not Impossible She?' I asked.

'Oh, a sensible sort of person,' he said vaguely.

'Somebody who would help you in your work?' I suggested. 'Somebody with a knowledge of anthropology who could correct proofs and make an index, rather like Miss Clovis, perhaps? '

'Esther Clovis is certainly a very capable person,' he said doubtfully. 'An excellent woman altogether.'

'You could consider marrying an excellent woman?' I asked in amazement. 'But they are not for marrying.'

'You're surely not suggesting that they are for the other things?' he said, smiling.

That had certainly not occurred to me and I was annoyed to find myself embarrassed.

'They are for being unmarried,' I said, 'and by that I mean a positive rather than a negative state.'

'Poor things, aren't they allowed to have the normal feelings, then?'

'Oh, yes, but nothing can be done about them.'

'Of course I do respect and esteem Esther Clovis,' Everard went on.

'Oh, respect and esteem – such dry bones! I suppose one can really have such feelings for somebody but I should have thought one would almost dislike a person who inspired them. Anyway, Miss Clovis must be quite a lot older than you are, and then she looks so odd. She has hair like a dog.'

Everard laughed. 'Yes, so she has.'

I now felt ashamed at having made him laugh by an unkind criticism of the excellent Miss Clovis, so I tried to change the subject by commenting on the other inhabitants of the restaurant in what I hoped was a more charitable way. But he would not agree with me that this woman was pretty or that one elegant, and we lapsed into an uncomfortable silence which was broken by a voice behind me saying my name.

It was William Caldicote.

I introduced him to Everard and then William took command of the conversation.

'Thank goodness *some* of one's friends are unfashionable enough to be in town in August,' he said, 'then one needn't feel *quite* so ashamed, though I suppose nowadays women don't feel that they must go about veiled and in dark glasses and sit in their houses behind drawn blinds.'

'No, I think there are a good many people who have to stay in London during August,' I said, remembering the bus queues and the patient line of people moving with their trays in the great cafeteria.

'Yes, even people like ourselves,' William agreed. 'But *what* my poor mother would have said!'

I thought for a moment of old Mrs Caldicote sitting comfortably in the ugly drawing-room of her villa in a Birmingham suburb, but I did not remind William of how she had liked to visit London in August – her 'annual jaunt' she called it – to stay at one of those garishly decorated hotels which used to be, and perhaps still are, the Mecca of provincial visitors, especially when the tips were often included in the bill and they were thus saved that embarrassment. My father had preferred a quiet depressing hotel near the British Museum, where he could be near the reading-room and perhaps meet another clergyman who had been up at Balliol in the very early nineteen-hundreds.

'Yes, August is not a pleasant month in London,' said Everard stiffly. 'So many libraries and museums seem to be closed.'

'One's club is being cleared,' chanted William, 'so inconvenient.'

'But Lyons Corner House is always open,' I reminded him, trying to remember which was William's club or even if he really had one. He could hardly be on his way there now, for I noticed that he was carrying two rolls in his hand.

'Bread for my pigeons,' he explained. 'I feed them every afternoon; Mildred knows the ritual. Well, Mildred, I suppose you will be going on your holiday with Dora, as usual. We must have luncheon together when you get back,' he added, with a suspicious glance at Everard.

In the autumn? I thought and nearly said it aloud, for our annual luncheon was always in March or April.

'Yes, that would be nice,' I said. 'Dora and I will send you a postcard.'

'Oh, I do like to be the kind of person people send postcards to,' said William, 'those anonymous "views" with too much sea or too many mountains, or your window marked with a cross, or even those rather naughty ones of fat ladies on donkeys.' He waved the roll at us and hurried away.

'Who was that?' asked Everard politely.

'The brother of a school friend of mine. He's a civil servant in some Ministry. I've known the Caldicotes for years.'

'I thought he might be a friend of the Napiers. Have you any more news of them?' he asked rather too casually.

'Oh, Rocky is in the country and Helena has gone to her mother in Devonshire,' I began, 'but I've already told you that. And I have had to write letters about furniture and arrange for it to be moved.'

'There is no question of any – er – proceedings?' he asked delicately.

'You mean a divorce? Oh, I don't think so. I certainly hope not.'

'No, one doesn't approve of divorce,' said Everard, rather in William's manner. 'But it seems a bad sign, all this moving of furniture, if it's only a temporary quarrel.'

'Oh, dear, perhaps the remover's men will have to bring it all back again – I hadn't thought of that. And perhaps this time the worm-eaten desk really will fall to pieces.'

Everard looked puzzled.

'When they came to move Rocky's desk it was all worm-eaten at the back,' I explained. 'I nearly telephoned your mother to ask her what to do.'

'Oh, my mother has been in Bournemouth for the past fortnight,' said Everard quickly, as if he could not bear that any of the Bone family should be associated even with the Napiers' furniture.

'Then it would have been no use my telephoning her,' I said, putting on my gloves and gathering up my bits and pieces. 'Thank you very much for my lunch.'

'It has been so nice seeing you,' he said, rather too politely to be sincere, I felt. 'We must meet again after you come back from your holiday. I hope you will enjoy it.'

I thanked him but did not offer to send him a postcard, for Everard, unlike William, did not seem to be the kind of person one sent postcards to. Although, I reflected, if one should happen to come across something of anthropological or archaeological interest, some stone circle or barrow or curious local custom, perfectly serious, of course, no jokes about windows marked with a cross or fat ladies, it might be quite well received.

CHAPTER TWENTY-ONE

'Of course it rains a great deal in Austria and Switzerland in the mountains and even in Italy at certain times of the year,' said Dora cheerfully, as we stood at the window of the hotel lounge gazing at the steady downpour.

'And in Africa and India, too,' I added.

'Yes, but there the wet and dry seasons are carefully defined,' said Dora in a schoolmistress's tone. 'It depends on the monsoons and other things.'

'We might go and look at the Abbey this afternoon,' I suggested, 'as it's so wet.'

'Oh, well, I suppose so,' said Dora, who did not really like looking at buildings but was an indefatigable tourist. 'We can go on the bus.'

The bus stop was just outside the hotel and there were already a few people waiting when we got there. A crowd of little black priests from a nearby Roman Catholic seminary came and waited in the queue behind us. Dora nudged me. 'Like a lot of beetles,' she whispered. 'I hope we don't have to sit near them. I bet they'll try and push in front of us.'

The bus was half full when it came and some of the priests were left behind. Dora looked down gloatingly from our superior position on the top deck. 'Serve them right,' she said. 'The Pope and all those Dogmas of his!'

'Oh, poor things,' I protested, pitying the dripping black priests who would have to wait another twenty minutes. 'It's not their fault.'

'I suppose the Abbey will be swarming with priests and nuns,' Dora went on, with a fierce gleam in her eye.

'Well, naturally there will be a good many. After all, it must be like a kind of pilgrimage for them and it's certainly rather wonderful to think that the Abbey was built by the monks themselves. I expect there will be quite a number of ordinary tourists as well, though.'

After a ride of about half an hour we got off the bus and found ourselves in what seemed to be open country with no sign of an Abbey anywhere. A woman came up to me and asked me the way. 'I think it must be somewhere along here,' I said, indicating what seemed to be the only path.

'Oh, thank you,' she said. 'I hope you didn't mind my asking, but you looked as if you would know the way.'

I pondered on the significance of this as we walked along in a straggling file, led by Dora and me. Even the priests had accepted our leadership. This seemed a solemn and wonderful thing.

'You'd think they'd have a signpost saying "This way to the Abbey: or an arrow pointing,' grumbled Dora in a satisfied way. 'I wonder if we'll be able to get a cup of tea there? I expect they'll have thought of every way of making money.'

As we rounded the next bend in the lane we came upon a rather new-looking building of an ecclesiastical appearance.

'That must be it,' said Dora.

'Yes, I think so,' I said, relieved that it had shown itself at last, for it would indeed have been a dreadful thing if I had led priests astray. 'I suppose we can join a conducted party.'

'Oh, if you like,' said Dora, 'though I'd rather poke about by myself. You can be pretty sure they won't want to show us everything,' she hinted darkly. 'Like those tours of Russia.'

Parties of tourists arriving in cars and buses or on foot filled the space in front of the Abbey. There was a large car park and Dora nudged me and pointed to a notice which said LADIES and another which said TEAS. 'I told you the whole place would be commercialised,' she said.

I did not answer, for by now we were inside the Abbey and I was almost overwhelmed by the sudden impression of light and brilliance. The walls looked bright and clean, there was a glittering of much gold and the lingering smell of incense was almost hygienic. Not here, I thought, would one be sentimentally converted to Rome, for there was no warm rosy darkness to hide in, no comfortable confusion of doctrines and dogmas; all would be reasoned out and clearly explained, as indeed it should be.

A neat-looking monk with rimless glasses took charge of our party or rather the group of people in which we found ourselves, for we were an ill-assorted company – a few young soldiers in uniform, a priest or two, middle-aged and young 'couples', a cluster of what seemed to be Anglo-Catholic ladies of the kind who might advertise their services as companions in the *Church Times*, and a crowd of nondescript or unclassifiable bodies, among whom I supposed I should have to include Dora and myself, though I dare say I should have been quite happy with the Anglo-Catholic ladies.

We moved from place to place with reverence and admiration while our guide explained the history and meaning of this or that in a kind patient voice.

'I don't suppose any of you are Catholics,' he said smoothly, 'so you may not understand about Our Lady.'

I saw the Anglo-Catholic ladies gather more closely together, as if to distinguish themselves from the rest of the group. They seemed to be whispering indignantly among themselves and one looked almost as if she were about to protest. But in the end, perhaps remembering their manners or the difficulty of arguing with a Roman, they calmed down and listened patiently with the rest of us.

Dora was looking particularly fierce, though for different reasons, and I was afraid that she might challenge our guide at any moment and start an argument, but evidently she too thought better of it and moved sulkily on to the next point of interest.

'Of course it's no use saying anything to them,' she muttered. 'They've got it all off pat and just recite it like parrots. I'm tired of being led round like this. I'm going to explore on my own.'

When we had finished our tour I found her waiting outside the Abbey, her eyes gleaming triumphantly.

'I hope you didn't put any money in any of those boxes,' she said. 'They've got a shop round the corner to sell rosaries and images and all sorts of highly coloured junk. I can't imagine why anybody should want to buy such stuff.'

I tried to explain that Roman Catholics and even non-Romans found these things comforting and helpful to their faith, but Dora would not be convinced.

'Parts of the place are roped off,' she said in a low voice.

'One certainly isn't allowed to see everything here. I wonder what goes on *there?*'

'That must be the monks' enclosure,' I said. 'One would hardly expect to be able to go in among them.'

'Oh, I shouldn't want to,' said Dora huffily. 'Nothing would induce me to.' She grasped her umbrella and waved it like a sword.

'Well, then, we may as well find somewhere to have tea. After spiritual comes bodily refreshment.'

'I'm afraid I didn't get any spiritual refreshment,' said Dora. 'Quite the reverse, the smell of that incense made me feel quite ill. It would probably penetrate into the tea place here and anyway I don't fancy the look of it. Could we find somewhere on the way back, do you think?'

'Yes, there's a nice village we came through,' I suggested. 'It's where Helena Napier's mother lives, as a matter of fact, and Helena is staying with her now. Don't you remember that black and white café we saw from the bus?'

'Oh, Ye Olde Magpie? Yes, we might try that.'

'You never know,' I ventured, 'we might even see Helena.'

'Oh, you can't keep away from those Napiers,' said Dora good-humouredly. 'Though somehow I don't think it's *Helena* you really want to see.'

I could think of no suitable answer to make to this, so let Dora think what she liked. Rocky's easy and obvious charms were in themselves a kind of protection, for no sensible person could be supposed to feel anything for him. I had to admit to myself that the thought of seeing Helena did not please me particularly, but it seemed a kind of duty to Everard Bone to find out what was happening to her and what, if any, were the latest developments.

I had hardly expected to come upon her as quickly as we did, standing outside Ye Olde Magpie with a shopping basket.

After we had greeted each other with suitable exclamations of surprise and even a certain amount of pleasure, she said, 'Mother sent me out to buy cakes. The vicar is coming to tea.'

'That will be a nice change for you,' said Dora brightly, and, I thought, impertinently.

'Oh, but didn't you know? I get on splendidly with clergymen. Father Malory was quite taken with me – wasn't he, Mildred? – and asked me to let him know if there was anything he could do for me.'

'They always say that,' said Dora, 'and hope to goodness there won't be. It's part of their duty.'

'Oh, come,' I said, but feebly, I'm afraid, 'Julian Malory certainly does a lot of good and so do many other clergymen. He would even have taken Helena out for a drink if that was what she really wanted.'

'Only it happened to be his boys' club night and it always would be something like that, wouldn't it?' asked Helena rather sadly. 'Mother is a real holy fowl. She and Mildred would get on splendidly.'

'Like a house on fire,' said Dora inevitably.

'Won't you come in here and have a cup of tea with us?' I suggested. 'It's only a quarter to four and I don't suppose the vicar will be punctual,' I added, with no possible means of knowing.

'You should really come to tea with us,' said Helena, hesitating, 'but it might be a little embarrassing. Perhaps I will just have a cup, then.'

We went into the café and sat down at an unsteady little

round table which was just too small for three people. After what seemed a long time, a young woman with flowing hair and dark red nails came to take our order.

Helena ignored Dora and began questioning me. Had I seen Rocky? Had he written to me? Had I visited him at his cottage? I answered 'No' to all these questions, and added, 'he did say something about my going to see him, but nothing has been arranged yet.'

'Oh, I expect he has forgotten all about it,' said Helena. 'That would be just like him.'

'Yes, I expect he has forgotten.' I bowed my head and peered into the teapot. It had been assumed that I should pour out and until the young woman brought us more hot water I could not have a full cup of tea.

'You must go and see him,' said Helena, 'or at least you must write. We really must make up this stupid quarrel or whatever it is. You can't imagine how bored and miserable I am here.'

'I expect your mother is glad to have you,' I said helpfully.

'Oh, yes! Nothing has been touched in my old room, so terribly depressing. The girlish white-painted furniture and the hollyhock chintz – even photographs of old loves on the mantelpiece.'

'I think white-painted furniture is nice in a bedroom,' said Dora. 'Do try a piece of this sandwich cake. It's really good.'

'Imagine finding photographs of old loves on the mantelpiece after all these years,' Helena went on, refusing the cake.

'Yes, it must be a little unnerving,' I agreed, seeing as usual Bernard Hatherley's face, the sepia print a little faded behind the glass, yet not faded enough to be romantically Victorian. 'Didn't you think of putting them away in a box or a drawer before you left home? It would seem quite decent and suitable to find them there.'

'Oh, you know how it was in the war. Things did get left.' Helena stood up. 'I must go now. Look, there's the vicar already. He must be on his way to our house.'

I looked through the window and saw a round jolly-looking little man hoisting himself up on to a bicycle. 'Does he,' I began, 'I mean, will he – have been told about things?'

'Oh, Mildred, your delicacy is wonderful!' Helena laughed for the first time that afternoon. 'I am sure Mother has already told him all. She can never keep anything from a clergyman.'

'Well, they are often able to help, as I've said before.'

'Oh, you can help much better than any vicar. Promise me that you will write to Rocky *soon* and tell him about me.'

I said I would try to do this.

'But *soon*, Mildred. I may already have lost him to one of the Wren officers. And think how noble your position will be, a mediator, a bringer-together of husbands and wives.'

I agreed that it certainly did sound noble, but like so many noble occupations there was something a little chilly about it.

Dora and I sat in silence for a little while after Helena had gone.

'Well, well,' said Dora at last, in her comfortable manner which seemed to dispose of difficulties, 'some people don't seem to know when they're well off. It sounds delightful, I think.'

'What sounds delightful?'

'Her room with the white-painted furniture and the holly-hock chintz. Of course at school we have bed-sitting-rooms so one can't have anything really dainty-looking, but I was think-ing of getting a new divan cover this autumn and possibly curtains to match. I've got a brown carpet, you remember, and my colour scheme has usually been blue and orange. What do you think, Mildred?'

'Oh, hollyhock chintz would look charming,' I said absently.

'You don't think it would be too much? Having curtains as well?'

'Oh, no, of course not.'

'I might not be able to get hollyhock, though I shall have to see what there is, of course.'

'Yes, you will have to see what there is.'

'There seems to be a little garden at the back here. Shall we go out and look at it?' said Dora, springing up from the table. 'It seems to have stopped raining now.'

We walked out through the back of the cafe into another room, also full of unsteady little round tables, but empty now. It was damp, cold and silent and the tables needed polishing. On one wall there was a spotty engraving of a Byronic-looking young man who reminded me of Rocky. The room led out into a romantic little garden, shut in with high walls covered with dripping ivy.

'Oh, what a gloomy place!' exclaimed Dora. 'You'd think they could brighten it up with a few striped umbrellas.'

'Oh, we do have umbrellas in the season, madam,' said the waitress in an offended tone. She had followed us in with our bill, as if fearing that we might escape without paying for our tea. 'But of course we aren't doing many lunches and teas now, you see, the season's really over.'

Yes, I thought sadly, the season was really over and in the little garden I could see the last rose of summer. 'This must be an old house,' I said, 'almost Elizabethan.'

'I don't know about that, madam, but of course it's called Ye Olde Magpie, so it must be *old*,' said the girl. 'It's a pity they don't spend a bit of money on it and make it more modern. The kitchen's terrible.'

'I don't feel like going in that garden,' said Dora. 'It looks a bit damp to me. You don't want to go out, do you?'

'No, not really.' I could see a little lawn and a stone cupid with ivy growing on it and it seemed rather too melancholy. 'I wonder if they have any picture postcards of this garden?'

'Oh, to send to William, you mean?'

'Yes, perhaps to William, but I've already sent him one.'

'Oh, you mustn't overdo it, or he'll think you're running after him.'

I agreed that I mustn't and imagined William's beady eyes, round and alarmed. But there were no postcards of Ye Olde Magpie at all, and even if I had been bold enough to send one to Rocky I should not have been able to say anything about the last rose of summer and the ivy-mantled cupid.

'We should just catch the five o'clock bus,' said Dora, 'if it isn't too full of those awful priests.'

When we reached the bus stop we were a long way behind in the queue and when the bus came it took only half a dozen people. I noticed a group of priests looking down on us from the upper deck and I felt that somehow the Pope and his Dogmas had triumphed after all.

CHAPTER TWENTY-TWO

A week later I sat at my desk trying to compose a letter to Rocky. It was one of those sad late September evenings when by switching on a bar of the electric fire one realises at last that summer is over. I had been sitting for over half an hour, listening to the heavy rain falling outside rather than writing, for I did not know what to say. It had been difficult enough to write about the furniture but it seemed infinitely harder to know how to tell Rocky that Helena regretted their quarrel and that they must come together again, that he must take her back. And yet, who was to take who back? That was the point, for I had forgotten, if I had ever really known who was to blame. The inability to wash a lettuce properly, the hot saucepan put carelessly down on the walnut table . . . it seemed now as if it had been nothing more than that. But there was Everard Bone – where did he come into it? His position now seemed to be merely that of an anxious onlooker, who did not want to become involved in any 'unpleasantness'. I smiled to myself as I remembered the carefully worded postcard I had sent him. A Dolmen on Dartmoor – at least the title was pleasing. 'We walked here today – I wonder if you know it? A lovely spot. Luckily it was a clear day so we had an excellent view. All good wishes – M. Lathbury.' With that ambiguous signature, which was one I never normally used, I might have been man or woman, though the wording of the card was perhaps not very masculine. William Caldicote had been luckier in my choice for him, a fine picture of the Diamond Jubilee bandstand, with a few little jokes which it would be tedious to repeat here. I had not been able to find a suitable card for Rocky.

'Dear Rocky . . .' I turned back to the letter with determination and wrote on a fresh sheet of paper. 'I have just come back from my holiday in Devonshire and happened to see Helena there.' That was a good clear beginning. I would say that she seemed unhappy and bored, then I might ask how he was and what he was doing. The next thing would be to introduce a more personal note – 'You may think it very interfering, but it does seem to me . . .' What seemed to me? I wondered, listening to the rain which had suddenly become heavier, and why should he take any notice of what I said?

The shrill sound of my door-bell made me start as if somebody had fired a pistol shot at my back. Who could be calling now? Not that it was very late – barely half past nine – but I could not think of anybody likely to visit me unexpectedly and on such a wet night. I went down to answer the bell rather unwillingly, but hearing the rain drumming on a sky-light I hurried, realising that whoever it was must be getting very wet standing by the door.

I had just started to turn the handle when I heard my name being called. It was Winifred Malory's voice. I had certainly not expected it to be her, for I had imagined that she and

228

Julian and Allegra would all be cosily together in the vicarage, from which I felt myself to be somehow excluded these days.

'Oh, Mildred, thank goodness you're in!'

I drew her quickly into the hall and saw that she was soaking wet. Then I noticed that she was wearing only a thin dress without a hat or coat and that on her feet were what looked like bedroom slippers, now sodden with rain.

'Winifred! Whatever are you doing dressed like that? You must be mad coming out without even an umbrella.' I suppose I must have spoken sharply, for she drew back as if she would go out again and I saw that she was crying. So I led her up to my sitting-room and put her in an armchair in front of the fire. I found myself turning on the second bar and plugging in the electric kettle for a cup of tea, almost without thinking what I did.

'I couldn't stay in the house a minute longer with that woman!' Winifred burst out.

'What woman?' I asked stupidly, thinking as I did so how melodramatic Winifred sounded, talking about 'that woman' as if she were in a play or a novel.

'Allegra Gray,' she stammered in a burst of tears.

I was so astonished that I could think of nothing to say, but wondered irrelevantly if I was to be caught with a teapot in my hand on every dramatic occasion.

'But I thought you were such friends . . .' was all I could say, when words came out last.

'Oh, we were at first, but how was I to know what she was really like? It's such a terrible thing to be deceived by a person, to think they're something and then find they're not.'

Of course it all came out then, all I had always felt myself about Allegra Gray but with apparently no justification. It seemed that the friction between her and Winifred had started quite a long time before they went on holiday together.

'You remember those flowers Lady Farmer sent for the church at Whitsuntide?'

'Oh, yes, lilies, weren't they?'

'Yes. Well, Allegra and I were doing the altar and naturally I felt that the lilies should go there, but she had the idea of putting them on the floor at the side and having peonies and delphiniums on the altar. I told her we never had peonies on the altar and naturally Lady Farmer would expect the flowers she sent to be used for the altar . . .'

I suddenly felt very tired and thought how all over England, and perhaps, indeed, anywhere where there was a church and a group of workers, these little frictions were going on. Somebody else decorating the pulpit when another had always done it, somebody's gift of flowers being relegated to an obscure window, somebody's cleaning of the brasses being criticised when she had been doing them for over thirty years . . . And now Lady Farmer's lilies on the floor and peonies on the altar, an unheard-of thing! But here, of course, there was more to it. The little friendly criticisms, the mocking which had gradually become less good-humoured – 'Winifred, you really must do something about your clothes . . . Have you made any plans for when Julian and I are married? Where are you going to live?' And then the suggestions flung out, the settlement in the East End, the religious community – 'Dear Winifred, you're just the kind of person who would have a vocation, I feel' – or the cheap and comfortable guest house in Bournemouth, full of elderly people . . .

'But Mildred, I'm *not* elderly! I'm only a year or two older than she is.' Winifred's voice came at me plaintively and I reassured her that of course she was not elderly.

'I'd always thought we could live together so happily, the three of us. I never imagined any other arrangement. Julian never gave any hint of it.'

'No, he wouldn't, of course,' I said. 'This may sound a cynical thing to say, but don't you think men sometimes leave difficulties to be solved by other people or to solve themselves? After all, married people do like to be left on their own,' I said as gently as I could. 'Didn't it occur to you that perhaps you ought to find somewhere else to live after they were married?'

'No, I'm afraid it didn't, but then I haven't known many married people. And it never occurred to me that Julian would marry. Men are so strange,' she said, in a pathetic puzzled way, as if she were finding it out for the first time. 'He always said he would never marry. You see, Mildred, I always used to think it would be so nice if you and he . . .'

'Oh, there was never any question of that,' I said quickly. 'Where *was* Julian when all this happened this evening? Surely he didn't let you run out of the house in the rain?'

'Oh, no, it's his boys' club night and he went out immediately after supper, otherwise Allegra would never have said the things she did. She was always nice to me when he was there. He thinks she has such a sweet nature.'

'Yes, men are sometimes taken in. They don't ever quite see the terrible depths that we do.' The Dog beneath the Skin, I thought, and then remembered that it was the name of a clever play William Caldicote had once taken me to, so perhaps it didn't apply here.

We sat in silence for a while and I thought of the unfinished letter to Rocky lying on my desk. 'What time will Julian be back?' I asked. 'I had better come back to the vicarage with you when you're quite sure he will be there.'

'Oh, but, Mildred, I hoped I could come and live with you,' said Winifred with appalling simplicity.

For a moment I was too taken aback to say anything and I knew that I must think carefully before I answered. Easy excuses, such as the difficulty of finding a whole pair of clean sheets that didn't need mending, would not do here. I had to ask myself why it was that the thought of Winifred, of whom I was really very fond, sharing my home with me filled me with sinking apprehension. Perhaps it was because I realised that if I once took her in it would probably be for ever. There could be no casting her off if my own circumstances should happen to change, if, for example, I ever thought of getting married myself. And at the idea of getting married myself I began to laugh, for it really did seem a little fantastic.

Winifred noticed my amusement and smiled a little uncertainly. 'Of course it may be too much to ask,' she faltered, 'but you've always been so kind to me. I should pay, of course,' she added hastily.

The truth was, I thought, looking once more at the letter on my desk which could not now be finished tonight, that I was exhausted with bearing other people's burdens, or burthens as the nobler language of our great hymn-writers put it. Then, too, I had become selfish and set in my ways and would surely be a difficult person to live with. I could hardly add that the bed in my spare room was hard or that Dora might want to come and stay with me. I must obviously make a gesture towards helping Winifred.

'But of course you must stay for a night or two,' I said, 'at least until we see how things are going to turn out.'

She thanked me and then we were both silent for a time, as if thinking over the implications of the last part of the sentence.

I felt better after I had made this offer and together we looked out a pair of sheets and some blankets. We had just finished making up the bed in the spare-room, when the front door-bell rang again, urgently and impatiently.

I went down and found Julian Malory outside the door, He was hatless and had flung round his shoulders one of those black speckled mackintoshes which seem to be worn only by clergymen. He looked worried and upset. I could not think why he should be carrying a couple of ping-pong bats in his hand, until I remembered that it was his boys' club night.

'Where's Winifred?' he asked sharply. 'Have you seen her this evening?'

'Oh, yes, she is here,' I said. 'She is going to stay a night or two with me – after what happened,' I added, feeling awkward.

'That's quite impossible,' said Julian quickly. 'You must see that it is.'

We were walking upstairs and as I switched landing lights on and off I racked my brains to discover why it should be impossible for Winifred to stay a night or two with me.

'Don't you see,' he went on, 'Mrs Gray and I cannot stay alone in the vicarage. It would be most awkward.'

'But she could keep her own flat, surely?' I said, wondering why he was calling her 'Mrs Gray' and not 'Allegra'.

'Even so, we are still under the same roof.'

'Oh, don't quibble so,' I said, impatient of his talk of roofs. 'Nobody would think anything of it. You are both respectable people, and after all you *are* engaged to be married.'

'The engagement is broken off,' said Julian flatly, laying down the ping-pong bats rather carefully on the kitchen table.

I hardly know what happened next, but eventually we were

all sitting down and I was trying to console both Julian and Winifred, who seemed to be in tears again. It occurred to me that I might have to put them both up for the night and I began to wonder how it could be managed. I should have to sleep on the narrow sofa in the sitting-room, unless I used one of the Napiers' beds.

Julian did not tell us very much about what had happened. It appeared that he had come in and asked where Winifred was and then the whole story had come out. I should never know exactly what had passed between him and Allegra Gray. There are some things too dreadful to be revealed, and it is even more dreadful how, in spite of our better instincts, we long to know about them. I found myself worrying about irrelevant details – who had actually done the breaking off, had she given him back the ring, and how did it come about that he was still carrying the ping-pong bats, which he had presumably taken from the boys' club to the vicarage, when he came to my flat? Had he perhaps been holding them in his hand all the time the dreadful scene was going on? I knew that things like that *could* happen . . .

At that moment the telephone rang. It was Mrs Jubb who looked after the Malorys at the vicarage. I handed the receiver to Julian and heard him say 'Yes' and 'No' once or twice in answer to what seemed like a great flood of conversation from the other end.

'Well, she's gone,' he said, turning towards us. 'She left the house ten minutes ago with a small suitcase. Mrs Jubb thought I ought to know.'

Winifred gave a kind of moan and began to cry again.

I looked at Julian questioningly and he nodded.

'Come, Winifred,' I said, 'you've had enough for tonight.

You must go to bed and I'll bring you a hot drink and something to make you sleep.'

She came with me willingly enough and when I had settled her as comfortably as I could, I returned to Julian, who was sitting despondently by the electric fire.

'Where will she have gone at this time of night?' I asked, almost fearing that the bell might ring and I should find her outside my own door.

'Oh, she has a friend in Kensington who will put her up. I expect she has gone there.'

'What sort of a friend?'

'Oh, an unmarried woman with her own flat. A very sensible person, I believe.'

I lay back and closed my eyes, for I was very tired. I wondered if Mrs Gray's friend was tired too. I imagined her in the tidy kitchen in her dressing gown, just putting on the milk for her Ovaltine and being startled by the front door-bell ringing and wondering who on earth it could be calling so late. And now she would have to sit up half the night, listening and condoling.

'What does she do?'

'What does who do?' asked Julian rather irritably.

'This friend with the flat in Kensington.'

'Oh, I'm not sure. She is a civil servant of some kind, I believe. I think she has quite a good job.'

'I suppose Mrs Jubb knows what has happened?'

'Oh, I imagine she will have gathered that something is wrong. I suppose everybody will know tomorrow, but these things can hardly be concealed.'

'Are you going to put an announcement in *The Times*?'

'Oh, does one do that?' asked Julian vaguely. 'I should hardly have thought it was necessary.'

'Well, it might save embarrassment, and there is nothing dishonourable about it, I mean nothing to be ashamed of,' I said. 'It is much better to have found out now rather than later.'

'Yes, that's what people say, isn't it? I suppose one must bear the humiliation of having made a mistake. I obviously had no idea of her true character. You see, I thought her such a fine person.'

She was certainly very pretty, I thought, but I did not say it. I could not add to the burden of his humiliation by pointing out that he may have been taken in, like so many men before him, by a pretty face.

'Of course it was mostly my fault,' Julian went on. 'I can see that now.'

'Well, I imagine there are always faults on both sides, though one person may be more to blame than the other. But I'm sure you need not reproach yourself for anything you did.'

'Thank you, Mildred,' he said, with a faint smile. 'You are very kind. I don't know what we'd do without you.'

'Perhaps clergymen shouldn't marry,' I said, realising that Julian was now a free man again and that we ladies of the parish need no longer think of ourselves as the rejected ones. But the thought did not, at that moment, arouse any very great enthusiasm in me. Perhaps I should feel differently in the morning when I was less tired.

'Some seem to manage it very successfully,' said Julian rather sadly.

I could think of nothing to say beyond suggesting that he could always have another try, but this did not seem to be quite the moment to say it.

'I know the kind of person I should like to marry,' he went

on, 'and I thought I had found her. But perhaps I looked too far and there might have been somebody nearer at hand.'

I stared into the electric fire and wished it had been a coal one, though the functional glowing bar was probably more suitable for this kind of occasion.

'*I cannot see what flowers are at my feet,*' said Julian softly.

Nor what soft incense hangs upon the boughs, I continued to myself, feeling the quotation had gone wrong somewhere and that it was not really quite what Julian had intended.

'That's Keats, isn't it?' I asked rather bluntly. 'I always think *Nor What Soft Incense* would be a splendid title for a novel. Perhaps about a village where there were two rival churches, one High and one Low. I wonder if it has ever been used?'

Julian laughed and the slight embarrassment which I had felt between us was dispelled. He stood up and began to make preparations for going. He put on his speckled mackintosh, but seemed to forget about the ping-pong bats on the kitchen table, nor did I like to remind him. I went to bed immediately after he had gone, but I did not sleep very well. In my dreams Allegra Gray came to my house with a pile of suitcases, Rocky stood by the electric fire and asked me to marry him, but when I looked up I saw that it was Julian in his speckled mackintosh. I woke up feeling ashamed and disappointed and made a resolution that I would take Winifred her breakfast in bed.

CHAPTER TWENTY-THREE

There was a kind of suppressed excitement about Mrs Morris's manner next morning and she went about her work smiling and almost nodding to herself, occasionally glancing at me and then at Winifred with an expression of triumph on her face. I could see that she was longing to get Winifred out of the way and when, after we had drunk our mid-morning cup of tea, Winifred asked if I would mind if she went over to the vicarage to see if Julian was all right, I was almost as eager as Mrs Morris to see her go.

'*Well*, Miss Lathbury, *now* what've you got to say?'

She stood with her back to the sink, her hands on her hips. I felt unequal to the note of challenge in her voice, as if I were about to perform before a critical audience and was certain that I should not fulfil expectations.

'It's all been so sudden,' I said feebly. 'I hardly know what to say.

'Ah, but that's how it goes. Getting engaged and breaking it off. One minute it is and the next it isn't.'

I had to agree that this was certainly so.

'I hardly know what really happened,' I said.

'Oh, well, if that's it,' she said comfortably, 'I've had it all from Mrs Jubb. She heard every word.'

'Oh, dear, I do hope she wasn't listening at the door.'

'Listening at the door? Goodness, you could hear it all over the house. Mrs Gray, that is, not a word out of the vicar. Only a sort of muttering, she said. Oh, it was terrible!'

I was glad that Julian had preserved his dignity, as, indeed, I knew he would, even with the ping-pong bats in his hand.

'She said she'd had quite enough being married to one clergyman, and something about them not knowing how to treat women and no wonder.' Mrs Morris paused, a little puzzled. 'I don't know what it was no wonder about, Mrs Jubb didn't say. And then she went on about Miss Winifred, oh, it was shocking the things she said.'

'What kind of things?' I found myself asking.

'Oh, well, Mrs Jubb didn't say exactly or maybe she didn't hear but she said it sounded something terrible. Not *bad* words, you know,' said Mrs Morris, lowering her tone and looking at me a little fearfully, 'if you see what I mean. Not the kind of things with bad swear words, but dreadful things. And then Mrs Gray ran screaming upstairs to her flat and *he* went out of the house very quickly. And then *she* came running down again with a case packed and went away somewhere, Mrs Jubb didn't seem to know where.' Mrs Morris looked at me hopefully to supply this missing information.

'To a friend in Kensington, I believe,' I said, thinking that although I shouldn't be talking like this to Mrs Morris, it was better that she should know some of the truth.

'*Kensington, well,*' said Mrs Morris, sounding more Welsh

than usual in her excitement. 'And when Mr Malory, Father Malory, I should say, got back he looked *terrible*, Mrs Jubb said. I should think he'd been walking the streets, distracted,' said Mrs Morris, adding something of her own. 'I shouldn't be surprised if he hadn't been down by the river.'

I could hardly believe that sitting quietly by my electric fire could have given Julian such a terrible appearance, unless, of course, he had not gone straight home when he left me. 'He was here with Miss Malory and me,' I said.

'Oh, he knew who to turn to,' said Mrs Morris, beaming. 'Didn't I tell you, Miss Lathbury? He knew who his true friend was, the poor soul. A pity he didn't see it before. But a thing often happens like that, some terrible calamity and we get some kind of a revelation. Like St Paul, isn't it?'

'Well, perhaps, not quite . . .' I began, but I was unable to stem the flow of her Welsh eloquence.

'The scales fell from his eyes and he saw her for what she really was and you for what you really was, and oh, the difference! To think he'd been so blind all this time, *groping* in darkness . . .'

'I hardly think . . .'

'Not knowing black from white, but a lot of men is like that. And a clergyman's just the same as other men, isn't he, only he wears his collar back to front, that's all, really, isn't it?'

I did not think it worth pointing out that there were perhaps more subtle differences between clergymen and others than the wearing of the collar back to front.

'Well, look at us, this won't get the work done, will it, Miss Lathbury?' she said suddenly, seizing the wet mop and swilling it vigorously in the bucket. 'But I'm not surprised at this. I saw it coming.'

I was not quite clear as to what it was that Mrs Morris had seen coming, but I decided that we had talked enough about it. Was I then to marry Julian? Was that what she had seen coming? Would he propose to me, after a decent interval, of course, and should we make a match of it and delight the parish? It sounded ideal, but somehow morning had not brought any more enthusiasm than the night before. I still thought of myself as one of the rejected ones and I could not believe that he loved me any more than I loved him. Of course I liked and admired him, perhaps I even respected and esteemed him, as Everard Bone did Esther Clovis. But was that enough? In any case, it was indecent, wicked, almost, to be thinking of such things now. There must surely be some practical help I could give. What was to happen to Mrs Gray's furniture and possessions? Was a go-between needed, or a letter-writer? Letter-writing reminded me of the unfinished letter to Rocky Napier which was still lying on my desk. Gritting my teeth, as it were, I determined to get it out of the way, and sat down there and then and did it. I hardly knew what I wrote and spent no time on subtleties. I told him the news about Julian and Mrs Gray and made that an excuse for my careless writing.

When I had posted the letter, I walked towards the shops to buy some things to eat. I was walking back with my string bag full of uninteresting food, when I saw Sister Blatt advancing towards me on her bicycle. She lowered herself carefully off it and blocked the pavement, so that I could not help stopping and talking to her.

'Well, well,' she said, waiting for me to begin.

'Well,' I repeated, 'there really seems to be nothing to say. It's all very upsetting, isn't it?'

'Oh, I'm sorry for Father Malory, of course, though I never liked the woman, but good comes out of everything.'

'Yes, I suppose it does,' I said uncertainly, for although I believed that it did I thought that it was surely a little soon for any to be apparent yet.

'I am to have Mrs Gray's flat,' said Sister Blatt triumphantly. 'A friend of mine from Stoke-on-Trent is coming to work in Pimlico, so near, you see, and we have been wanting to get a place together and now this has happened.'

'A ram in a thicket, in fact,' I said, feeling like Mrs Morris and St Paul.

'Exactly.' Sister Blatt nodded vigorously. 'Just what I said to Father Malory this morning. I went to the vicarage as soon as I heard the news. You see, I realised that it might be awkward for them being under the same roof, so I put forward my idea as a solution to the difficulty. As it happened, she had gone away.'

'To a friend in Kensington,' I murmured.

'Yes, much the best thing for all concerned. You're looking tired,' she said suddenly. 'Your face is quite grey. You must take care of yourself.' And with these encouraging words, she swung herself up on to her bicycle and rode majestically away.

I am tired, I said to myself, as I walked upstairs, and my face is quite grey. Nobody must come near me. I would have a rest this afternoon, for Winifred had gone back to the vicarage and was comforting Julian. I felt a little sorry for him, surrounded as he would be by excellent women. But at least he would be safe from people like Mrs Gray; Sister Blatt would defend him fiercely against all such perils, I knew. Perhaps it might after all be my duty to marry him, if only to save him from being too well protected.

I made myself what seemed an extravagant lunch of two scrambled eggs, preceded by the remains of some soup and followed by cheese, biscuits and an apple. I was glad that I wasn't a man, or the kind of man who looked upon a meal alone as a good opportunity to cook a small plover, though I should have been glad enough to have somebody else cook it for me. After I had washed up I went gratefully to my bed and lay under the eiderdown with a hot-water bottle. I had finished my library book, and thought how odd it was that although I had the great novelists and poets well represented on my shelves, none of their works seemed to attract me. It would be a good opportunity to read some of the things I was always meaning to read, like *In Memoriam* or *The Brothers Karamazov*, but in the end I was reduced to reading the serial in the parish magazine, and pondering over the illustrations, one of which showed a square-jawed young clergyman in conversation with a pretty young woman, as it might be Julian and Mrs Gray, except that Julian wasn't square-jawed. The caption under the picture said, 'I'm sure Mrs Goodrich didn't mean to hurt your feelings about the jumble sale.' I finished the episode with a feeling of dissatisfaction. There was some just cause or impediment which prevented the clergyman from marrying the girl, some mysterious reason why Mrs Goodrich should have snubbed her at the jumble sale, but we should have to wait until next month before we could know any more about it.

I turned back to the parish news. There was a warning from our treasurer about our financial position. Julian's letter to his flock was short and uninteresting. The servers had had a very enjoyable day at Southend; all those who had brought gifts and helped to decorate the church for Harvest Festival were thanked; there was to be a working party to mend the cassocks, 'commencing on the first Tuesday afternoon in October'. I was distressed that Julian should use the word 'commence', but I suppose I must have dropped off to sleep somewhere here, for there was a long gap between the announcement about the cassocks and my next conscious thought, which was that I was thirsty and that it must be teatime.

I was just finishing tea when the telephone rang. I let it ring for quite a long time before I lifted the receiver warily and held it to my ear, wondering whose voice would come out of it and what it would ask me to do. It was a man's voice, a pleasant voice, but for the moment I could not think whose.

'Hullo, Mildred. This is Everard.'

I was instantly suspicious. I had hardly even realised that we called each other by our Christian names but I supposed that after all this time we probably did, though I was not conscious of ever having called him Everard.

After a few formal preliminaries, during which each asked how the other was, and gave and received an answer, there was a pause. What does he want? I wondered, and waited for him to say.

'I rang up to ask if you would come and have dinner with me in my flat this evening. I have got some meat to cook.'

I saw myself putting a small joint into the oven and preparing vegetables. I could feel my aching back bending over the sink.

'I'm afraid I can't tonight,' I said baldly.

'Oh, I'm sorry.' His voice sounded flat and noncommittal, so that it was impossible to tell whether he really minded or not. 'Perhaps some other time?' he added politely.

feeling uneasy and yet not quite knowing why. I had not wanted to see Everard Bone and the idea of having to cook his evening meal for him was more than I could bear at this moment. And yet the thought of him alone with his meat and his cookery book was unbearable too. He would turn to the section on meat. He would read that beef or mutton should be cooked for so many minutes per pound and so many over. He would weigh the little joint, if he had scales. He would then puzzle over the heat of the oven, turning it on and standing over it watching the thermometer go up . . . I should have been nearly in tears at this point if I had not pulled myself together and reminded myself that Everard Bone was a very capable sort of person whose life was always very well arranged. He would be quite equal to cooking a joint. Men are not nearly so helpless and pathetic as we sometimes like to imagine them, and on the whole they run their lives better than we do ours. After all, Everard knew quite a lot of people he could ask to dinner and was probably even now ringing them up. If I could not come, no doubt somebody else would be only too glad to. But then another thought came into my mind. Why had I assumed that I was the first person he had telephoned that evening? I might very well have been the last. There must be many people whom he knew better than he did me and with whom he would rather spend an evening. For some reason that I could not understand, for I believe I have always had a modest opinion of myself, I found this a disturbing thought. It seemed as if it was necessary for me to know that I had been the first choice, but I did not see what I could do about it. I did not look forward to my evening at home, and all the useful and half-pleasant things I had planned to do, like ironing and sewing and listening to the wireless, seemed uninteresting and unnecessary. In the end I decided to go over to the vicarage to see if there was anything I could do there.

CHAPTER TWENTY-FOUR

'Mildred, *darling* . . . how wonderful to see you!'

I was quite unprepared for Rocky's effusive greeting and embrace. I was unprepared for his appearance at all at that moment, for I had had no answer to the letter I had written to him some time ago, and I had begun to think that I had offended him by my well-meaning efforts to bring him and Helena together again. It is a known fact that people like clergymen's daughters, excellent women in their way, sometimes rush in where the less worthy might fear to tread.

'Hullo, Rocky,' was all I could say.

'You don't seem very pleased to see me.'

'Oh, I am, but it's so unexpected . . .'

'Surely nice things always are?' He stood looking at me, confidently charming. I noticed that he was holding a bunch of chrysanthemums.

'These are for you,' he said, thrusting them at me. I saw that the stems had been broken very roughly and that they were not tied together at all.

'Are they out of your garden?' I asked.

'Yes; I snatched them as I was hurrying for the train.'

Somehow they seemed a little less desirable now. He had not chosen them, had not gone into a shop for that purpose, they had just happened to be there. If he had gone into a shop and chosen them . . . I pulled myself up and told myself to stop these ridiculous thoughts, wondering why it is that we can never stop trying to analyse the motives of people who have no personal interest in us, in the vain hope of finding that perhaps they may have just a little after all.

'Helena said that I must bring you some flowers and these happened to be in the garden,' he went on, leaving me in no doubt at all.

'Thank you, they're lovely,' I said. 'Is Helena with you, then?'

'Yes, of course. After getting your letter, I wrote to her and we met.'

'I hope you didn't think it interfering of me?'

'Of course not. I know how you love contriving things,' he smiled. 'Births, deaths, marriages and all the rest of it.'

Perhaps I did love it as I always seemed to get involved in them, I thought with resignation; perhaps I really enjoyed other people's lives more than my own.

We were standing in one of our usual talking places, the entrance to my kitchen. I could feel Rocky looking at me very intently. I raised my eyes to meet his.

'Mildred?'

'Yes?'

'I was hoping . . .'

'What were you hoping?'

'That you might suggest making a cup of tea. You know how you always make a cup of tea on "occasions". That's one of the things I remember most about you, and surely this is an "occasion"?'

So he did remember me like that after all – a woman who was always making cups of tea. Well, there was nothing to be done about it now but to make one.

'Oh, certainly,' I said. 'And anyway it is nearly teatime, I mean, the conventional hour for drinking tea.'

'You never came down to visit me at my cottage. Why?'

'Well, you didn't ask me.'

'Oh, but people mustn't wait to be asked. Other people came.'

'Did any of the Wren officers come?' Had they had luncheon in the wild garden with a bottle of some amusing little wine? I was very much afraid that they might have done.

'Wren officers?' Rocky looked puzzled for a moment and then laughed. 'Oh, yes, one or two. But of course they weren't in their uniforms, so one regarded them as human beings. Oh, lots of people came. I was very social. Had you imagined me there all alone?'

'I don't know, really. I didn't think.' I was unwilling to remember or to tell him how I had imagined him. 'Of course, men don't tend to be alone, do they? I think we talked about it before some time.'

'Oh, surely! Haven't we tired the sun with talking on every possible subject?'

The tea was made now and it was as strong as it had been weak on the day Helena had left him. I wondered why it was that tea could vary so, even when one followed exactly the same method in making it. Could the emotional state of the maker have something to do with it?

We sat in silence for a while, brooding over our strong tea, and then I began to ask him about the furniture which had been moved and whether he was going to have it all brought back again.

'Oh, no, we have decided to settle in the country,' he said. 'We don't really like this place very much.'

'No; I suppose the associations . . .'

'The rest of the stuff can quite easily be packed up and sent after us, can't it?'

'Oh, yes, that can easily be arranged,' I said in a consciously bright tone. 'I wonder who will take your flat?'

'Somebody respectable, I hope, as you have to share the bathroom. Couldn't you advertise in the *Church Times* for a couple of Anglo-Catholic ladies? That's really what you want.'

'Yes, I suppose it is.' I hoped I did not show how depressed I felt at the idea of this future. But then I remembered that it was not within my power to decide who the new tenants should be. The landlord would arrange that, though I supposed that had I known anyone in need of a flat I could put in a word for them.

'What news?' asked Rocky, taking the last chocolate biscuit. 'Has anything exciting happened in the parish?'

'Julian Malory has broken off his engagement,' I said. 'I think I told you that when I wrote.'

'Oh, of course, the vicar, *your* vicar. But that's splendid; now he can marry you. Isn't that just what we wanted?'

'If he had wanted to marry me he could have asked me before he met Mrs Gray,' I pointed out.

'Oh, not necessarily. It often happens that a person is rejected or passed over and then their true worth is seen. I always think that must be very romantic.'

'It could be romantic if you had been the person to do the

rejecting, but one doesn't like to be the person to have been rejected,' I said uncertainly, feeling that I must be giving Rocky the impression that I really did want to marry Julian. 'Anyway, there has never been any question of anything more than friendship between us.'

'How dull. Perhaps you could marry the other one, the curate?'

I explained patiently that Father Greatorex was not really suitable, not the kind of person one would want to marry.

'Let me stay as I am,' I said. 'I'm quite happy.'

'Well, I don't know. I still feel we ought to do something,' said Rocky vaguely.

I got up and took the tea tray into the kitchen.

'Have you seen our friend Everard Bone at all?' Rocky called out.

Immediately he asked this, I realised that there had been a little nagging worry, an unhappiness, almost, at the back of my mind. Everard Bone and his meat. Of course it sounded ridiculous put like that and I decided that I would not mention it to Rocky. He would mock and not understand. It made me sad to realise that he would not understand, that perhaps he did not really understand anything about me.

'I had lunch with him some time ago,' I said. 'He seemed very much as usual.'

'I imagine he will be both relieved and disappointed when he knows that Helena and I have come together again,' said Rocky complacently. 'I think he found the situation a little alarming.'

'It was rather awkward for him,' I said. 'Or it might have been.'

'Poor Helena, it was one of those sudden irrational passions women get for people. She is completely disillusioned now.

When he should have been near at hand to cherish her she found he had fled to a meeting of the Prehistoric Society in Derbyshire! Do you know how that happens?'

'You mean being disillusioned? Yes, I think I can see how it could. Perhaps you meet a person and he quotes Matthew Arnold or some favourite poet to you in the churchyard, but naturally life can't be all like that,' I said rather wildly. 'And he only did it because he felt it was expected of him. I mean, he isn't really like that at all.'

'It would certainly be difficult to live up to that, to quoting Matthew Arnold in churchyards,' said Rocky. 'But perhaps he was kind to you at a moment when you needed kindness – surely that's worth something?'

'Oh, yes, certainly it is.' Once more, perhaps for the last time, I saw the Wren officers huddled together in an awkward little group on the terrace of the Admiral's villa. Rocky's kindness must surely have meant a great deal to them at that moment and perhaps some of them would never forget it as long as they lived.

Rocky stood up. 'Well, thank you for my tea. Helena is coming back at the weekend. I must go and do some shopping at the Army and Navy Stores before they close. What are you doing this evening?'

'I have to go to a meeting in the parish hall to decide about the Christmas bazaar.'

'To decide about the Christmas bazaar,' Rocky mimicked my tone. 'Can I come too?'

'I think it would bore you.'

'Why do churches always have to be arranging bazaars and jumble sales? One would think that was the only reason for their existence.'

'Our church is very short of money.'

'Perhaps I should give it a donation as a kind of thank-offering,' said Rocky lightly. 'Though I should really prefer to give something more permanent. A stained-glass window – the Rockingham Napier window – I can see it, very red and blue. Or some money to buy the best quality incense?'

'I'm sure that would be most acceptable.'

'Well, perhaps I will. I must hurry now – goodbye!'

After he had gone I stood looking out of the window after him. I seemed to remember that I had done this before, and not so very long ago. But my thoughts on that occasion, though more melancholy had been somehow more pleasant. Now I felt flat and disappointed, as if he had failed to come up to my expectations. And yet, what had I really hoped for? Dull, solid friendship without charm? No, there was enough of that between women and women and even between men and women. Of course, if he had not been married . . . but this suggested a situation altogether too unreal to contemplate. In the first place, I should probably never have met him at all, and I should certainly not have enjoyed the privilege of preparing lunch for him on the day his wife left him or of making all those cups of tea on 'occasions'. This thought led me to worry again about Everard and his meat and how I had refused to cook it for him, and it was a relief when the church clock struck and I realised that it was time to go to the meeting in the parish hall.

CHAPTER TWENTY-FIVE

Perhaps there can be too much making of cups of tea, I thought, as I watched Miss Statham filling the heavy teapot. We had all had our supper, or were supposed to have had it, and were met together to discuss the arrangements for the Christmas bazaar. Did we really *need* a cup of tea? I even said as much to Miss Statham and she looked at me with a hurt, almost angry look, 'Do we *need* tea?' she echoed. 'But Miss Lathbury . . .' She sounded puzzled and distressed and I began to realise that my question had struck at something deep and fundamental. It was the kind of question that starts a landslide in the mind.

I mumbled something about making a joke and that of course one needed tea always, at every hour of the day or night.

'This teapot's heavy,' she said lifting it with both hands and placing it on the table. 'You'd think one of the men might help to carry it,' she added, raising her voice.

Mr Mallet and Mr Conybeare, the churchwardens, and Mr Gamble, the treasurer, looked up from their business, which they were conducting in a secret masculine way with many papers spread out before them, but made no move to help.

'I see it is done now by the so-called weaker sex,' said Mr Mallet. 'I think Miss Statham has got everything under control.'

'Come on now,' she said, 'make room for your cups of tea. You've got the table so cluttered with papers and your elbows on it too. You'll be knocking something over. Anyone would think you weren't interested in having a cup.'

'Oh, we are that, all right,' said Mr Conybeare. 'Just you pour it out, Miss Statham, and we'll soon make room.'

Miss Statham and I served the men and the other ladies and then sat down ourselves. Winifred Malory was at home with a bad cold and Julian had not yet arrived, which added considerably to the enjoyment of all present, as the broken engagement could be discussed freely and without embarrassment. It was the first time since it had happened that there had been any kind of parish gathering.

'Of course a man can carry it off with more dignity, a thing like that,' said Miss Statham, putting a knitted tea-cosy on the teapot. 'Anyone who wants a second cup can help themselves. A man doesn't feel the shame that a woman would.'

'After all, he can easily ask somebody else – after a decent interval, of course,' said Miss Enders.

'Once bitten, twice shy,' said Mr Mallett. 'I should say he was well out of it. Not that she wasn't a charming lady in her way. But if he's got any sense Father Malory won't go asking anyone else in a hurry. He'll know when he's well off.'

'Really, Mr Mallett, it's a good thing your wife isn't here,' said Miss Statham indignantly. 'Whatever would she think to hear you talking like that?'

'My good lady leaves the thinking to me,' said Mr Mallett, amid laughter from the men.

'What does the vicar want with a wife, anyway?' asked Mr Conybeare. 'He's got his sister and you ladies to help him in the parish.'

'Oh, well, what a question!' Miss Statham giggled. 'He's a man, isn't he, and all men are alike.'

There followed some rather embarrassing badinage between Miss Statham and the two churchwardens in which I was quite unable to join, though I envied her the easy way she had with them. Their joking was broken up by the arrival of Sister Blatt, looking very pleased with herself.

'*Well*,' she said, sitting down heavily and beaming all over her face, 'it's a disgrace, I never saw anything like it.'

We asked what.

'The way Mrs Gray left that kitchen in the flat. You know the remover's men have been in today to take away her furniture. Oh, my goodness, there was food in the larder, been there weeks! And dishes not washed up, even!'

'She left in rather a hurry,' I pointed out. 'I don't suppose she thought of washing up before she went.' People did tend to leave the washing up on the dramatic occasions of life; I remembered only too well how full of dirty dishes the Napiers' kitchen had been on the day Helena had left.

'But, Miss Lathbury, dear, that wouldn't account for the mess there was. Tins half used and then left, stale ends of loaves, and everything so *dirty* . . . I never thought she was the right wife for Father Malory and I often said so too. I'm afraid she was a real viper.'

'In sheep's clothing,' added Mr Mallett. 'Now, is the vicar going to honour us with his presence tonight or is he not?'

'I dare say he's forgotten and is playing darts with the boys next door,' said Miss Statham. 'Would anyone like to go and see?'

I said that I would, and, bracing myself to meet the pandemonium went into the main part of the hall, where Julian, surrounded by a crowd of lads, was playing darts. It seemed a pity to interrupt the game and drag him off to our dull meeting and the cold stewed tea and he seemed to come rather unwillingly.

'What is it, Mildred?' he asked. 'The bazaar meeting? Good heavens, I'd forgotten all about it!'

He took his place at the head of the table and accepted a cup of the stewed tea absent-mindedly. Everybody was quiet now as if out of respect for Julian's new status brought about by the broken engagement.

'I'm sorry to have kept you waiting,' he said. 'Now, what exactly is the purpose of this meeting?'

'It might have been to decide on a wedding present from the parish,' whispered Sister Blatt to me. 'What a good thing we hadn't started to collect the money!'

The treasurer cleared his throat and began to explain.

'Ah, yes, the Christmas bazaar,' said Julian lightly. 'Well, I suppose it will follow its usual course. Do we really need to have a meeting about it?'

There was a shocked silence.

'He's not himself,' whispered Miss Statham.

'Why not let us decide about the bazaar?' I suggested boldly. 'Why don't you go back to the boys? I could see that you were having a very exciting darts match with Teddy Lemon.'

'Yes, I was beating him for once, too,' said Julian. 'If you'll excuse me, I think I will go back.' He got up from the table and went off, leaving his tea unfinished.

'Well, really, I've never heard of such a thing,' said Miss Statham. 'The vicar has always presided at the meeting to arrange about the Christmas bazaar – it's been the custom ever since Father Busby's time.'

'Well, Miss Statham, if you can remember what went on in the eighteen-seventies when Father Busby was vicar, the rest of us must retire,' said Sister Blatt genially.

'But it's so irresponsible,' protested Miss Statham, 'especially when you consider how important the bazaar is in these days.'

'I am reminded of nothing so much as the Emperor Nero fiddling while Rome is burning,' said Mr Mallett.

'Now then, Mr Mallett, who said anything about Rome?' said Sister Blatt. 'We're not there yet, you know.'

'Not like poor Mr and Mrs Lake and Miss Spicer,' said Miss Enders.

There was a short silence as is sometimes customary after speaking of the dead, though in this case the people referred to might have been thought to have met with a fate worse than death, for they had left us and been received into the Church of Rome.

'Oh, well, I was speaking metaphorically, as is my wont,' said Mr Mallett.

'One might say that Father Malory's conduct this evening reminds us of the behaviour of Sir Francis Drake, going on and playing bowls when the Armada was sighted,' suggested Mr Conybeare.

'But that was supposed to be a good thing, a brave thing,' said Miss Enders.

'I think perhaps Father Malory is doing a good thing,' I said.

'But he didn't even finish his cup of tea,' protested Miss Statham.

'Well, it was rather stewed,' said Sister Blatt.

'Perhaps this unfortunate affair has turned his head,' said Miss Statham mysteriously. 'We shan't know what to expect now.'

'He might take it into his head to enter a monastic order or to become a missionary,' said Miss Enders, almost gloating at the prospect.

'People often do strange things when they've had a disappointment,' agreed Miss Statham. 'He might ask the Bishop to put him in the East End.'

'Or in a country parish,' said Miss Enders.

There seemed to be no end to the things that Julian might do, from making a hasty and unsuitable marriage and leaving the Church altogether to going over to Rome and ending up as a Cardinal.

'Well, ladies,' said Mr Mallett at last, 'what about this bazaar? Isn't it the purpose for which two or three are gathered together?'

'Oh, well, as Father Malory said, it can just follow its usual course,' said Miss Statham rather impatiently. 'I imagine the stall-holders will be as usual?' There was a note of challenge in her voice as she looked round the table, for it was known that she herself had always taken charge of the fancy-work stall, which was considered to be the most important.

'Oh, yes, we leave it to you ladies to fight all that out,' said Mr Mallett, recoiling in mock fear. 'We men will just do the hard work, eh?'

'Of course we could ask Father Greatorex to preside,' said Miss Enders doubtfully.

'Oh, that man! A fat lot of good he'd be,' said Sister Blatt. 'I think we've really done quite well on our own.'

'Without benefit of clergy,' said Mr Conybeare.

'But we don't really seem to have *decided* anything,' I said. 'When is the bazaar to be? Have we settled the date?'

'Oh, well, it will be when it always is,' said Miss Statham.

'When is that?'

'The first Saturday in December.'

'Is it always then?'

'Oh, yes, it always has been as long as *I* can remember.'

'Since the days of Father Busby, eh?' said Mr Mallett jovially. Miss Statham ignored him, perhaps she was tired of his joking or considered the date of the bazaar to be no matter for joking.

'It is not a movable feast, then?' asked Mr Conybeare.

'Well, there isn't any better date, is there?' said Miss Statham sharply. 'It must be on a Saturday and a week or two before Christmas.'

We agreed that no better date than the first Saturday in December could be imagined, and I felt rather guilty for having raised doubts in anybody's mind. But I still felt dissatisfied, as if the evening had been wasted. Surely there was something we could discuss, some resolution we could carry?

'What stall shall I help with?' I asked.

They looked at me with such surprise that I began to think that perhaps I had been infected by Julian's strange behaviour.

'Why surely you will help me with the fancy stall?' said Miss Statham. 'Like you did last year and the year before. Unless you'd prefer to do anything else?'

I hesitated, for there was an uneasy feeling in the air, as if umbrage were about to be taken. 'Of course I will help you,

Miss Statham,' I said quickly. 'I was only wondering if there was anything else that needed doing. The hoopla or the bran tub,' I suggested feebly.

'But Teddy Lemon and the servers will look after that sort of thing,' said Miss Statham, as if it were beneath our dignity; 'they always do.'

'Yes, so they do. I'd forgotten.'

'Money needs to be spent,' said Mr Gamble, making himself heard for the first time. 'You must bring some of your rich friends, Miss Lathbury.'

'I dare say that Mrs Napier could afford to spend a bit of money on us,' said Miss Statham.

'I've often seen her smoking cigarettes in the street *and* going into the Duchess of Granby,' said Miss Enders, in a mealy-mouthed sort of way.

'Well, why shouldn't she?' I burst out. 'You can hardly expect her to come and spend money at our bazaar if that's the way you feel about her.'

'Oh, I didn't say anything, Miss Lathbury,' said Miss Enders huffily. 'I'm sure I didn't mean to offend.'

'I suppose these cups should be washed,' I said, standing up.

'Oh, yes, and the big urn ought to be refilled. The lads will want something,' said Miss Statham.

The men went on smoking and chatting while we gathered the cups together and struggled to fill the heavy urn between us. They belonged to the generation that does not think of helping with domestic tasks.

'Poor Father Malory. I suppose it was all for the best,' said Sister Blatt, waiting with a drying-cloth in her hand. 'We are told that everything happens for the best, and really it does, you know.'

'When one door shuts another door opens,' remarked Miss Statham.

'Yes, of course. Perhaps a door will open for Father Malory.'

At that moment a door did open, but it was only a group of lads headed by Teddy Lemon coming out of the hall. When they saw that we were washing up they withdrew hastily, with some scuffling and giggling.

'Perhaps he will throw himself into the boys' club,' suggested Sister Blatt. 'After all, it is a splendid thing to work among young people.'

I found myself beginning to laugh, I cannot think why, and turned the conversation to Sister Blatt's friend, who was to share the vicarage flat with her.

'I wonder if Father Malory will get engaged to her?' said Miss Statham in a sardonic tone.

'Oh, no, my friend isn't at all the type to attract a man,' said Sister Blatt with rough good humour. 'There won't be any nonsense of that kind.'

'Well, well, then everything will be as it was before Mrs Gray came, then.'

'Nothing can ever be really the same when time has passed,' I said, more to myself than to them, 'even if it appears to be from the outside. And didn't I tell you, the Napiers are leaving? So there will be new people in my house and things won't be at all the same.'

'Oh, I wonder who they will be?' asked Miss Statham eagerly.

'I don't know yet. Somehow I think they will be women who will come to our church.'

'Then there might be danger there,' said Sister Blatt in a

satisfied tone. 'I shall have to keep my eye on Father Malory.'

'That's right, Sister,' said Mr Mallett, overhearing the tail end of our conversation. 'Where would we be, I'd like to know, if you ladies didn't keep an eye on us?'

CHAPTER TWENTY-SIX

It was easier saying goodbye to Rocky the second time. He and Helena seemed almost sorry to be going and were very nice to me. They asked me down to their flat the evening before they were to go and Rocky opened a bottle of wine. Seeing them together, gay, frivolous and argumentative, made me feel smug and dull, as if meeting them had really made no difference to me at all.

'You must look after poor Everard Bone,' said Helena. 'Oh, how he needs the love of a good woman!'

'I'm glad you are not claiming that your love was that, darling,' said Rocky flippantly. 'Personally, I can't imagine anything I should like less than the love of a good woman. It would be like – oh – something very cosy and stifling and unglamorous, a large grey blanket – perhaps an Army blanket.'

'Or like a white rabbit thrust suddenly into your arms,' I suggested, feeling the glow of wine in me.

'Oh, but a white rabbit might be rather charming.'

'Yes, at first. But after a while you wouldn't know what to

do with it,' I said more soberly, remembering that I had had this conversation about white rabbits with Everard Bone.

'Poor Mildred, it's really rather too bad to suggest that the love of a good woman is dull when we know that she is so very good,' said Helena.

'And not at all dull,' said Rocky in his expected manner. 'But Mildred is already pledged to the vicar, and after his unfortunate experience you must surely agree that he has first claim.'

'Oh, he's surrounded by good women,' I said.

'I think he's nice,' said Helena, 'but it always seems to be his boys' club night, so one would never get taken out for a drink.'

'He and I had a drink together once,' said Rocky. 'We had a long talk about Italy.

> *Because it is the day of Palms,*
> *Carry a palm for me,*
> *Carry a palm in Santa Chiara,*
> *And I will watch the sea . . .'*

He began pacing round the room, touching the bare walls and looking out of the uncurtained windows. 'I wonder who will be sitting in this room a month from tonight?' he mused. 'I wonder if they will feel any kind of atmosphere? Should we carve our names in some secret place? One longs to have a bit of immortality somewhere.'

'You were going to give a memorial stained-glass window to the church,' I reminded him.

'Yes, but that's rather an expensive way of doing it. Besides, I feel it would be such a very hideous window.'

'Well, then you said you would give some money to buy incense.'

'Good heavens, so I did.' He took out his wallet and handed me a pound note which I put away quickly in my bag.

'That won't make you remembered,' said Helena; 'it will go up in the air and be lost. I suppose we should write something on a windowpane with a diamond ring. Here, Rocky,' she took a ring from her finger, 'try with this.'

'When my grave is broke up again
Some second guest to entertain,'

chanted Rocky, 'but perhaps a line of Dante would be better, if I could remember one.'

'I only know "abandon hope all ye who enter here,"' I said, 'which doesn't seem very suitable, and that bit about there being no greater sorrow than to remember happiness in a time of misery.'

'Ah, yes,' Rocky clapped his hands together, 'that's it!

Nessun maggior dolore,
Che ricordarsi del tempo felice
Nella miseria.'

'It seems an unkind way to greet new arrivals,' I said doubtfully.

'Oh, don't you believe it – people love to recall happiness in a time of misery. And anyway, they won't know what it means.'

'Quite a lot of people who were in Italy during the war must have learnt Italian,' I pointed out.

'But not Dante! The noble Allied Military didn't get much further than a few scattered imperatives, but they might have got as far as asking if dinner was ready and they probably knew the names of a few wines.'

'Unless they had Italian mistresses,' said Helena.

'Oh, then they domesticated them and taught them English,' said Rocky coolly.

'I don't suppose the new tenants will understand it anyway,' I mumbled quickly.

'Of course I haven't the patience to do this really properly,' said Rocky, looking at what he had written, 'the lettering isn't very good, but at least we shall feel we've left something to be remembered by.'

'But you don't need to. People aren't really forgotten,' I said, not wanting to be misunderstood but certain that I should be.

Rocky gave me one of his characteristic looks and smiled.

'What will you *do* after we've gone?' Helena asked.

'Well, she had a life before we came,' Rocky reminded her. 'Very much so – what is known as a *full* life, with clergymen and jumble sales and church services and good works.'

'I thought that was the kind of life led by women who *didn't* have a full life in the accepted sense,' said Helena.

'Oh, she'll marry,' said Rocky confidently. They were talking about me as if I wasn't there.

'Everard might take her to hear a paper at the Learned Society,' suggested Helena. 'That would widen her outlook.'

'Yes, it might,' I said humbly from my narrowness.

'But then she would get interested in some little tribe somewhere and her life might become even more narrow,' said Rocky.

We discussed my future until a late hour, but it was hardly to be expected that we should come to any practical conclusions.

The next day I saw them off and turned back a little sadly into the quiet empty house, wondering if I should ever see them again. Of course there had been the usual promises to write on both sides and I was invited to visit them whenever I liked.

It seemed that husbands and wives could part and come together again, and I was glad that it should be so, but what happened after that? It is said that people are refined and ennobled by suffering and one knows that they sometimes are, but would Helena have learned to be neater in the kitchen, or Rocky to share her interest in matrilineal kin-groups? It seemed as if this was at once too little and too much to expect from the experience they had been through, and I felt myself incapable of looking into their future. All I could do was to be prepared to receive Helena if she should ever appear on my doorstep with a suitcase, though perhaps that was Esther Clovis's privilege.

In the meantime, I began to think about Everard Bone and even to wish that I might cook his meat for him. I had a wild idea that I might join the Prehistoric Society, if only I knew how to set about it. It would probably be easier to belong to this than to the Learned Society, whose members must surely have some knowledge of or interest in anthropology. But any-body could scrabble about in the earth for bits of pottery or wander about on moors looking for dolmens, or so it seemed to me in my innocence. Then a more practical idea came into my head. I was supposed to keep Everard up to date with news about the Napiers; perhaps he did not know that they had become reconciled and left London to live in the country.

Why had he not telephoned me? Was it possible that he had gone away, or was lying ill, alone in his flat with nobody to look after him? Here my imaginings began to follow disconcertingly familiar lines. Well, at least I should see him in Lent, I told myself sensibly, at the lunchtime services at St Ermin's. I remembered that there was a poem which began *Lenten is come with love to town*, and with a feeling of shame I hastened to look it up in the *Oxford Book of English Verse*. But it was one of the very early ones, 'c. 1300', and although there was a glossary of unfamiliar words at the bottom of the page, the poem did not really comfort me.

> *Deowes donketh the dounes,*
> *Deores with huere derne rounes*
> *Domes forte deme;*

I read; that would teach me not to be so foolish.

Some days later I was walking near the premises of the Learned Society; in other words, I was doing what I had so often done in the days of Bernard Hatherley. The walk along Victoria Parade in the gathering twilight, the approach to 'Loch Lomond', the quick glance up at the lace-curtained window, the hope or fear that a hand might draw the curtain aside or a shadowy form be seen hovering behind it . . . is there no end to the humiliations we subject ourselves to? Of course, I told myself, there was no reason why I shouldn't be walking past the premises of the Learned Society, it was on the way to a dozen places. So I did not bow my head in shame as I approached the building but even looked up to see a bearded man step out on to the balcony, and Everard Bone and Esther Clovis coming out of the front door.

Esther Clovis . . . hair like a dog, but a very capable person, respected and esteemed by Everard Bone, and, moreover, one who could make an index and correct proofs. I felt quite a shock at seeing them together, especially when I noticed Everard taking her arm. Of course they were crossing the road and any man with reasonably good manners might be expected to take a woman's arm in those circumstances, I reasoned within myself, but I still felt very low. I decided that I would go and have lunch in the great cafeteria where I sometimes went with Mrs Bonner. It would encourage a suitable frame of mind, put me in mind of my own mortality and of that of all of us here below, if I could meditate on that line of patient people moving with their trays.

'Mildred! Didn't you see me?'

Everard sounded a little annoyed, as if he had had to hurry to catch me up.

'I didn't think you'd seen me,' I said, startled. 'Besides, you had somebody with you.'

'Only Esther Clovis.'

'She's a very capable person. What have you done with her?'

'Done with her? I happened to come out with her and she was meeting a friend for lunch. Are you going to have lunch? We may as well have it together.'

'Yes; I was gong to,' I said, and told him where I had thought of going.

'Oh, we can't go there,' he said impatiently, so of course we went to a restaurant of his choice near the premises of the Learned Society.

Naturally the meal did not come up to my expectations, though the food was very good. I found myself wondering how

I could have wanted so much to see him again, and I was embarrassed at the remembrance of my imaginings of him, alone and ill in his flat with nobody to look after him. Nothing more unlikely could possibly be imagined.

The conversation did not go very well and I began telling him about the people with their trays in the great cafeteria and suggesting that it would have done us more good to go there to be put in mind of our own mortality.

'But I'm daily being put in mind of it,' he protested. 'One has only to sit in the library of the Learned Society to realise that one's own end can't be so very far off.'

After that things went a little better. I told him about the Napiers and he invited me to go to dinner with him at his flat. I promised that I would cook the meat and I felt better for having done so, for it seemed like a kind of atonement, a burden in a way and yet perhaps because of being a burden, a pleasure.

Just as we were leaving the restaurant two men came and sat down at a table near us. I did not need to be told who they were.

'Apfelbaum and Tyrell Todd,' said Everard in a low voice. 'I dare say you remember who they are.'

'Oh, yes, you and Helena met them once at one o'clock in the morning and you were all so surprised. I often think of that – it makes me laugh.'

'Well, nothing came of it,' said Everard rather stiffly. 'I suppose it was amusing, really. I expect they will be more interested to see me with somebody they don't know. You must come and hear Todd talking about pygmies some time.'

'Thank you – I should like that very much,' I said.

I went home rather slowly, imagining myself having dinner

with Everard at his flat; then I saw myself at the Learned Society, listening to Tyrell Todd talking about pygmies. I was just getting up to put an extraordinarily intelligent and provocative question to the speaker, when I realised that I was nearly home and that there was a furniture van outside the door. As I approached it I was able to take note of some of its contents which were lying forlornly in the road. There were some oak chairs and a gate-legged table, an embroidered fire-screen and a carved chest, the kind of 'good' rather un-interesting things that people of one's own kind might be expected to have. I guessed that the owners were probably a couple of women like Dora and myself, perhaps, though I had no means of knowing if they were older or younger.

I walked quietly up the stairs, not wanting to meet them yet, but I was just passing what I shall always think of as the Napiers' kitchen when a sharp but cultured woman's voice called out, 'Is that Miss Lathbury?'

I stood transfixed on the stairs and before I had time to answer a small grey-haired woman, holding a tea caddy in her hand, put her head out of the door.

'I'm Charlotte Boniface,' she announced. 'My friend Mabel Edgar and I are just moving in – as you can see.' She gave a little laugh.

Another pair of women, I thought with resignation, feeling a little depressed that my prophecy had come true, but telling myself that after all they were the easiest kind of people to have in the house.

'Edgar!' called Miss Boniface into the other room. 'Come and meet Miss Lathbury, who lives in the flat above us.'

A tall grey-haired woman holding a hammer in her hand came out and smiled in a mild shy sort of way.

'Come in and have a cup of tea with us, Miss Lathbury,' said Miss Boniface.

I went into the sitting-room which had a carpet on the floor and a few pieces of furniture spread about in an uncertain way. Miss Edgar was standing on a stepladder hanging pictures, dark-looking reproductions of Italian Old Masters.

'Do excuse me,' she said. 'I always have to hang the pictures because Bony can't reach. These walls don't seem to be very good, the plaster crumbles when you knock nails in.'

'Oh, dear,' I said conventionally, feeling relieved that there was nothing I could do about it. 'I hope you will like this flat.'

'Oh, it will be wonderful to have a home at last, to have our own things around us,' said Miss Edgar. 'And I think we shall be happy here. We have found an *omen*,' she lowered her voice almost to a whisper and pointed in the direction of the window.

I saw Rocky's lines from Dante scratched on the glass.

'What is it?' I asked.

'Our Beloved Dante,' said Miss Boniface reverently. 'Could anything be happier? Those wonderful lines.' And she quoted them with a rather better accent than Rocky had managed.

'Whoever engraved them has made a small mistake,' said Miss Edgar. 'He or she has written *Nessun maggiore dolore* – it should of course be *Nessun maggior dolore*, without the final "e", you see. Still, perhaps this person was thinking of Lago di Maggiore, no doubt it was the memory of a happy time spent there. It would be interesting to know how the lines came to be engraved on the window – there must be a story behind it.'

I decided that I could not reveal the circumstances and the conversation turned to other things. I learned that Miss Boniface and Miss Edgar had lived in Italy for many years and were now eking out their small private incomes by teaching Italian and doing translations. They fired questions at me, speaking sometimes individually and sometimes, or so it seemed, in unison. I told them of a laundry, a grocer and a butcher where they might register, and we went on to discuss the bathroom arrangements in some detail. They were much more businesslike than the Napiers had been and insisted that we should have a rota for cleaning the bath.

'All right,' I said; 'shall I do it one week and you the next?'

'Oh, no, there are two of us. We shall do two weeks and you will do one, and so on.'

The question of the toilet paper was not openly discussed as it had been with Helena, but I noticed later that a new roll had appeared, hung in a distinctive place. It seemed as if Miss Boniface and Miss Edgar were going to be very pleasant and cooperative, a real asset to the parish, in fact.

'And where is the nearest Catholic church?' asked Miss Edgar.

'Oh, very near, not two minutes' walk away,' I said. 'Father Malory and his sister are friends of mine. He was engaged to be married, but it was broken off,' I added chattily.

I thought they looked a little surprised at this, and then it suddenly dawned on me that perhaps they meant *Roman* Catholic, so I hurried to explain myself.

'Oh, well, mistakes will happen,' said Miss Edgar pleasantly. 'Of course we know about Westminster Cathedral, but there must surely be a church nearer than that.'

'Oh, yes, there is – St Aloysius, and Father Bogart is the priest there. I believe he is a very nice man.' 'A lovely man' was how Mrs Ryan had described him at the jumble sale and I had often seem him on his bicycle, a fresh-faced young

Irishman, waving to a parishioner or calling out 'Bye-bye now!' as he left one after a conversation.

I gathered that they had 'gone over' in Italy, which seemed a suitable place to do it in, if one had to do it at all.

'There was really no English church where we were,' said Miss Boniface almost apologetically, 'or at least, it was just a room in a house, you know, not at all inspiring.'

'There was an altar at one end, I suppose it was the east,' said Miss Edgar doubtfully, 'but you could see that it was just a mantelpiece with the fireplace below it.'

'We didn't care for the priest either – Mr Griffin – he was very *Low*,' said Miss Boniface.

'And the congregation was rather snobbish and unfriendly,' said Miss Edgar. 'You see, Bony and I were governesses and they were mostly titled people living in Italy for their own pleasure.'

'Oh, yes, I can understand that,' I said obscurely, and I did understand their feeling although their reasons appeared to be hardly adequate; no doubt there had been other and deeper ones, but I could not expect to be told about those.

'I do hope you will let me know if there is anything I can do for you,' I said, as I got up to leave. 'Perhaps I can lend you cooking things and have you got bread and milk?'

It seemed that they had everything, but we parted on very cordial terms. I could see us having interesting religious discussions, I thought, as I went upstairs to get ready for supper with Winifred and Julian Malory.

'It seems a strange coincidence,' I said, 'but I remember coming to supper here just after Helena Napier moved in.'

'Yes, and Julian had just received the anonymous donation for the restoration fund,' said Winifred.

'Did you ever find out who gave it?' I asked.

'Oh, it was Allegra Gray,' said Julian lightly. 'Didn't I tell you?'

'No, I don't think I ever knew. And I don't think I should have guessed. I thought she was supposed to be poor,' I added, remembering the extraordinarily delicate conversation about the rent which Julian had reported to us.

'That made the giving all the more praiseworthy,' said Julian.

At this moment an unworthy thought occurred to me. Supposing *I* had given an anonymous donation of, say, twenty pounds, would Julian have got engaged to *me*? Had Allegra Gray regretted the donation when the engagement was broken off or had she simply not thought of it? Perhaps she was one of those generous people who do not remember when they have given money or think about it when it is gone . . . I stopped suddenly, remembering Rocky thrusting a pound note into my hand on the evening before they left. I supposed I must have put it into my bag and forgotten all about it.

'Julian,' I said, 'I've done a terrible thing. Rocky Napier gave me a pound, he said it was to buy the best quality incense, and I forgot about it!' I rummaged in my bag and found that it was still there folded up among a jumble of ration books, shopping lists, old letters and the other things that collect in bags.

'How nice of him,' said Julian. 'I thought him a charming fellow. I'm so glad he made up that silly quarrel with his wife – she was very charming, too. Do you know, Mildred, I met her when I was coming out of church one evening and we went and had a drink together.'

'She never told me that. She complained that it was always

your boys' club night,' I said, admiring Helena for having managed it. 'I shall miss them. The new people seem quite nice, though, two middle-aged spinsters.'

'Ah, yes, very suitable.' Julian nodded and became rather clerical again. 'Churchgoers, I've no doubt.' He seemed resigned to the prospect of them.

'I'm not sure about that,' I laughed. 'You'll have to ask Father Bogart about it.'

'Bogart, is it now? Are they after being Romans?' asked Julian, his relief making him break into an Irish brogue.

'I'm afraid so,' I said, almost as if it were my fault. 'But you wouldn't grudge him a couple of gentlewomen, I'm sure. He hasn't many such in his flock.'

'I thought they looked very nice,' said Winifred. 'I happened to be passing when they were down talking to the furniture men. I hope we shall be able to be friends.'

'They've lived in Italy for many years,' I said.

'Italy! Oh, how lovely!' Winifred clasped her hands and I heard the familiar note of enthusiasm in her voice. Looking forward a little, I could almost imagine a time when Winifred might want to become a Roman Catholic and I wondered if I should be there to help with the crisis. That was something that had not so far fallen within my experience of helping or interfering in other people's lives, and I wondered whether I should be capable of dealing with it.

CHAPTER TWENTY-SEVEN

Some time before the evening when I was to go to dinner at Everard Bone's flat, the idea came into my mind that of course Esther Clovis would be there. It seemed the most likely thing in the world, especially as Everard was writing an article for a learned journal and was also busy on a book about his field-work in Africa. I should find her there correcting proofs or making an index, and the idea did not please me. I decided that I would try to make myself look like the kind of person who could not possibly do either, but it was not very easy. My normal appearance is very ordinary and my clothes rather uninteresting, but the new dress I had bought showed an attempt, perhaps misguided, to make myself look different. It was black, a colour I had never worn before except when I was in mourning after my parents' death. I had often seen Helena in black, but her fair hair and complexion set it off better than my mousy colouring, and she had the knack of enlivening it with some brilliant touch of colour or 'important jewel' as one was told to do in the women's magazines. I had no important jewels except for a good cameo brooch which had belonged to my grandmother, so I fastened this at the front of the little collar, brushed my hair back rather more severely than usual and looked altogether exactly the kind of person who would be able to correct proofs or make an index. Still, I reflected, Esther Clovis, with her dog's hair, would probably be wearing a tweed suit and brogues. At least I should provide a contrast.

As I was going out of the house, I met Miss Statham walking towards the church.

'Hullo, dear,' she said, peering at me with a doubtful expression on her face. 'What've you done to your hair?' she asked at last.

'I don't know,' I said feebly. 'Nothing, really.'

'It looks sort of scraped back as if you were going to have a bath,' she said cheerfully. 'If you don't mind my saying so, it looked better the way you did it before.'

'How did I do it before?'

'Oh, I don't know, really, but it was softer somehow, more round the face.'

Well, it was too late to do anything about it now and perhaps Miss Statham's opinion was not worth bothering about. Softer, somehow, more round the face . . . who wanted to look like that? Certainly she herself was no oil-painting, as Dora would say.

Suddenly she moved towards me and took my arm. 'I *knew* I had something to tell you,' she said. 'I just popped into Barker's on Saturday morning and who do you think I saw? You'll never guess!'

'Mrs Gray?' I suggested.

'There, and I thought I'd surprise you! Well, anyway,' she went on, recovering quickly from her disappointment, 'I felt a bit awkward and was going to walk past – she was looking at some underwear, you see – but, oh no, she came after me and began asking me what news in the parish and all about everybody and Father Malory, even – I didn't know what to say.'

'Well, you could have told her about the Christmas bazaar.'

'Oh, I did and she said she might even come to it! You'd think she'd have a little shame, wouldn't you? Anyway, it seems that she's found a flat already, in the *best part of Kensington*, that's what she said – oh, a *much* higher-class district than *this*. And there are three or four Anglo-Catholic churches, all within ten minutes' walk and less.'

'An *embarras de richesse*,' I said.

'What, dear? Anyway, the one she's decided to go to has a vicar and *two* assistant priests and they're none of them married! She told me that. They all live together in a clergy house.'

'Goodness me, I suppose they need to band together to protect themselves and each other,' I said.

'That's what I thought,' said Miss Statham. 'I'd almost feel like warning them to look out.'

'Oh, I expect she's tired of clergymen,' I said. 'To have been married to one and engaged to another, isn't that perhaps enough?'

'Well, I suppose you get a liking for a particular type of man,' said Miss Statham tolerantly, 'though they aren't all as nice as Father Malory, I must say.'

The bell started to ring for Evensong and Julian hurried out of the vicarage into the church.

Miss Statham clapped her hand over her mouth and giggled. 'Talk of the devil,' she exclaimed, and hurried into church after him.

I went on my way feeling a little less confident than when

I had set out, though the interest of hearing about Allegra Gray helped a little to take my mind off my appearance. I felt more kindly disposed towards her now that she was removed from us and I did not grudge her the flat in the best part of Kensington or the three unmarried priests. I had no doubt that she would eventually marry one of them.

I got off the bus and turned into the street where Everard's flat was, only to find that I had walked straight into William Caldicote.

'Why, it's Mildred,' he said, 'but I hardly recognised you. You have a rather more *triste* appearance than usual – what is it?' He stood back and contemplated me. 'The hair, perhaps? The sombre dress?' He shook his head. 'Impossible to say, really.'

'Do you think it an improvement?' I asked apprehensively.

'An improvement? Ah, well, I should hardly presume to express that kind of an opinion. You mean an improvement on the way you usually look? But how do you usually look? One scarcely remembers. Where are you going now? Were you perhaps coming to see me?'

I thought I detected a note of alarm in his voice, so hastened to reassure him.

'Ah, perhaps it's just as well. I should not have been able to entertain you as I should have liked. I have a small bird *en casserole* in the oven, but it is such a *very* small bird, and now I am hurrying to my wine merchant, who should still be open, because I have just discovered, to my chagrin, that I have nothing but white wine in my little cellar!'

'How dreadful,' I murmured. 'I suppose you will buy a bottle of Nuits St Georges?'

'Well, possibly. He has one or two quite drinkable burgundies.

My only fear is that it will scarcely be *chambré* by the time I shall want to drink it.'

'Well, why don't you put the bottle by the fire or into some hot water for a few minutes?' I suggested. 'That should warm it up.'

'Warm it up! Mildred, my dear, you *mustn't* say such things. One can't stand the shock. I might have expected such a remark from poor Dora but never from *you*.'

I felt obscurely flattered. 'If you are dining alone,' I suggested, 'nobody need know about it.'

'Yes, you're right, of course. There's sometimes quite a pleasure in secret vice. One can feel really rather wicked and at the same time have the satisfaction of not harming anybody else – if that is a satisfaction.'

'Oh, surely,' I said. 'And now I really must go. I'm supposed to be having dinner with somebody and I shall probably have to help with the cooking.'

'How very anxious for you,' said William. 'I always like to have *full* control of a meal or no part in it at all. I'd rather not *see* people adding Bovril to the gravy and doing dreadful things like that.'

We parted with mutual expressions of anxiety about the meal which each of us was going to eat, though William seemed a little complacent about his bird, I thought.

When I rang the bell at Everard's flat, I realised that I was late. Miss Statham and William had each delayed me a little, but it was better than being too early and having to walk slowly past the house in the dark, hoping I should not be seen from an upper window.

'Oh, there you are,' Everard said as he opened the door. Not exactly a welcoming speech but I knew him well enough now to realise that he never did appear pleased to see any-body.

'I'm afraid I'm a little late,' I said, taking off my coat and hanging it in the hall which had, I noticed with a slight shock, several fierce-looking African masks hanging on one wall. There was no looking-glass, which was just as well, and I waited with resignation for Everard to make some comment on my appearance. But to my relief none came, and after a time I realised that he evidently did not think I looked any different from usual. Unless, of course, he was too polite to say anything.

He led me into a sitting-room where I noticed a decanter of sherry on a low table and a bottle of red wine by the gas fire. I suppose I must have looked at it rather pointedly, remembering my conversation with William, for Everard commented on it.

'I know what you are looking at,' he said, 'and I know it's one of the unforgivable sins. I can only hope you'll forget what you have seen and let it be a secret between us.'

'I think perhaps that everybody puts wine by the fire secretly,' I said. 'I don't think I should ever have known it was wrong if William Caldicote hadn't told me, But what about the meat? Oughtn't it to go in the oven?'

'Oh, the woman got everything ready for me. She has put something in the oven,' he said vaguely. 'A bird, a chicken or something. I expect it will be all right. Perhaps you would help to take it out – at about half past seven, I believe.'

'Is it in a casserole?'

'Oh, would it be? Then I dare say it is.'

'And is there an oven cloth?'

He looked a little worried for a moment but then a smile

broke through. We sat down by the fire and he gave me a glass of sherry.

'It should be hanging on a nail by the cooker, shouldn't it?' he said. 'I seem to remember that.'

Not an inspiring conversation, I thought, but it would do. We sat quite peacefully drinking sherry until I suddenly remembered about Esther Clovis. No doubt she would be arriving just before dinner, when I was taking the casserole out of the oven. No woman is at her best when taking something out of the oven, and I couldn't even correct proofs or make an index.

'Where is Miss Clovis?' I asked.

He looked surprised. 'At home, I imagine. Where else should she be?'

'I thought she might be coming to dinner.'

'To dinner? Would you have liked me to invite her? I'm afraid I didn't think of it.'

'I thought you respected and esteemed her.'

'Oh, certainly I do, but that doesn't mean that I should want to ask her to dinner.'

There was a silence, during which I looked round the room, which was pleasant but in no way remarkable or unusual. There was a large desk, a great many books and papers, but no photographs and nothing interesting on the mantelpiece, apart from a card announcing the autumn programme of the Learned Society.

'How is your mother?' I asked.

'Oh, quite well, thank you.'

'And Miss Jessop?'

'Miss Jessop?'

'You know, the person who was in the room that evening when I had dinner with you.'

'I'm afraid I don't know anything about her.'

'I think it may be time to see to that casserole,' I said, getting up. 'It's just on half past seven.'

It turned out to be a very nice bird and I am sure that even William's could not have been better. The red wine was perfectly *chambré* and our conversation improved quite noticeably, so that by the time we were sitting drinking coffee by the purring gas fire the atmosphere between us was a pleasant and cosy one.

'I should be interested to see the article you said you were writing for the Learned Journal,' I said.

'Oh, it's very dull; I shan't inflict that on you.'

'Well, what about your book, then? How is it getting on?'

'I have just had some of the proofs and then of course the index will have to be done. I don't know how I'm going to find time to do it,' said Everard, not looking at me.

'But aren't there people who do things like that?' I asked.

'You mean excellent women whom one respects and esteems?'

'Yes, I suppose I did mean something like that.'

There was a pause. I looked into the gas fire, which was one degree better than the glowing functional bar into which I had gazed with Julian.

'I was wondering . . .' Everard began, 'but no – I couldn't ask you. You're much too busy, I'm sure.'

'But I don't know how to do these things,' I protested.

'Oh, but I could show you,' he said eagerly; 'you'd soon learn.' He got up and fetched a bundle of proof sheets and typescript from the desk. 'It's quite simple, really. All you have to do is to see that the proof agrees with the typescript.'

'Well, I dare say I could do that,' I said, taking a sheet of proof and looking at it doubtfully.

286

'Oh, splendid. How very good of you!' I had never seen Everard so enthusiastic before. 'And perhaps you could help me with the index too? Reading proofs for a long stretch gets a little boring. The index would make a nice change for you.'

'Yes, it would make a nice change,' I agreed. And before long I should be certain to find myself at his sink peeling potatoes and washing up; that would be a nice change when both proofreading and indexing began to pall. Was any man worth this burden? Probably not, but one shouldered it bravely and cheerfully and in the end it might turn out to be not so heavy after all. Perhaps I should be allowed to talk to Mrs Bone about worms, birds and Jesuits, or find out who Miss Jessop really was and why an apology had been demanded from her.

'It should be interesting work,' I said rather formally and began to read from the proof sheet I was holding. But as I read a feeling of despair came over me, for it was totally incomprehensible. 'But I don't understand it!' I cried out. 'How can I ever know what it really means?'

'Oh, never mind about that,' said Everard, smiling. 'I dare say you will eventually. But don't you remember the late President's wife?'

'Why, of course, that's a comfort,' I said, seeing myself once more in that room at the Learned Society where the old lady was sitting in a basket chair in the front row with her knitting. The lecture flowed over her head as she sat there, her needles clicking and then dropping from her hand as her head fell forward on to her breast. She was asleep, but it didn't matter. Nobody thought anything of it or even noticed when her head jerked up again and she looked about her with unseeing eyes, wondering for the moment where she was. After all, she was only the President's wife, and she always went to sleep anyway.

JANE AND PRUDENCE

Barbara Pym

'Barbara Pym is the rarest of treasures; she reminds us
of the heartbreaking silliness of everyday life'
Anne Tyler

If Jane Cleveland and Prudence Bates seem an unlikely pair to
be walking together at an Oxford reunion, neither of them is
aware of it. They couldn't be more different: Jane is a rather in-
competent vicar's wife, who always looks as if she is about to
feed the chickens, while Prudence, a pristine hothouse flower,
has the most unsuitable affairs. With the move to a rural parish,
Jane is determined to find her friend the perfect man. She learns,
though, that matchmaking has as many pitfalls as housewifery . . .

'Over the years, as Barbara Pym replaced Nancy Mitford,
Georgette Heyer, even Jane Austen, as my most loved author,
I devoured all her books, but *Jane and Prudence* remains my
favourite. Even an umpteenth reading this weekend was
punctuated by gasps of joy, laughter, sympathy and
wonder that this lovely book should remain
so fresh, funny and true to life'
Jilly Cooper

virago

To find out more about Barbara Pym
and other Virago authors,
visit our websites

www.virago.co.uk
www.viragobooks.net

for news of forthcoming titles and events,
exclusive interviews and features, competitions
and our online book-group forum.

And follow us on Twitter @ViragoBooks